THE

Q

UESTION

BOOKS BY AUSTIN CLARKE

FICTION
The Survivors of the Crossing
Amongst Thistles and Thorns
The Meeting Point
Storm of Fortune
The Bigger Light
When He Was Free and Young and He Used to Wear Silks
When Women Rule
The Prime Minister
Nine Men Who Laughed
Proud Empires
In This City
There Are No Elders
The Origin of Waves
The Question

NONFICTION
Growing Up Stupid Under the Union Jack
A Passage Back Home
Pig Tails 'n Breadfruit: Rituals of Slave Food

SELECTED WRITINGS
The Austin Clarke Reader

THE QUESTION

Austin Clarke

Canadian Cataloguing in Publication Data

Clarke, Austin, 1934-
The question

ISBN 0-7710-2128-3

I. Title.

PS8505.L38Q47 1999   C813'.54   C99-931640-0
PR9199.3.C52Q47 1999

The quotations on pages 166, 212, 234, and 235, are from the poem
"The Sand O'Dee" by Charles Kingsley. The retelling of Odysseus's
encounter with Polyphemus on page 152 is from *Nelson's West Indian
Readers, Book Three*, compiled by J.O. Cutteridge (London: Thomas
Nelson and Sons, Ltd., 1943). Reprinted by permission of the publisher.
The paraphrase of lyrics from Leonard Cohen's song "Suzanne" on page
178 appears by permission of Leonard Cohen Stranger Music, Inc.

We acknowledge the financial support of the Government of Canada
through the Book Publishing Industry Development Program for our
publishing activities. Canadä

We further acknowledge the support of the Canada Council for the Arts
and the Ontario Arts Council for our publishing program.

Typeset in Sabon by M&S, Toronto

Printed and bound in Canada

McClelland & Stewart Inc.
The Canadian Publishers
481 University Avenue
Toronto, Ontario
M5G 2E9

1 2 3 4 5   03 02 01 00 99

Speak of me as I am; Nothing extenuate,
Nor set down aught in malice

— SHAKESPEARE
  Othello

THE QUESTION

S HE AND I WERE SITTING on the wooden deck. Thirteen other men and women were in the garden. We were at the house of the woman who had made the deck herself, she told me soon after I had sat down beside her. "Fuck-all job, don't you feel?" she said to me, as if she wanted to put some distance between herself and the woman. I did not know the woman. "Isn't it a shitty job?" She had this manner of raising her voice, as if asking a question, even though she was making a statement. Her statements were clear, and blunt, and filled with opinion, and spoken in an aristocratic voice, declarations of confidence.

She and I were the only ones sitting and talking, and behaving as if we had been friends before this afternoon, as if we were now seducing each other with the words passing between us, from one lip wet with the red wine, from her reddened lips to mine, back and forth, but more from her lips. And we knew it. We knew what we were doing.

A small dog was lying at our feet. It was hearing her words about the deck, and the words that sounded like jabs, like sparring, daring and venturing into a relationship – words passing between us. The dog raised his ears once or twice, and then he ignored the two of us. He then looked as if he was sleeping; and then he looked as if he was dead. Or almost dead. I do not like this dog: I did not grow up liking dogs.

But she and I were not, in spite of the words flying between us, building a relationship with those words.

Neither the words that were spoken, nor the acknowledgement of those words, had any real meaning. At least to me. It was just talk. It was summer. Strawberries were in glass bowls of sour cream, sliced watermelons like clotted wedges of blood, with small round black bones in them, were in platters with ice on them, and champagne was in the hands of most of the other guests standing on the lawn, amongst the beds of red and pink impatiens. It was summer. And frivolous. And we had time. Although this summer, like all summers, is short. But we had time.

It was as if we were moving over a vast interminable body of water that was blue, with white clouds low over the water, and were taking our time to travel and saunter in our conversation, and make our words have the life of the waves in the tropical water, never-ending in this journey that was meant to be long and logged with pleasure and with curiosity.

"Do you know, I don't know *five* of the people here," she said, and then behaved as if she hadn't spoken.

But I could feel that even though it was a journey of imagination and not of acquaintance, of getting to know her, and her getting to know me, making up a bed to lie in, it was not going to be all fun and gaiety, placid water and peace. Perhaps it was even one of those journeys with no destination. The words that passed between us, cut off from the rest of the party, in our secret journey were themselves longer, deliberately longer than the words spoken by the other guests who were now standing in knots on the grass which seemed wet, as if they were standing in dew. Some of them seemed as if they were getting ready to leave. But it was only their nervousness and their discomfiture, as if they too did not know any of the other guests. Without uttering a word, she and I knew it would be good if they were to disappear and leave us alone on the deck.

The two of us were going to remain on the wooden deck, with our conversation, with the uneven slabs of cedar, with the heads of nails jutting from the floorboards biting into our thin summer shoes; one woman passed us from the kitchen with a pile of white plates with blue rims, and shrieked, and stopped to look at the sole of her right foot, and saw the spot of blood. She said, "What could this be?" and looked at us; and that seemed to convince us that we were going to sit together on this same dangerous deck, and would see the end of the warm night through the journey of our words. We would be happy, in spite of the lingering dog which has just risen as if from the dead, and has run his tongue over my ankles, and then jumped into my lap. I try to ignore it. This dog cannot think in my terms, may not even be able to think, has no mind like mine. But something about his behaviour tells me that he has a mind of his own. A mind conditioned by the way its owner behaves with it. Who is its owner? Perhaps it is a trained mind, in a trained dog.

This woman I am sitting beside has reddish hair, and when she lifts her glass, I can see thin hairs under her arms, like thin lines drawn without precision; and her lips are full and the smear of lipstick makes them seem wet and red to suit the colour of the wine she is drinking. I can see her legs, for she crosses her legs each time she makes a point, each time she ends her statements with the raising of her voice. If we should stand up, she would reach to my neck. She could be five-foot-eight. Her skin is darkened with the sun of summer in a back-yard much like this one, on a chair of unpainted wood and blue canvas, like those that the English sit in in parks. But it is her breasts, and their shape, and their size, which I am always coming back to, as I try to admire them, focus on them, without being caught, and then have to blush about doing this, as if it is wrong, incorrect to fall in love with a woman's breasts before I know something about her mind. I have been sitting, before this afternoon, alone in a room, the smallest room in my large house, with music and no lights, painting pictures, through frustration and want, of the exact kind of woman I would like to choose, to know, to love and live with: draw her shape, her skin, her legs, her education, her feel when I am lying beside her, and her breasts. Now, from this afternoon, I may not need to draw any more portraits of fantasy. Her breasts. It is always her breasts that give me focus, that pull the artist's way of seeing from me. I think now of my favourite fruit at this time of the year when they have their own rich colour, and how at the first bite the juice or the water comes bursting into my mouth like the freshness of rainwater back in the island. I fill her blouse with two of them, and then I have to feel them because, if I do not, they may be not be ripe enough for easy release of the water. And I am ashamed immediately afterwards for this freshness, as we say back in the island. But her breasts remind me of the peaches I buy in dozens from a store on Front Street which sells them for a higher price than I can get them for, by walking an extra mile, to Kensington Market. This laziness, which costs me money, is the same laziness I know I suffer from by sitting and drawing pictures of women I would like to know, instead of sitting in a bar, and wishing . . .

This woman I am sitting beside is not one of those pictures I have imagined in my dark, music-filled room of fantasies. That is an eccentricity I shall have to put aside.

Perhaps this dog is a trained dog. He has for the second time jumped into my lap. He is making small, jerking movements with his small body against my zipper fly. I move him from the area of my fly. The zipper of my white linen trousers was slightly damaged when I got them from the cleaners earlier today. But I am larger than he, and his smallness embarrasses me and puts me at a disadvantage.

She ignores what he is doing to my linen trousers. So I place the dog, as I would remove a rotten golden leaf in October from my shoe heel, with one hand gently back onto the wooden deck, onto the nails that rise from the uneven cedar planks. A space of one inch separates each plank, running the length of the deck; but this is not enough space for the dog to fall through. And the nails do not bother him.

It is a dog of some breeding. I can see this from the colour of its hair and the sheen of its coat, and from the shape of its body, and from its collar and the three tags, like medals of pedigree and performance.

She said she liked dogs. Two times, so far.

"Won't live without pets," she has said. "Especially dogs. Never *trust* a person who doesn't like dogs, doesn't have dogs as pets. What do you say to that?"

And it was this that caused me to look at the dog with different eyes, and see the shiny hair, and to see the woman, through a cloud of cigarette smoke, in a different light.

A few guests were leaving. Most still held champagne in their hands.

Rover was the name of my dog. But I cannot remember who gave it to me, or who gave it its name. It was a she-dog. There were other dogs in the neighbourhood, and most of them were he-dogs. Rover never came into the house, would not dare, knowing her place, "dogs amongst doctors," because my mother would kick it back outside into the yard, the place for dogs and doctors, with her shoe, or strike it with a broom, or with a chair if it was not too heavy. Rover never ate food from a can, unless it was a tin of Fray Bentos corned beef which we had already emptied and cooked, and thrown the tin at the dog in the yard. Dogs were not spoon-fed, or can-fed, and were supposed to find their own food. But there was something about my dog Rover that I liked.

It was during a certain time of the year, a certain time when the heat of the night was in the air, covering us with a second skin of tight closeness, when the moon was full as a smiling face, and bright, when all the dogs in the neighbourhood and within barking distance would come around our house, and there would be fights and screels and growls as if one dog was being mauled by all the other dogs. And then there would be no noise, just the soft shaking of the leaves in the shack-shack tree after the sun had gone to bed for the night, leaving a taste of the heat from the sun on the breath of the night, and the flowers round our house and round the other houses to the left and to the right and across the narrow lane would whisper with their multiplying strong fragrances and colours; and they would lose their greenness for the black of passion. It was this time of silence and purity, and shining moons, as if nature were about to perform some action of final chastisement, that the barking would change to wailing, soft and smooth.

It was not that I was not loving to the dog. It was not that I had not ever patted the dog. Or bathed it. Or combed its white short, tough hair. The dog was given to me, in the same way of giving, as when my mother looked out into her large backyard and said, "That bardrock hen is yours. You want the three li'l leghorn chicks, too? They is yours." The dog was given to me in that same way of apportionment. Everyone else had had their gifts.

And it was this sudden sinful silence that took me to the front window to look out into the golden brightness of the full moon and the lingering heat, to see why it was so still so early in the night. The hour of ghosts and of men with two heads and duppies and fowl-cock thieves had not even come. It was early in the night, early and so still.

And the stillness was ruptured by noise and growling. I counted six snarling dogs. Rover was amongst this pack. She was trying desperately and silently to escape from the clutch of sex that kept her stuck to her lover-dog after she had satisfied him. But had she satisfied him? They were still stuck, going in opposite directions, like policemen from the island and sailors from English ships, going this way, and then that, in a tug of war. Rover would pause for breath, and then tug. And her mate would pause, and then tug. They both made no ground. And remained stuck. She was pulling him in one direction, perhaps to hide under the cellar, but the other dog was pulling her in the opposite direction, perhaps to run to his master. She was heading, or trying to head, towards her own backyard, but the other dog was trying to run away to his home. The male lover-dog was a coward, like some of my friends who would never stand and fight, but would run home crying for their mothers. Rover was stuck to an unknown, cowardly dog. All four or five other dogs, which I knew by name because they were the noise-making mongrels that belonged to the neighbours on the left and on the right and across the lane, and who always played in our backyard, were just standing around, like unfaithful friends, watching and doing nothing. They were just looking on, as I was looking.

My mother had just reached the front-house and was going through the door, holding her large black Bible with the torn leather binding close to her right breast, as if it were a lover. She was dressed in a white pleated sharkskin dress, her favourite, which reached to her shins. I had seen her grease her shins with coconut oil, after she was fully dressed and just before she threw my father's old black jacket over her shoulders. She would wear this black jacket at night, for warmth when it was chilly, for protection when she had to walk the half-mile from church alone, in the dark night, to give the impression she was a man, wearing the old black jacket just as I had seen Italian movie stars wear jackets in movies about guns and love and *la-dolchee-vituh* in the tight leather seats of the Olympic Theatre in Town; my mother had just reached the front steps.

She saw more than I did. More than she wanted me to see. And what she saw made her stand on the coral stone step in dumbfounded embarrassment. For just one moment. Long enough for a reprimand.

"Close your eyes, boy!" she said. She was not sure whether to put anger, or the embarrassment we both shared, into her reproach.

But I had seen more than she wanted me to see, though I had seen it many times before: riding my bicycle through areas where there were as many dogs as men and women, in the poor areas, where men sat and talked and played cards and drank rum and threw dice, and in the rich districts where you would not see even a single man sitting in front of a house, but only dogs who chased you from their district, and when they caught you, gave you the penalty for this trespassing, a bite, with a big tear in your school-uniform pants, leaving their teeth in your pants and in your arse, always in the shape of an L. And you would need iodine and Jays Fluid to recover from the bite, and not "catch *tettinnus*." I had seen dogs locked like this in sexual tug-o'-wars before; but Rover was never one of them. Now, I had seen enough.

By this time, my mother was outside, beside the house. And in her hand was a bucket of water. The water was not hot. It was cold. This kind of water, tossed into the low-hanging branches of fruit trees to chase culprits and thieving boys, this kind of christening water, must be cold, always cold. Cold water was also for cooling passions and for ensuring chastity and cleanliness.

When she threw it on the two stuck dogs, it struck them just like the waves at Gravesend Beach.

The dogs were still glued in their silent, ambivalent tug-o'-war. The witnessing, cowardly other dogs, tasting the cold water not meant for them, ran.

My mother came back with a second bucket of water, of the same temperature, and did the same thing with it.

"And I am getting my damn shoes wet!"

The dogs remained stuck.

I was looking at Rover, feeling her sorrow, and, by accident, found her eyes. My dog was looking into my eyes, the plaintive eyes of her glance covered by a film of grief. I felt that Rover knew that I was her owner, her father – "Look, dog!" my mother told Rover, once. "Look to your blasted father, your rightful owner! Not to me!" – someone responsible for her. Someone who had not warned her about this thing that was happening to her. And I felt embarrassed for my negligence. And I felt angry.

"I could poison this dog for behaving in this way, you don't know!" my mother said. She placed the empty bucket closer to the side of the house, near the gate to the backyard. She pressed the black Bible closer to her side where her heart is. And she shrugged her shoulders to make the old black jacket fit her anger more comfortably. "What you expect from a damn salmon-tot retriever? This dog don't have any breeding, boy!"

I no longer had any love for Rover, liked her even less than before, and did not offer her a drink of water all the next day.

This worried me so much even then, my meanness to a dog, that I did not sleep at all the first night after that night of the tug-o'-war, because in our village, in our custom, the least kindness anyone could offer a beggar, or a stranger, or to a dog, was a glass of water. "My God!" I had heard my mother say, many times, talking about other things, about big things, about things that only big people understood, "Mistress Barnes, with all her money, is so damn mean, she won't even offer a drink o' water to a dog!"

And when I heard these words, in my mind, I started to cry, and then I went into the backyard and poured from the drum a clean tin of water for my sweet dog, for Rover. I stood and watched her as she lapped and then looked up at me, lap and look, lap the fresh crystal drops from the sardine tin which me and my mother had eaten many weeks before, and did not then even offer Rover a piece of the skin, or a sardine bone from the fish that came all the way from the Grand Banks of Newfoundland, all the way up in Canada.

Rover was a salmon-tot retriever. It had no breeding, not like this sausage of a dog that is lying now on the uneven cedar floor, as if it were dead, beside my brown suede shoes, on this Toronto summer afternoon. But Rover was my dog.

The impatiens were deep and red. Some were more than one colour. They ran around the edges of the garden beds, in and out of larger plants, green bushes, and amongst rocks large as coral stone front steps back in the island, and like thick weeds. They were so fragile that when the breeze hit them, some of their leaves trembled and fell off and were blown away. They were luscious, like bridesmaids at the roots of the other plants in the garden. Marigolds, zinnias, and geraniums were the only flowers I could identify. But there were white ones, too, thick and round like gigantic roses, and fluffy, and giving off that special scent you find in funeral parlours. They were giving off this powerful scent, which increased as a few more of the guests were leaving. Perhaps it was someone's perfume, or aftershave lotion, and not the fragrance of these gigantic rose-like flowers I was smelling.

Flowers and sea and deep blue water are always present at moments like this, as on nights when Rover and her friends would play. Back then, flowers were red and rough and tossing, and they lunged, through a sense of freedom, or liberality, my mother called it, from the background of our lives right into the front row, into the dress circle of the Olympic Cinema.

Now, they are placid, the impatiens and the flowers and the green plants in the rock garden. And the dog. Almost artificial, although I can see that they are alive and growing. The sea is sometimes a memory now, a past I have bathed in, and once nearly drowned in. Only the skies above this wooden deck in summer are the same as a summer there.

"What I like about summer," she has just said, "is the price of cut flowers. I can keep them longer. Even after they are *dead*. I put them in vases. And between the pages in *books*."

Champagne bottles without corks sit in a large pail with pieces of ice floating in water, like battleships in a sea with icebergs. Wine bottles are placed in a pail like that with the champagne, an unpainted galvanized pail, with cubes of ice packed round them. And the red, in bottles lined up like toy soldiers, their labels looking like shields, are standing on a plastic cloth that covers a wooden table. This is what she and I are drinking. Large black flies and dark brown flies crawl and flit round the mouths of these bottles, helping us drink it.

I have just picked one fly, with my thumb and index finger,

out of my glass, and snapped it on the head of a large nail; and another time, I poured a few drops from a bottle before I tipped it into the crystal glass that she held out to me, as if I were measuring a portion, a libation on the black soil, the ground, in honour of some ancestor who, like the custom, had come from Africa, and whom I did not know but was told I had to remember. A fly was drowned in that bottle. The fly, still floating, came out as a larger drop when I poured a glass. I flicked it out. When it hit the head of the nail, its body did not move.

This woman I am sitting beside smiled when the drops struck the unpainted, sturdy wood of the floor of the deck.

"What the fuck did you do *that* for?" And she laughed, and covered her face with her hands, and the harshness of the profanity was softened; her gesture had caused her summer dress to be raised a little higher above her knees, more than she wanted to do, showing me more than she intended to show me. "I like how you did that," she said, making it sound as if she was asking me a question. She did not ask for an explanation, at first, but added, "Is that some custom from the islands? You're from the islands, aren't you? Your friend that's on the Bench with you said so." I did not say anything to her. The dog did not move, although a drop of wine had struck him in the head.

She does not tell me whose birthday party it is. And I do not ask her for the name. A little less than half the guests are still here.

But birthday parties that I have attended back in the island were times when there were balloons blown to bursting point and explosion, and music loud as the bangs, whenever that happened.

Birthdays in this city are such sombre gatherings when they

are held; and sometimes they are not held at all. And sometimes women tell me, "I hate holding my birthday!"

The woman beside whom I am sitting said earlier, "Me? I don't even want to know how old I am." She said it as if she were asking a question, as if she were asking me for approval to make the statement. She is telling me too much in this short time.

We have not yet exchanged names, but I already know many things about her: she is a civil servant, and she hates her job; and she likes to write things, "like poems"; she is unmarried, she hates being single, and she has no children, but wants to be a mother, although she says she wouldn't like caring for children, even her own, and she hates childbirth and "all that blood that goes with childbirth"; and she has a mother who lives in Kingston – "Kingston? The penitentiary capital of this country? Ever heard of the Kingston Pen?"; she lives in a large two-bedroom "apart-ment" on the penthouse floor with a solarium. I have never seen a solarium. And she really hates high-rises; "The place I live in only has eight floors"; and she loves travelling, but hates planes.

I know all these things about her, but they do not tell me much, nor give me as much focus as those pictures I sometimes dream about, dreams of women I think I might want to come into my life. But still I wonder if I could spend time with this woman and sit in a room that faces a garden, and watch the darkened plants and the skies no different from the darkness inside the room, with the music of Miles Davis, "Someday My Prince Will Come," playing loud.

The woman I am sitting beside has just said, "Where do you live?"; and before she hears my answer, she says, "I live a twenty-dollar taxi ride from here."

Yes, birthdays back there and then were spread from mouth to mouth like a fire in the sugar-cane fields, and friends and strangers would be covered with the ashes that fell from these informal invitations, and there would be pots of peas and rice and curried chicken and pork chops that were large and oily and stiffened on the outside with a line of skin and fat and breaded and tough and tasty, and large buckets of rum punch, and the rum itself would flow like the River o' Jordan; and the birthday girl – or the birthday boy – would be dressed in Sunday-go-to-meeting clothes; and the funny hats and noise-makers and streamers the colour of rainbows and sunsets, and balloons, would transform the house into a merry-go-round, into a circus, into a carousel. The boys would hold drinking races, pouring huge quantities of Coca-Cola in huge glasses and mixing it with one or two drops of Mount Gay Rum, and then pretend they were inebriated and imitate the stutter and the stammer, the walk and talk of the village drunk, to give themselves a history with drink, bright and early the following Monday morning at school.

But during the birthday festivities there would be speeches, made in the style of classical orators reminiscent of consuls and proconsuls in the Senate at Rome, or in the Sanhedrin in the New Testament. Churchill would be imitated.

"Ladies and gentlemen, we are gathered here this auspicious evening to celebrate the anniversary, the *annus natu* . . . the *annus mirabilis* . . . the birthday of . . ."

And the house would erupt in cheers and laughter and applause, and nobody would remember to ask, "How old you is, this birthday?"; but they would all sing the birthday song, as they stood around the cake, a white crypt of marble blazing in the middle of a table covered in white damask, with the red, white, and blue candles that told the right age.

"Undoubtedly, and sententiously, as is my *modus operandi*, I do not think this is the proper occasion on which to divulge to this felicitous gathering of friends . . . old friends, new friends – and fair-weather friends! – ah-hem! ah-hem! . . . the number of years I have had the distinguished pleasure to have known the guest of honour! Suffice it to say that I knew her before she born!"

And after this, not much of the speeches given by the birthday boy or birthday girl, or by the master of ceremonies, would be heard. It was all laughter now. And not many of the words of the succeeding speeches, not limited to the felicitations of friends and family, brothers and sisters, would be listened to.

We all made speeches at the same birthday party, because it was ours to celebrate. At different times, throughout the long night. And there was always music and dancing. But here in this backyard in this suburb – Pickering? Scarborough? Am I in Willowdale? – with its wealth and enormous house and beautiful gardens and freshly constructed wooden deck, there is only me and there is this woman, and as I look into the garden, I see a few straggling guests in a hurry to leave.

One of them said, "We have to go, my dear. We have another party to go to."

Back there and then, at birthday parties, we screamed while dancing, "This party *can't* can't can't done!"

The temperature now feels as if it is more than twenty-nine degrees. It is getting hot.

On her neck is a mark. I see in this blemish the mark of a hand that wrapped its five fingers round her throat, a colour of darker hue than the rest of her body. Her tan will be erased soon by the fierceness of the cold and winter. She will live under lights, day and night, and recapture her true colour. And the same dark hue, her summer colour, the tan, is settled too, in the crux of her arms and round her knees, as if the person who laid a hand on her has deliberately chosen these delicate, vulnerable joints on which to emphasize his anger. But the colour, even though it reminds me of such savage blows, still adds to her beauty and desirability. I am imagining all this about her, as I sit and sip my share of red wine, as she talks with an unending familiarity about personal matters: ". . . and I was six when I started the piano. Taking lessons from a man who pushed his finger up my . . ." The dog starts to bark at a bird. ". . . I was six. Six, and still wetting my bed?"

Her skin and her complexion look as if her blood is about to pour through these spots, these blemishes that are drawing me, compelling me into some kind of passionate competition with all the men who have touched her body, in love and in anger, and while teaching her music. I do not know music. Cannot play an instrument.

It is hot. She is sitting now out of the area of shade from the tree that grows on the neighbour's side, but which spreads its shade over part of this wooden deck. She is trying to keep the quality of the tan she already has in shape. And I describe in this semi-shaded light the sun and the heat on her body the way I do because of the burning sensation the temptation and the temperature have on my body. It is burning hot.

Back there in the island, this kind of heat can kill a man, and does. It is hotter than a man's passion for a woman.

I am looking straight ahead at the neighbour's deck, evaluating her choice of flowers, trying to gauge her wealth and social status in the arrangement of her hanging plants. All her hanging plants are green. It must be the glare of the light on their branches that gives this deep, dull monotony. I do not like hanging plants, plants that hang. In that island with the sun and the sea the colour of bluish green and the colour of the sky also monotonous but blue, plants that hang contain in their branches lizards that are the size of baby crocodiles, and bugs that can reach the stature of squirrels, and other crawling things that can bite you, and leave a sting that can kill you.

The colour of the skies and the sun coming through the branches makes the flowers in the neighbour's hanging baskets into kaleidoscopes. But the danger continues to hang.

The dog has now chosen another guest, who lingers with her regrets and goodbyes, to make love to her white summer sandals. She does not look down at the dog, just flicks her left leg, and the clutching dog is sprattled against the vertical slats of the railing of the wooden deck, and lies there, for a long moment, long enough to raise doubts about its life, as the woman passes me and the woman sitting beside me and enters the house.

"I *hate* that," she says to the man beside her. "Don't you?"

The man does not answer. He is standing beside the woman who built the wooden deck, just inside the sliding glass door, and he does not know who is the owner.

"Why don't they train their bloody animals?"

She takes a fresh pink Kleenex from her handbag, stoops in front of the woman who built the wooden deck, whose hand is outstretched to take hers to say goodbye and thank you; and this woman tainted by the dog's intentions wipes her white sandal, but the wrong one, for it was the left that the dog had tried making love to, and stands up, and puts the Kleenex back into her handbag, and smiles and says, "It was a lovely party." The woman who built the deck does not smile and does not answer.

17

The dog is still on the floor of the deck, beside the same vertical slat against which his body had been kicked. And the
woman sitting beside me does not move, does not say a word
of reproof. I like her for this. This is not her dog. Perhaps it is
the hostess's dog, and this is why she did not respond to the
guest who was leaving.

This woman beside whom I am sitting is young, and is viva-
cious in her speech, and bright. She has a woman of today's
confident female independence, something like feminism and
feminist militancy – although I do not know what that means.
She is well dressed, in a quiet, expensive way, and I can
imagine her attending to each strand of hair and each dab of
mascara. She is wearing a black silk dress that is loose round
the body and loose and long round her waist. A gold chain
reaches down to the tip of her cleft. I do not know this word
too well, for back there we called it her "creft." But I might be
inventing. We called it also the gorge that defines the breasts,
in which they sit.

This gold chain has heavy links and it sits with satisfaction
both to the eyes and to her colour, with its weight of solid
breeding. She is expensive and tasteful in her attire. You can
tell that she spends hours and many dollars on her appearance.

I feel that if I should get to know this woman, although at
the moment I do not want to know her any better, and certainly no more intimately, that something about the way she
appears to me now, acceptable and challenging, will be my
undoing. And probably hers. And the undoing of the young
love that would have sprung up. I am looking at the beds of
pink impatiens. There is this unspoken challenge, just like the
ease with which I used to paint fantasies. The challenge lies in
the unnatural way in which we find ourselves, imagining
things, and then are surprised when our fantasies turn into the

granting of hopes and wishes. And then, disaster. We are talking about things I reserve for stronger, older relationships.

And I think, as I listen, that this is probably the way it should be, this honesty of declaration, although neither she nor I should have to believe in the words being spoken. Perhaps this is the way of big places, cities and large land masses the size of continents. In the island, we are too close, too numerous, and live too thick, one upon the other, to have anything that is personal and secret to say to each other. Perhaps this way of speaking to a stranger is a gift. The gift of superiority.

It is summer. And it is hot. The wine is like blood, deep and red. And the sun makes the flowers more violent in their richness and growth, like splashes of blood itself. And I am back in that island. Looking into her face burnished by a different sun, or by a different slant of the same sun, sitting on this deck with the uneven cedar boards and heads of nails that punch the feet, like stones in that road, I am really not here. The blood is hot.

She has now moved close to me. And now her leg is on my linen trousers. I had this very afternoon taken them out of the cleaners at the corner of Davisville and Yonge, where a West Indian woman works behind the counter.

When I first descended the three concrete steps to this woman, I remembered that the week before she had lost three of my white summer shirts.

Her hair was plaited in braids. They lay flat on her skull, and rose all the way down her neck like reddish brown snakes. Each time she spoke to me, the snakes in her hair rattled. They gave me their hissing message in each look and gesture of the true meaning of space between a woman's teeth. But that common knowledge about space and islands was the very warning I would take to keep us far apart. Look, but don't touch. And don't so-and-so feel up my things!

But when, minutes later, I mounted the same three steps, there were pieces of paper larger than the pages advertising discounts for this week's cleaning, leaves from the *Toronto Star* newspaper which had travelled the farther distance from their boxes, or from littering hands, from across the street at the entrance of the subway station at Davisville.

I walked on the crackling newspaper pages, and crushed my precipitous attitude towards that woman from the islands; and when I got to the level of the street, I wiped off my prejudices, as I would wipe my shoe, as I would wipe the dying golden and yellow leaves from the falling maple trees in October from my feet.

Before I left, she had said, "Man, I real sorry about those three shirts that get loss, you don't know!"

My eyes touched the rich, soft material of my linen trousers, shimmering through the cellophane bag, and I saw the zipper slightly damaged, and looking rusty. I thought of the pain it would cause if it stopped suddenly while zipping and climbing up the front on the thick hairs it was supposed to protect and hide from the public.

The trousers were spotless, in the brilliant sunshine. Going home on the southbound subway, the car was full, and new women were around me: Chinese, Pakistanis, West Indians, Koreans, Indians, Filipinos, and Canadians, and I retouched all of them, their legs, their breasts, their bodies, their colours, trying up until that time to paint the model I had dreamed so much about in the room without lights and with the loud music of "Someday My Prince Will Come." With all these new images, it was my way of forgetting the woman from the islands in the cleaners. And I had to wonder why I would travel all the way from College Park on the subway, north to Wellesley, to Bloor, to Rosedale, to Summerhill, to St. Clair, and to Davisville, to the cleaners, when there are so many that are closer?

Now, her leg is resting on the trouser leg, across the crease, cutting it in a manner that brings out the meaning of her own leg on mine, destroying the crease put there by the cleaners where the woman from the islands works, her behaviour emphasizing the innuendo in her voice.

She passes her tongue across her lips, and closes her eyes at the same time, for just one second. But it is a second of long, interminable sexual arousal and violence. She is taunting me. She does this a second time, and continues talking, and her voice drowns out the woman from the islands, erases everyone and everything I had been thinking about; and this new danger I take into my own hands with each minute I sit here, as with each time I descend those three cement steps six subway stops from where I live, each time I would have painted a picture of the woman with the long black hair, every time I kneel beside the woman from the Philippines saying her prayers, in all this time that I sit here sipping red wine and looking at the travelling clouds moving away from me into the direction of the lake, like her words.

"Children?" she has just said, raising her voice, making her statement a question, an argument and a consideration. I do not know, and could not guess, her precise age. "This friend I have? We talked about it already." My mind races to that friend. "I never voted." She says this with pride. "In all my adult life, I've never thought of voting, wasting my time voting for the bastards that run this province. Or this country?" She passes her tongue across her lips, and I think of the man who kisses these lips. The wetness of her tongue that now passes over her lips and over her lipstick the colour of peaches adds a stronger seductiveness to her face. When she closes her eyes at the same time as she passes her tongue over her lips, the hotness of the afternoon becomes cool like the wind off the sea at Gravesend Beach at five; and the breeze comes through the branches of the large tree in the neighbour's backyard, here on my right hand, and scatters her hair like leaves in October.

"This is my country," she says. "And I intend to keep it Canadian. *Fuck* the French! Those Frenchies?"

I am not sure what she is talking about, for Frenchies back in the island are prophylactics; and I am sure she is not talking about these.

"The way all these people are coming into Canada now," she says. I cringe. "I don't see why I should stand for that crap, should I? What I mean is that I have nothing against these people coming into my country, but they should remember that they are not born here, and like they should *adapt*."

I cringe again. She is looking up into the sky. The sky is blue. I follow her gaze, and I see the coconut palms and hear the waves nearby, and see the screeling boys in the waves that are blackened by their cries of joy . . . and I see the postman, on his bicycle, ringing his bell to bring the woman to the window.

"Something come. It feel like a money order. . . ."

This woman is sitting before me, on a chair that is lower than mine. The drawing room in my mother's house, back in the island, contains chairs that are masculine and chairs that are feminine; and before my pee could foam, declaring and then delivering me into manhood, my place was always in a low chair, lower even than the one my mother sat in, as she made with crochet and wool little landscapes and dark clouds, stubby chimneys with smoke pouring out of them like orange explosions from a sugar-cane fire, and trees that did not grow in the island, which she called cypresses. She held the page from *Illustrated Country Life* beside her, and that was resting on a small table, half the height of the female chair, and showed me one more time the English countryside reproduced on the shiny page and being transferred by her to the painstaking small wooden circle filled with the results of her constantly moving hands.

"The Victorians, boy!" she told me once, when she had me hold the glossy landscape painted by Turner. "The Victorians."

"You and me?" I asked her.

"These are the Victorians," she said on that occasion, moving her finger with the gold wedding ring on it, over the faces of women who wore the same long white pleated dresses, buttoned or pinned at the neck for "decentness," but who did not have the benefit of sun and sea to take the pallor from their faces. "We pattern our lives after them."

The champion cricket team of the village was called the Victorians. And this young woman sitting before me on the lower, female chair is beautiful and frightened. She is about nineteen, but you can never with certainty tell age in the faces of women who come from that part of the world where she says she was born, and raised, and had to flee from. . . .

My chair is really a Bench. Beside me is another man, a minister of the cloth, of the Anglican Church, sitting on his half of the Bench. This young, fragile, and frightened woman is holding one of her hands in a fist that is placed in the other hand, that is tight one moment and relaxed the next. And if I look carefully, as I have been doing, I can see that her fingers are marking out circles of confusion and hesitation and fear on her palms and then on the backs of her hands. Gold runs in three layers of bangles on her left hand; and on her right hand they cover about one inch of the wrist. There is gold round her neck. But she does not touch this, or hang on to it, in her nervousness.

She has been telling me, and telling my colleague, her age, her name, the place in that far-off country where she was born and went to school; and she has just given us the names of five brothers and six sisters, names that sound like poetry, names that ramble and run like rivers in that land, names of her family, wide as the flowing waters themselves that are born also in that far country somewhere in the East.

Beside her, on her left hand, is a lawyer who is her lawyer. Behind her, silent, and shifting at each word she says, are two men who look as if they could be two of the five brothers she has told us about. "Family members" the translation tells us she calls them. And beside her, on her right hand, is an older man, also from that same country, speaking her words, and who tells us in English what the weeping woman is telling him in another language. We listen. We lean over the broad desk that is a Bench, to catch the words spoken to us in English but with an accent that makes the English almost identical to the foreign language coming from the young, beautiful woman's quivering lips.

I look at this woman, and I am drawn closer to her by the pure silk of her garment, and I follow the way it folds and falls and covers her frail build, but even its folds and the protection it provides exposes her body to my prying eyes, and discloses to me the smoothness in the shape of her limbs and the soft roundness of her belly that are concealed by her sari. The garment is like a wind ruffling her entire body as she rubs her palms and then rubs the backs of her hands, as she constantly adjusts the fit of her bracelets, and the fit of her words to suit the evidence she wants my colleague and me to believe. She is a woman without a land.

I am not trained to notice these details of limb and torso, only to seek out what is true in her story, and mine from the ore of her words the "credibility" buried there. But I am a Judge who is first a man.

". . . and they take me and carry me in a Jeep," she is saying, "and they take . . . took me to a deserted place, like a bush . . ." And after she has spoken her words in her own language these words, this repetition is what the man sitting beside her, the interpreter on her right side, is telling us.

Someone asks, "Who are they?"

The huge Canadian flag, with its red maple leaf, is still. And stiff. It stands in this room that lets in no air from the street below. And there is a lawyer who is not her lawyer but the lawyer of the court, who sits silent, reacting with jerks of her body to the story we are listening to; and there is my colleague who shifts in his seat, scraping the elongated platform on which we sit with his thick-soled black Rockport brogues, and he does this more dramatically and noisily each time the woman's story takes one more deep, downward path, through the luscious green landscape of trees and rivers and running water and jungles and degradation, and soldiers that terrify her.

". . . it was the peacekeeping forces, soldiers with guns, and one of them hit me in my face with the end of the gun . . . ," she says.

"End? End of the gun?" someone says.

"Butt!"

"Gun-butt."

No one but me is looking into her eyes. I am looking into her eyes, not for the tears that fall from them, but for that sign, that flicker of an eyebrow, that tremor of lip that will tell me if what I am hearing, in this second-hand language of interpretation, is exactly what the "peacekeeping forces" had done to her.

Her skin is soft and brown, and I feel that if I touch it, it will bruise. I have never held a gun in my hand. I am trying to imagine her experience of that touch of cold steel and toughened hardwood on her brown flesh in that distant, mysterious land I had read about in so many books back in that small island, when I was even younger than her age, and what I learned here, in this half-continent, from documents and propaganda and the United States Congressional reports and on CNN. I know her country like the back of my hand, mainly through the romance of books about caves and elephants and luscious green fields with flowers of greater and more numerous colours than the ones I have been looking at in this other garden sitting beside this woman on this wooden deck, and through the slithering of deadly snakes, and from large brown chests, made stronger against assault by robbers by means of ribs of iron and steel, these brown chests which contain rubies and gold and precious stones.

". . . here, on my head, is where the gun-butt struck me. . . ." This young woman who should be touched with garlands of feathers from the peacock, who should be kissed lightly on the cheek, and perhaps, if it is not against her religion and culture, just one inch beside the red dot in the middle of her forehead. But it is her garment, moving with laziness, in spite of the terror and the shuddering breaths she has to take to speak out her story, it is her garment that draws my compassion from the sound of her words to the shape of her body beneath the tale of Indian terror. I see her breasts heave each time a new terror comes from her lips.

But this is not something I have been trained to do, or think about. And if even my colleague, who is a priest, or the supervisor, or this woman's own lawyers should read my mind, they would want my hide. So, I banish the comparison of breasts to mangoes from my thoughts. But I have to wonder what turmoil is boiling in the mind and in the sinews of the man who sits next to me on this elevated Bench, tapping his desk with his fountain pen, for emphasis in her words. He is a priest in the Church, and might want my confession. The windows of this court are not open. No fresh air can come in. I cannot clear my lungs and inhale the other breeze or wind coming up from the hot, dusty street below, from Front Street. The buildings facing me, on the other side of the same street, are too high to allow a wind through this concrete gorge. But I hear a car honking, and I can barely see the top of a passenger bus, trying to move into a space which from my elevation looks too small to accommodate this huge, smoke-belching vehicle.

My attention is inside this court, once more, where there is not the same impatience. Only the soft, quivering voice of this young woman who does not feel at home in the country of her birth, who cannot be at home, not yet, not so fast, in this country of her refuge, not without the trampling of many procedures, and the cutting up of many ribbons that are red, tape that barricades easy entry, who cannot feel at home even in this room, in this court, where she is assured of human rights, fairness, and the possibility of a two-bedroom apartment subsidized by the federal government. And a Canadian passport.

". . . and after the peacekeeping forces hold me in their barracks for two weeks, and they *torture* me every day for two hours in the morning, and two more hours in the evening, I was crying and they did not give me much food to eat. And my father, who is still in the same village, and my mother too, do not know where I am, as I had to flee and leave my home, without going back home, and I could not get a message to my brothers and my sisters to tell them where I am. Where I was."

Her eyes were now filled with the tears of her story; and I think of those streams, rivulets which I could see running down the sides of mountains, and across plains that hold and cultivate rice in waterlogged paddy fields . . . I can hear the pen scratching the notepad of my colleague. I can hear the breathing of the two men sitting at the back of the court; and I can hear the intake of breath from the interpreter who earlier had stood beside me outside at the front door, by the street, to take a smoke.

"An interesting case, sir," he said, knowing that these things are never discussed.

"An interesting case," I said, knowing the exact regulation.

Then, suddenly, the interpreter's voice is affected by a deeper intake of breath. It is like a sound that comes from a man who has bronchitis. His voice gets worse, is losing some of its clarity, as he reproduces for us the coming on of the climax of her story. . . .

No wind comes through the windows. No ventilation comes from the vents in the ceiling, which pour only dust that is invisible, along with a strong smell of asbestos, upon our heads. It is quiet. Very quiet, while the interpreter talks, like in those childhood books, when the wild animal is approaching, and the people in the tent are sleeping, and the wind across the corrugated, parched, prairie flatness of the land takes on the configuration of lines in a woman's palm, and the danger about to rip apart the heart and the heavy canvas roars in its momentary assault.

"And they *rape* me."

Her age now came into my mind, not the nineteen years she had said it is, as it is written in her file, which I had read a few hours before I arrived at the birthday party and am now sitting with this woman on the wooden deck; in my mind, she is much younger. She is a child. Unprotected, fragile, and innocent. And the voice of this young child takes over my imagination, showing me her ripped garment and her bruised limbs, her breasts and her belly which the garment could not protect then, but which it hides now. I am faced with the rawness of depravity.

The depravity screams in my mind as loud as the charging cries of the peacekeepers of force, those peacekeeping soldiers. I can see them dressed in white robes that billow in the speed of their chase, stirruped on Arabian steeds that gallop over the parched steppes, in clouds of dust, in white turbans and long beards that flap like flags and pennants in the assaulting breeze.

". . . and I did not tell my family because back home . . . for me to admit as a woman that I was . . . raped, raped . . . the only thing left for a woman in my custom . . . is to kill myself."

"*Herself*," the interpreter says, in correction.

She is saying this when my colleague sitting closer to the door leans towards me and whispers into my right ear, in a voice that is too loud and too hissing to be a secret.

"Do we need to hear any more of this?"

And he scrapes his chair, and puts down his fountain pen, and scrapes the platform with his large black Rockports, and I know that we are heading for the door.

The room is plunged into quiet, into the silence of confusion. They do not know why we are leaving in the middle of hearing the evidence. And they probably feel that our withdrawal is caused by some serious, technical point in law, unknown to all of them sitting in the court, some disadvantageous complication, our exit is so sudden.

The last I saw of the young weeping woman was her fingers fumbling the three gold bracelets on her left hand, and the water coming down her cheeks. Someone passed her a white tissue from the jumbo Kleenex box.

"Those bastards, eh?" my colleague says.

We are standing in the corridor, with our backs leaning against its cream wallpaper.

"I could kill those bastards myself! Such a young, lovely girl! You want to hear more of her evidence? If we finish now, we could have a longer lunch. Those bastards! Did you see the way her sari was heaving as she was reliving her trauma . . . ?"

It was a numbing story. And I had had enough.

"I can't take much more o' this," he said. "It is worse, much worse, than hearing certain confessions. Once, I heard the confession of a man who told me he had just killed his mother. I knew him and I knew his mother. And he was telling the truth!"

My colleague, the Judge, is a priest in the Anglican Church. I sometimes visit his church at Church and King Streets on Sunday. Last Sunday, he preached a sermon about sin and greed, and I sat in the back of the large church, resplendent as the Sin-Michael's Cathedral back in the island, following his words hitting against the nave and the ornate ceiling, off the portraits of Christ in various stages of the annunciation of His birth, proselytization, betrayal, passion, crucifixion, and resurrection in the dramatic stained-glass windows. His words cut through my body and mind like small swords peeling away sin from my sinews; and then with this absolution, in his pointing sermon, I experienced the comfort that peace brings. The expiation of the sinner. That Sunday, I felt almost as a Christian, to be in his company. That morning was a sacred Sunday.

And he gathered up his robes, and as we sat in his small Honda car, he roared off farther down Church Street to his townhouse, for a lunch of ackee and salt fish, prepared by his maid. He had taught Christian Ethics in Jamaica, at the Mona campus of the University of the West Indies, for five years. When he returned to Canada, he brought his Jamaican maid with him.

"Why don't you give the Decision orally? You're good at giving oral decisions. And we can get outta here, and go to lunch," he says to me now.

We open the door, and catch them unawares. Back inside the court, it is very quiet. The young woman who had been telling us about her rape by the peacekeeping soldiers, in a monotone of her soft voice that quivered, is now entertaining the two lawyers and her brothers with a story, perhaps from the East. And she is speaking in perfect English. The interpreter is laughing, too. They see us. Our presence cuts short their hilarity, and aborts her new story of joyfulness. As we sit on the Bench, her appearance and countenance take on, once more, the reflected abomination in the country where she was born, and from which she wants to be a refugee.

Dust from another passenger bus comes up to the large windows, like confetti tossed in a parade; and the noise of cars honking at the congestion disturb the quiet and the lingering unhappiness in the court.

I do not look at her as I begin to talk. She holds her head down all this time, and the man giving us the English to match her native language looks at me, straining to follow my words, and to paint the picture of my words exactly; and I see that he is, at the same time, wondering what I am about to say.

". . . and we have no reason to doubt that what you told us this morning did in fact happen, as we have read the documents pertaining to your country, and to your claim . . ."

My words were not making her cease her convulsion of tears and the grabbing of her wrists adorned with the gold bangles.

". . . your treatment at the hands of the peacekeeping forces is, from your story, believable, and you have a well-founded fear of persecution . . ."

I am not listening to my own words. She is not following my words either. I feel she is far away from this court, back in her land, rollicking in green grass, perhaps, even in the grass in High Park in the west end of Toronto. My words are compounded by the legalistic smear that is meant to cover them, and by the stiffness of the second-handedness of their interpretation.

". . . and congratulations. Welcome to Canada."

It is some time before my words sink in upon her. And when they do, and their meaning spreads like a warm wind, then everyone except my colleague, the Anglican priest, and I is smiling and laughing and patting one another on the back. And in that short space of time, we the Judges have ceased to exist.

Five minutes later, at the bar in Vines Wine Bar, we lift the glass of Pommard, twirling the large glass, and taste the peppercorn pâté and munch on biscuits thin as the Communion wafers I took from his hand at the altar rail one Sunday when he preached about love and loving your neighbour.

"Those bastards!" he says now.

It takes me a while to put his disgust into context. The Pommard clutches my palate. I do not even remember the name of the Indian woman who was raped.

That Sunday when I kneeled at the altar rail, contrite for the length of the moment of sanctity in the taking of Communion I had experienced years before in that small island, on that Sunday, I was nervous about receiving the wafer from his hand.

And when the silver chalice passed in front of my lips, I remember, as I am sitting now beside this woman on the wooden deck, that my lips received it, just as her own lips seem to receive her tongue which she passes across her own lips to irrigate the burning dryness from the hot afternoon.

"Do you believe in the Holy Ghost?" he asked me as I was kneeling before him, as if I were a complete stranger.

"Yes, Father."

Yes! Her views about abortion and pregnancy, and politics and foreigners clogging up her country, are like two sets of waves, two different waves and sentiments that are strong enough to smash the ship we are travelling on.

"We could be at two different parties, from the way that group there in the garden is having their own thing, and we here, sitting down by ourselves, as if we don't know them, and they don't know us," she is saying.

I am following two clouds, two chariots that collide without noise, softly, and become one large long-distance truck with ten wheels.

"Something happens to me when I travel. No, I mean . . . when I travel. Just getting on the plane? And fastening my seat belt? The whole idea of taking off in such a heavy, huge thing like a jet, and going through air, going through air, nothing but air . . . space . . . and then . . . coming down out of the clouds, and landing *on a dot*. Landing on the smallest dot.

Like an island. On the map of the world, in my atlas, some islands are just as big as a dot. That's what I mean. Now, that is something!"

The cloud I am travelling on, and travelling with, has just collided with another, larger cloud, and I am now going through a thick, soft hill of snow, in an avalanche, and all of a sudden, there is more light, the sun is brighter and hotter, and the snow melts, the avalanche becomes sprays in the sea, and I am let down, suddenly and finally.

"Do I talk too much?" she is saying. "Do I? I do, don't I?"

It is she who has been talking ever since I first sat beside her to receive the light from her gold Dunhill lighter. But it is summer. And the breeze is touching my blood. And the waves are no longer as high as they can be in that other place where they crash against the iron pipe, blackened by age and by ancient cockles and sea-beefs and the occasional crustacean. We eat these crawling, hard-shelled beasts straight from the sea.

She loves to travel. She tells me so, many times. She is holding her head high, letting the wind blow her hair into her eyes. Her words are meant to repaint and recapture those journeys. To Mexico, Thailand, Venezuela. "And the Bahamas, where it is not *really* better." To all parts of Canada, "which is shit." And especially to New York and Las Vegas. "Gimme Vegas, any time! I inherited that from my mother." She emphasizes this predilection by closing her eyes again. And she runs her tongue across her lips, and I can taste both her love for Las Vegas and her lips themselves. "Just love to travel, just *love*," she says.

She was born in bigger circumstances than I, in half a continent, and she has snow and winter as godparents, can exchange one extremity for another, as the whim passes over her, as the wind combs her long, thick, reddish brown hair.

The Other Eye . . . a moment of water, of wind and light, a solitude of stars and dreams, other forces and presences inhabiting the spaces you often call your own; other selves and memories calling in the healing solidity of tree and rock and sand, in the glowing verge and quietude of mountains, in wooded pathways and trails that go up and down thunderous foaming rivers of time and timelessness. . . .

The Other Eye is the eye that sees beyond, it is the third and invisible eye that gives meaning to sight, it is the reflective seeing eye, the eye of meditation and transformation, of visions of place and presence . . . this is the poem I would write her, if only she were one of the women I used to imagine and create in fantasy. But she is not the one I want to love, the one I want to love in reality.

I am talking about women who do not move too far beyond the distance of an island, and who stay within shouting distance of the shore. Women who do not dwell in the house, for the house is too small for two. I cannot imagine a house large enough for the two of us. But I am not thinking of a house, or partnership.

If these women do not wade out too far, to that point where the wave reaches up to their breasts, and into the danger of the rolling waves with white crests on them, then . . .

I do not have the courage to tell her this. This kind of sentiment lays too solid a groundsill and foundation on which to build even a casual meeting. Besides, it is a party. A birthday party. And it is July.

She is talking to me again. Her tongue has just travelled across her lips, leaving a thicker veneer, this third time, of a suggestive glow.

"To travel?" she begins. "To get away from this damn place, Toronto? I can spend my very last dollar on a plane ticket. Just to travel? And I've done it, too. Many times?"

The wine is making her generous with emphasis, giving every other word a deeper meaning. She is obsessed by emphasis.

"I go sometimes without paying my bills, even," she has just said. "Even without paying my Visa. I live on my Visa. Just to take a *trip*?"

And instinctively, I pass my hand over my right breast pocket. My wallet is still there.

The hostess, the woman who built this wooden deck on which we are still sitting, passes beside us like a seagull over placid water. She has just told me that this woman is her best friend. But I am not introduced to her. And the two women hardly acknowledge each other. Throughout the long afternoon, this woman I am sitting beside is the only person I know. But I do not know her name.

It is my colleague, the Judge, who invited me to this party. He had promised to drive me here. He had promised to call. To tell me when to be ready. He did not come to get me. But he called to apologize. And to give me directions.

"I apologize. I have a little matter to attend to," he told me. This was five minutes before he said he would arrive. "Ecclesiastical," he explained. "But nothing to hear a confession over."

His sense of humour bubbles whether he is talking about the Church, or refugees, or red wine, or the court. And I am attracted to his intelligence and worldliness, and to the way he expresses his understanding of both, peppering his words with Biblical allusions and religious philosophy. They intrigue me, and I try to remember them and copy them to use in my own conversation. But since I am a man who is not too close to the Church, and am not sure if I like God, his allusions fascinate me, and overwhelm me. But a moment after they are spoken, they leave my memory.

Once, after we had welcomed another woman into Canada as a refugee, from that same part of the world where the first woman told us she had been raped by a peacekeeping soldier, he told me, "Do you believe in the power of the sari?" I did not answer. I did not see the point. "My boy," he then said, "the Lord giveth, and the Lord taketh away. Blessed be the name of the Lord." I wanted to laugh, for he had just mentioned something about the weaknesses of men in gowns and saris worn by certain ethnic women. His question comes close to my own fantasy which walks with me, like a twin or a shadow, and which looms before my eyes each time I sit to judge, to listen to similar stories, each time I sit in this court for refugees to paint my fantasies, and I think he is indeed near to God, and is able to read my mind, and the minds of women who sit before us, waiting for our judgment. "Blessed be the name of the Lord!"

He had said this on the telephone when he called to apologize. I could see him smiling through the telephone, just as he smiled when he first stood in front of me, over me, as I knelt on the long red stool that stretched the length of the altar, when he held the silver bowl containing the wafers, and handed me one thin, almost transparent, tasteless symbol of the body of Christ. It stuck in my throat for a moment. I did not have enough saliva to swallow it. He moved down the long stool, on my right hand, to the other kneeling communicants, and on his return trip – all the time I was smelling the robes he wore – he stood again, and held the large silver chalice close to my lips, almost taunting me. "This is my blood," he said. I thought of the Pommard at the Vines Wine Bar. And I thought I saw him wink just a little, making his round ruddy face crease at the eyes, like the mark of the feet of crows printed there. I took my sip, but he was still holding the wine at my lips.

"Do you believe?"

"Yes, Father."

When I had put the telephone down, after his apology, I knew that I would not enjoy myself at this birthday party.

"Oh, incidentally!" he had said just before putting the telephone down. "The lady whose house you're visiting, she's a member of my congregation . . . I think I officiated at her baptism. . . . Are you taking Room?"

"She doesn't like crowds."

"She's a wise woman! Neither do I . . . but I officiated, as I told you. She has a friend . . . hers, too . . ."

I was driven to this house by the woman in my life. The woman from the Philippines. From the southernmost island, Mindanao, in a little town, so little that I had to use a magnifying glass to see it in my *Oxford Atlas of the World*. She was born in Kiambo, this little town, not far from Sarangani Bay. When I look at her place of origin, and see its size, and place its size against the size of the place we are now, and against the size of the island, we laugh and call it a wonder that we are not, both of us, at the same time, catching sprats and minnows and ning-nings in those aquamarine clear beautiful tourist seas, almost the identical colour of blue-green as the page in the atlas on which I found her Kiambo. Yes, this is the woman in my life. The woman I am seeing at the present time. I touch her hand as we walk, and I can feel the passion and the heat of the music of the Philippines. But she is quiet, very quiet, and shy. Room.

I am not a man on the loose.

She has refused to come with me, because she does not like crowds. I plead with her, but she refuses to be invited; and as I wave to her, and start to pick my way along the cobblestones in the narrow lane on one side of the house I am visiting, and walk beside a bed of red impatiens and another of pink, the length of the house, I look back to see her and blow her a kiss; and she is still waving, and standing beside her car.

I am heading towards the noise and laughter in the back-yard, in the garden, wondering as I suddenly become lonely for her about the number of Filipinos who are born in the Philippines and are still living there, village by village, from Negra in the north close to the Babuyan Channel right down the infested green hills and plains to her Kiambo in the south, trying to understand what she has against crowds.

But I have no intention of forcing her into crowds against her wish. And certainly, it does not cross my mind that I will meet anyone here this hot afternoon, or would want to meet anyone, to take her place.

Certainly not. Not even this woman sitting beside me, who likes crowds and travel, and wine and dogs.

But my woman's dislike of crowds sometimes irritates me. She has such a strong dislike of crowds that, even at small dinner parties of four guests, she would let her resentment be known, that she prefers to have dinner with just the two of us – she and me.

"Why can't we be together? Alone? Just you and me? Why do we need company? Even three is a crowd!"

"Why don't you like crowds?"

"Because they are crowds!"

I would hold dinner parties at my house, for fourteen guests, and spend many hours preparing, peeling sweet potatoes, cooking food similar to the food she grew up with, and setting the table, gathering the wine and rum and Bombay gin, which is what my friends drink; and now that she is in my life, my guests have dwindled in number; but she would stand beside me, following every move, memorizing each step, helping even when I had told her she didn't have to, but smiling and putting her arms around my waist.

"It is not work that I dislike. Only crowds."

"Why don't you like crowds? Really."

So, planning to live with her sometime, soon, in holy matrimony, "or living in loving sin!" she says, I soon learned to accommodate her reservations and dislikes. After all, this kind of give and take is part of the ritual. For better and for worse.

It was she who first mentioned matrimony, and then mentioned "living in loving sin."

I would dream, all day, of her enjoying only my company, and I, hers. But there are times when I resent the monotony of her company only, and so often; always to be with her, only . . . and would yearn for variety, a few other faces and voices at the dinner table.

All the time, I am seeing what a strong woman she is, assured and self-confident, happy within herself. She is. I am always bored with my own company.

She is from Kiambo, near Sarangani Bay, in Mindanao, in southern Philippines. It is a country with millions of people. And still she does not like crowds. It is the surprise of this, the extraordinary thing about it, that intrigues me, and causes me to water down my resentment. She is from the southern Philippines. Not the north. I do not know if there is a difference: the Philippines was the Philippines to me.

"Are you kidding?"

Just this. This is what she says when I say that the Philippines is the Philippines.

Her name is Romula Lucena Maria Mandaros. But I call her Room.

Room worships at a Pentecostal church every Sunday morning. That is another surprise. I think of all Filipinos as people who go to a Catholic church, or a hall where Filipino immigrants would congregate. Room takes the subway north on Yonge Street, that street that can take you up into the cold, frozen, frostbiting north, through all the suburbs and municipalities that touch it, that travels and travels in the same long, monotonous direction. But her church is not so far as the North Pole.

Room goes all the long clanking journey where this interminable Yonge Street enters the suburbs. She does not drive her car to church. Her car is an old, large, American car made by Chrysler Motors.

Perhaps the church Room goes to is just around the corner from where I am now, at this birthday party. Every Sunday, she invites me to go with her to church; and every Sunday morning, I say, "Next Sunday." Sometimes, her invitation comes as a shock, when I am not prepared for it, and I have to invent a better reason. But I have now settled on the best reason, if not the most truthful.

"I have refugee files to study for tomorrow."

And that satisfies her. For she spends Friday, Saturday, and Sunday nights, from six o'clock until ten, grading examinations and preparing her classes in home economics and budget administration for the following Monday. She is diligent. She is a high-school teacher. Her father and her mother, who brought her here when she was fourteen, live in Thunder Bay.

41

Her father, Mr. Mandaros – as I call him – is an engineer; her mother, Mrs. Mandaros – this is how I address her – is a house-wife. Room apologizes, all the time, for being so thoughtless.

"Your work comes first," she says. Not an ounce of doubt or resentment can be traced in her voice and manner. "Even before church."

And this would make me feel guilty, and like those sinners and people of greed that my friend and colleague on the Bench, the priest, talked about, those people like Ananias and Sapphira, that one Sunday when he delivered a two-hour sermon on greed and sin.

Room prays every morning and every evening. When she is spending time at my house, she prays three times, but cuts her prayers short. But when she is home, in her basement apartment, she prays until she is satisfied that her prayers have been heard. Fifteen minutes of concentrated silence, mostly. Twice as long as she brushes her teeth. She does not wait to hear if they are answered, or ought to be answered. She just prays until she is tired of praying.

Room likes to pray. Just as this woman beside whom I am sitting likes to talk.

In her flannel nightgown, which she sleeps in when she is at her home, in summer and in winter, Room goes down on her bare knees, after she has raised the hem of the nightgown just above her knees, and remains on the slippery linoleum floor which she washes every Friday night, in her basement bed-sitter apartment on Huron Street, near the university campus, a few yards from the St. George subway station at Bloor. Huron Street is where we all lived in cold basements from 1955 uninterrupted all the way till 1979 – a lifetime. Now, Huron Street is no longer the street where people from the islands make their stamp. Now, there is only Room.

I would kneel beside her, beside her bed, on her side of the bed, and join her in her supplications.

The first night she allowed me to sleep in her bed, about five months after we met at a friend's house, after we were seeing each other, I prayed beside her.

But nothing came from my lips. The strong smell of incense, not from the sticks of Dragon incense or Lotus incense, which she did not burn, but which fragrance came from the perfume of her body odour, sweat, and underarm deodorant and Pritzia, beautiful scents, sexual scents of seduction transformed her small basement apartment into a temple. A temple of lust and love. I remained kneeling beside her, conscious of her body in the flannel nightgown, watching in the periphery of my vision the way her breasts moved as she mouthed in silence the things she was saying to God.

I wanted to place my hand on her shoulder as I had seen preachers on television do, when they knew that a woman was on the point of confession and conversion. But I did not need to convert her into any congregation or denomination. She was, already, the woman I loved.

But it was the silence, the absence of words, which created the powerful impetus that made me want to touch her. I was listening for her words, her words of acknowledgement and sincerity that would tell, and give me some normal indication, as words do, that she was incapable of handling her own life. She prayed in silence. Only her lips moved, but they did not disclose any secret.

She prayed for me. And for our love. That she did not know if she was doing the right thing. That she was not sure. That she couldn't decide if we should live in the Philippines or back in the island when we get married. That she wished God would intervene and tell her if our love should last. And if it would last. She prayed for strength. I could see her breasts move each time she touched a part of her uncertainty in her words to God. She did not hold her head aloft as I had seen my mother do when she knelt beside her bed, bombarding God with all the inequities of her life, with all the mischief I had committed during that day, with all the wrongs her neighbours had done to her. My mother prayed for me, that I would not be tempted by the lascivious acts of that dog, Rover, to cause me to gain too much of the carnal knowledge of the world before it was my age and my time to know these things. And after each session with God, Room told me she had prayed for me. And each time, I felt safer and holier.

At the conclusion, Room started to speak, very softly, as if she were saying things to herself, as if there were no one present.

"I think I want it to last," she said. And she said she said that in her heart, to God. "*Con todo mi corazón. Todo todo todo todo . . .*"

The heavens in which she believed descended and made me angry, and my anger started to dampen the passion that was raging through my body so close to hers in this kneeling supplication. And the moment I harboured those thoughts, the same moment I felt as a sinner would, the same way I felt after I had watched the Indian woman from another part of the East where numbers are large, that subcontinent and archipelago of Far Eastern sea-swept islands, that refugee woman in her red and gold-trimmed sari that moved over her covered body, and that was pierced by the fantasy of my eyes which knifed through it like a sexual assault.

It was my impatience, Room kept telling me, "*lente, lente, lente.*" My masculine hurry to circumvent the decentness of courtship and of love. She was always telling me I am too impulsive and impatient.

"If it is to be," she was saying, "it will be."

Her voice startled me. Most of her kneeling had been in silence. I was imagining the words that were in her heart. But now she was talking.

"I have to wait until you say that this is the right thing. I love him, but I must first hear from you, God."

We did not pray again, together, on our knees.

But I remember that she kept a box, an orange-coloured box of incense, marked "Original Healing Incense for Stress & Tension Relieving Inhalant Pure Tibetan Healing Incense." Made in Nepal.

When she spent the next night, Friday, and the whole weekend, at my house, she did not sleep in her flannel nightgown, although she brought it along, packed in an overnight bag made of cloth, although she knew before she came that she would be staying the weekend. She dressed herself for bed in a suit of green army fatigues. The sleeves were short, the trousers were baggy, and the mark of rank, four holes for the pips, were left in the epaulettes. It was the uniform of a captain in the army of the People's Republic of China. I bought the uniform at a yard sale in the Gerrard Street East district, in Chinatown East. She used three safety pins to protect the front of the pants, which had buttons instead of a zipper, and make it fit, protecting her pubic hair, and more pins to fasten the shirt, right up to her neck. She folded her white flannel nightgown on the stool at the foot of the bed, and left it there the whole weekend. I wished she liked colours that hold the fiery, bright, and passionate blood of the Philippines in her dresses, colours of life and excitement, flowers of red and yellow. But she did not. This night she dressed herself in the green uniform of the Chinese officer, after she had taken her shower for the night. But the moment we pushed our bodies between the sheets, and killed the cold in the bedroom, the first thing she did was take the pins out of the trousers and make them into a pillow; and then she stripped the shirt off, and then she threw the uniform on the floor.

I could feel her body, cold as a hand shaken in winter, as it writhed out of the pyjamas, like a contortionist, without removing the sheet or the blanket or the comforter. And then she formed her body into mine, fitted like one spoon into the curvature of another of the same size.

"I forgot my pills at home," she said. And then, afterwards, she laughed.

She reached in the darkness at the foot of the bed for the Chinese officer's uniform.

That Monday, the night following the weekend, in her bed-sitter, was the first time I slept with her. Slept in her. Made love with her. Slept inside her. We climbed into the bed already too small for one body, and squeezed our bodies, back to belly, with my arms round her waist, but high enough to touch her breasts, while she remained motionless, and breathing heavily, and whispering, "Do you think we are doing the right thing?" And then she said, "Let me take my pills, first."

I had no answer for her. The strong smell of her body, with the trace of incense, wisteria, and the beating of our two hearts which turned into one soft, sweet thudding, lulled me to sleep sooner than I had wanted. The last words I heard before I drifted off were, "I feel so safe now I've taken my pills, lying here." No woman, even the ones I once drew in fantasy, had ever said so beautiful a thing like that.

So, here I am now, in this garden, sitting on this wooden deck.

But before Room had left to make me face this strange crowd alone, she had insisted that I call her, no matter the hour; and she would drive all the way back into this Pickering darkness and distance, to take me home. That was the arrangement. She would come west, and then back along this never-ending street, called Yonge, that could take her into the farther wilderness of the north, in case she did not pay attention to the increasing numbers on the street, or missed a turn. Room would not fall asleep at the wheel.

She kissed me before I got out of her old Chrysler. She held her body through the window with the glass wound down.

"It is summer," she said, placing her hand on my shoulder, the way she always did when she wanted to reassure me that some action or behaviour of mine was not unforgivable. Patting me on the shoulder the same way my mother used to do, when I had dutifully attended to my chores, and had done a little more without being asked. She said, "It's a nice day. Go and enjoy yourself. You need to relax. You will find someone to talk to."

"I hope so!" I said.

She smiled and kissed me, and said, "I will, one o' these days. Join you and your friends. I love you."

"See you soon."

"I'll be back. Coming back is always shorter. . . ."

I walked away from her, going through the alleyway, walking the length of the beds of red and pink impatiens, hearing the conversations in the garden, the laughter and the noise of bottles and glasses. It took me the time to travel that short distance to realize that when she said, "You will find someone to talk to," that she had no idea how correct she was. But before I had fully turned the corner to face the crowd standing amongst the impatiens, I was ready to turn back and go home with her. Go back with her. I was beginning to share her view about crowds.

I tried not to think of the short life of this summer.

The leg of this woman sitting beside me has become heavy. She is now relaxed in my company. Her familiarity makes me relax too, and I think of her as my sister, and I am her favourite brother, or cousin, so free and platonic and fresh has our conversation caused our meeting to become.

I had always hoped, even with Room now in my life – and I admit that I have failed to convince Room that she should end her supplications to God concerning my constancy, and accept my promise – that I could enter a conversation, or a relationship, that contains no motive, that would develop no critical reaction to a woman's clothes or her body, that I would disregard a silver ring in the nose, or in the navel, or two rings in one ear, one silver, one red; a relationship that would have no ulterior intention at all. But this time, on this burning hot afternoon in July, I feel myself creeping closer to a carnal desire, the kind of passion that I once fantasized about in the room with no lights on, with the piercing dagger stabs of the trumpet of Miles Davis.

I am facing this other woman now who is being so accommodatingly talkative, and at times silent, cavalier with her trust, as she empties her heart and her mind in words. I know she cannot enter my life, through any artery of softness, in words or entreaty.

But there is something about this woman that makes me uncomfortable, and that intrigues me at the same time.

I can see her knees as she extends her legs across my white linen trousers. A long time has passed. She has made new creases. The marks caused by her legs criss-cross the work of the cleaners where the West Indian woman works. I must ask that woman who makes creases what is her name?

I can see her knees, and the expanse of the tanned flesh of her leg, one inch above that knee. I am beginning to miss some of her words. My mind is wandering over courts and saris and naked bodies, and Room praying on the cold floor covered by the shiny, slippery linoleum that smells of disinfectant.

If it is true that passion and desire and fantasy can be transmitted through parts of the body, through a limb, for instance, or an eye, a hand, a finger, or a touch, then I am certain that should the red wine last like the sun, and the guests continue to drift out into the closing afternoon and the coming on of darkness, saying, as they leave, as if they believe their own words, "I had a good time, but I have to go. Thank you very much," and walk slowly to their cars and to their own destinations and destinies worked out over drinks, then this conversation that I am having with this strange woman can exhaust all honourable words and intention, and take a plunge of brute passion and of blunt desire.

Room does not wear dresses that are so loose. Room's dresses are not so transparent, even to the wandering, penetrating eye. And she does not wear clothes that have any colour other than white and grey and black and brown. Room favours brown.

"It's very warm," she says. "My colours, what you call my colours . . . passion in my book . . . is on the inside."

We were lying on the floor one Friday night; and we were talking about the sacrifice of self that comes from living in a country where we were not born; and then I said that I would like to be married to her on the twenty-third of August, and in a church as big as St. James' Cathedral, the church of my friend the Judge, with choir and incense teeming and holy water and soloists, like those of Trinity College Chapel, which is on a smaller scale, and walk beside her up that bare, white sepulchre of an aisle, close, so close that I can feel her blood and the material she is dressed in, a long, flowing, richly embroidered Polynesian robe with pearls and jewellery on it, in colours of gold and crimson and with white piping; and instead of Bach or Steiner or "Jerusalem," ukuleles in the loft. . . .

She sprang up from the carpet. Sat upright and stiffened and said, "Never!"

I thought her reaction was caused by a mosquito.

"What do you mean by 'never'?"

"I'll never wear those colours! I have never worn them in Kiambo, in the Philippines. I will never wear those colours in Canada. Gowns, for God's sake, Malcolm! Not even for you. I shall never, ever put a Polynesian robe on my body, as you call it."

"A Filipino woman, and . . ."

"Don't say it! I am from Kiambo, southern Philippines. I never wore coloured robes there," she said. "And I don't believe in Canadian multiculturalism of colours and robes."

I never asked the question again.

It must have been her dislike of showing her body, in the flowing robe which somehow conceals so much and exposes so much at the same time, that caused her to sleep beside me, in her basement, dressed in her long flannel nightgown, and, at my house, in the green Chinese officer's uniform.

I have never in broad daylight seen her legs, except through the thick, bubbled glass of her shower, which shows her out of focus and larger than life. Or unless she is undressing. Or kneeling to say her prayers. And in those states, it is just a glimpse, and then she shuts the door.

This woman beside me now is giving me a private exhibition of her thighs. The breeze exposes her thighs each time it rises. The breeze and her flowing summer frock. The temptation caused by this breeze that I can feel is like the cool, rich wine going down my throat.

But I am not going to let it happen. Room will not be long. She is coming to get me.

Something about this afternoon and the red wine makes me want me to go back to my Room, and kneel beside her, beside her side of the bed, on the cold linoleum that has particles of dust on it that stick into my knees, and pray with her, and assure her that her doubt will melt, with time.

So I brush from my mind the crawling effect of this woman's legs and her skin and the wine itself.

I shall continue to enjoy the frolic with our words in conversation that is turning this time into flirtation that is more rich and wandering, and which now takes us on this hammered wooden deck with the heads of nails jutting into our flesh over water that is calm and that is rolling into waves of holiday and vacation, somewhere to the horizon which is itself moving away from us as we move towards it.

I have not asked her any question that is personal. And I do not intend to. I would be showing interest. Besides, in about two hours, Room will be heading back in this direction, to take me back down to her bedsitter. And even though the hour will be late, she will still kneel in her flannel nightgown, to say her prayers. And even though I shall not join her in any brotherhood of similar disposition, she will be beside me, just her and me, without crowds, and I will smell the incensed fragrance of her body. For my mind is full of the scent of incense: "Original Healing Incense for Stress & Tension Relieving Inhalant Pure Tibetan Herbal Incense." But she will have nothing to do with this "healing incense formula is a traditional Tibetan medication for stress and tension."

Then, without warning, our conversation begins to take in her life. And to take in mine. But hers more than mine. Evening is coming over the wooden deck. And with the evening are mosquitoes and bugs and flies.

The flowers are deeper and the breeze is blowing softly into our faces. Before this, when the sun was harsh and hot, she was a private and unknown woman, someone walking along in the same direction on the hard, hot, concrete pavement, but anonymous. Now, as the light is more oblique, hitting us at a milder angle, and with each new sip of red wine, I am losing that clear outline of her body, and my senses themselves are like the first shadows, mixing into the same shapelessness of indecision the process of getting to know her. And in this strange exchange of frankness which normally I am unwilling to allow to pierce my privacy, she is crawling under my skin and my protection, and is getting to know me.

I can smell the roses that are clinging to the unpainted cedar slats nailed against the side of the kitchen facing me. They are in the neighbour's backyard. I see their profusion gone wild. In this light, in this familiarity, everything is richer, deeper, darker, like splotches of blood. Except they are roses. I can taste the wind blowing off the sea water from the blue skies. I turn my eyes to see if the hostess has planted any roses this year. There are none. Only the impatiens and the zinnias and the geraniums. And plants whose names I do not know, planted in rocks, amongst rocks, growing out of rocks like worms. She leans over, takes the bottle from the seat of the aluminum deck chair next to her, and the two glasses, which almost slip through the space between the unpainted cedar slats of the deck, and she pours the two glasses right up to the rim. The sun, not quite dead yet, dances on the crystal and dances on the colour of the wine. I think of Communion wine poured by my friend the priest, and of drinking that consecrated, holier wine, as I was poised on my knees in the sacristy in his cathedral church, and of drinking that other wine in that other small church in the small island, in the hot shirt-sticking first Sunday of each month. I drank that wine, in that island, kneeling in the same posture, each such first Sunday of all my first nineteen years lived in that island. And then, at that tender age, thirty years ago, I came to live in this half a continent.

"Married?" she says.

The wine splutters out of my mouth. My white linen trousers are stained. The mark spreads around my fly. I will have to explain this to Room. The woman I am sitting beside takes a paper napkin, wraps it round a wine bottle to absorb the sweat, and then she applies the dampened napkin to my fly, moving it up and down.

"Gimme your handkerchief!" she says, continuing to move the soggy napkin up and down my pants, which is getting less red and more pink as she rubs.

"No. Are you?" I say. And I wonder what Room would say if she heard this answer. And what she would want me to answer.

"Thought of it."

She is laying stress on her words again.

She puts the napkin in the chair beside her.

"Do I look like it?" I say. And the moment I say this, it sounds stupid. And I feel a small betrayal of Room. I am like a man who is married who is making an excuse to delude a woman who wants to think he is not married. "No," I say, seeking to erase the deception, and the misunderstanding. "How does one look? Or is supposed to look? A married man, I mean."

I look at her. She sips her wine, and allows it to wet her lips, as if she is being careless. "You have to admit you have the look. The position, I suppose. The money, maybe? Well, yes. I'd say so, wouldn't you?"

The light is changing. The colour of her hair changes in this new light.

She knows something about me. I am beginning to like her emphasis. My friend the priest and Judge had mentioned something about a woman, a member of his congregation. I wonder if she is that person. She knows something about me.

"You?" I ask her. And before she answers, my mind goes back to her talk about travel and immigrants clogging up her country and using her Visa; and my hand goes back to my jacket breast pocket, to my wallet. "You?" I ask a second time.

"You asked me that already. Don't you ever remember what you say? Are you an absent-minded professor? Don't judges have to remember what people say or something?"

Her legs are the colour of rosé wine. The new light of the day shows me her new colours: the colour of her hair and the colour of her skin. And of her eyes. Her eyes are three colours. The balls are white, pure white. Her pupils are dark brown. And the pool of changing, telling circles that holds her pupils are grey. Her eyes show a deep kindness, a deep softness, a deeper treachery than the movements of her body, her gestures, a clearer picture of her soul than the words she has spoken all afternoon.

"You asked me that already," she says a second time.

I am beginning to like her abrasiveness.

"Children?"

"No."

"That's great!" she says.

I cannot understand her enthusiasm. I love children. I was an only child for four years; and then, without warning, six brothers and one sister dropped upon my sole possession of the few toys and the scoops of homemade Sunday ice cream, upon my absolute possession of the small playroom, all of them, this new sudden brood, in five short, screaming, bawling, peeing years. And there are twin brothers amongst this brood. Do I really like children? And do I really like my six brothers and my sister? Perhaps not.

But when she expresses her glee at my dislike for children, a smile breaks her face into a wider, softer roundness, and I can see her teeth; and I can see her eyes take on four colours, and become smaller, and softer, too; and her breathing is making her breasts heave, just a little, as if they are trying to penetrate her brassiere, through the light summer dress. She appears in that moment as if there is Chinese in her blood, and then that ethnicity disappears altogether, and is replaced with a broad-faced Inuit look, her eyes closing and the colour rising to her cheeks.

The way the sun is slanting and striking her body shows me the straps of her bra, the thin line edged in lace, and where it meets the curve of her breasts.

"Great!"

Her exclamation comes from nowhere, appearing out of the changing colour of the skies. She speaks in a low, melodious voice. Her words are soft and clear, but with a clip, and with a trace of an English accent, even though she says over and over that she is "only Canadian, pure Canadian."

My hope, or my fantasy – assuming that men have fantasies – comes back to me: I am searching for thirty years after the first nineteen, almost to the day, for a relationship of no doubt or depravity. A relationship with no question, or with no suspiciousness in it. For *one* relationship of love, based upon talk and touch and words; the touch of words.

"'Course these days you don't have to be married to have *children*."

"Or at any other time!"

I am teasing her. I want her to declare her thoughts once more. My own thoughts remain in my fantasy. If I can get to know her views, they will give me the confidence and the power to fail – or otherwise – without having to guide her thinking along the paths to my own beliefs, assuming that her own thoughts are not too liberal and frightening for my narrowed mind fashioned in an island.

Am I being jealous? Already? Bidding for control and supremacy? This talk and thought of power? Sexual power, they call it? Is it sexual? Like my interest in the Indian woman who sits before me in sari and rings and bangles on her arms and wrists and toes? And in her nose? No! I am a gentleman who is a Judge.

I cannot live now even within the comfort of my own fantasy. Is this the way a man born in an island is conditioned to think? And is supposed to think? My thoughts begin to shame me.

I continue to hold the glass, and do not think of drinking the red liquid in it. It is summer. And the wine is rich and red and its body is like blood. On her left wrist is a very expensive watch, and on the same hand, twinned with the Rolex, is a thin gold chain. Her fingernails look as if each has been dipped ineradicably into ten small vials of thick red wine, or thick blood, or thick nail polish. They have been flashing each time she moves her hands in emphasis for words and for speech.

All that light back in the island, so different from this, and with the glare thrown by the sun that seldom disappoints, slashing on the surface of the seas, making the eyes weak, and forcing the vision to fade in the shimmering brightness, that tropical light bathes me like sea water in a feeling of confidence that surrounds me now. Does she see this kind of light? And does the different colour in the island's sun – and does she meet this kind of light on any of her travels in the Far East and the southern hemisphere, and learn to know anything about it – does the island's sun show me to her in this light?

The dog lowers his penis. It is like a stem from one of the branches that holds the red begonias. The dog trots in this freshness of attitude to my left leg. I brush him aside. The heat is coming from the sun. I do not know dogs. Rover was my only experiment; and I treated her as a dog. "Dogs amongst doctors!" my mother had been saying for nineteen years in my hearing; and in all that time, I never understood the hidden meaning in this philosophy.

I have to move this dog a second time.

The woman pretends she does not notice the stem of greed growing between the dog's thighs. I wonder what kind of a dog trainer she is.

"I wish to have a child?" she says, as if she is asking a question. "Someday, you know?" I look at her body. At her stomach. I hope she does not know as much about dogs as I do. I can no longer see her clearly as in the earlier light, for the shade from the awning that covers the deck has fallen thick and is making the outline of her thighs softer and less pronounced. They are now, in this new light, less defined.

Her arms are well tanned in an even cover of velvet, and are heavy. Her legs remain the colour of rosé wine. They have not changed. I pass my eyes across her neck. There is a smudge there. I will learn, later, that it is a scar. It is the same colour, almost, as her skin. Her skin is covered with almost invisible, bodiless hair, like the hair that covers a ripe peach.

The woman who owns the house, and who has built this wooden deck on which we sail through our life into unknown adventure, opens the door to the living room to let a cat out. Before the dog scampers from the cat, it arches its back and pulls its stem in. And I have enough light to see the woman's neck, and see the scar that stretches across her collarbone, at a slant. It is three inches long. It runs down into the shape of the V, the shape of her bone structure and the shape of the space between her breasts.

The knife that made this scar was held in a man's hand. Perhaps his finger did it. She fell from the pillion of his motorcycle one night, going too fast, too dark, too drunk.

"*I* want to have children."

She had been drinking with him before she raised her skirt to mount the pillion. I am still in conjecture about the cause of her scar when she continues to speak about wanting children.

"One, perhaps? A girl?"

The wine makes her lips wet. I feel she does it purposely. It brings out the wickedness in her face, her eyes blaze and I see their three colours, and her mouth is wide and all her teeth show, are pulled back from her lips, and creases appear under her chin, a kind of wild virulence, a kind of daring common amongst some upper-class women is now painted on her face. The wine makes her eyes look wild. Not wild. But daring. Playfully daring. Perhaps, it is merely that the wine has slipped from her mouth or from her glass.

I hope that she is about to say that, even though we are still strangers, in her wish to have a child, I am being considered. And as I think of it, I regret it. Just for the ego of it, I thought it. But I do not mind having a child from her. Because, for that to happen, I will first have to know her, as the Bible says. Something like Bathsheba knowing David, and Solomon knowing Sheba. We read these passages in Scripture classes back there, and giggled and were mature and intelligent enough to see this trick the Good Book was trying to play on us, after the older boys, who had gone through these classes before us, and these truths, had told us the real, true meaning of the transitive verb "to know." They were bragging themselves with their superior knowledge, and in this boastful fashion handed it down to us in the lower forms.

I would like it said that I know her. And have a child with her. I hope she cannot read my thoughts.

"But not with a man like you, though," she says.

I am offended. And stunned. She can read my mind. And angry. In order to stave off further disappointment, I become disregarding and callous, defensive against further penetration. In order to guard against more assaults on my manhood, on my secretive nature, I think for a fleeting moment of going back to the fantasies of women I used to draw in the dark, small room, holding the pictures of their bodies in my hands, and becoming contented, filled, satiated, and climaxed with the muted trumpet of Miles Davis. "Someday My Prince Will Come." For with these portraits of women that I used to draw, no shape, no word, no dismissal, and no remonstrance could occur unless I had myself daubed the paint with one of these characteristics.

I have made up my mind that this woman is intelligent. But I still feel awkward for the recited expression of views and trained thinking, the sway this thinking has built, and my own silence and crippling reservation that the island has schooled me in, narrowly – or narrow-mindedly? – I am still ill at ease to face women and motherhood, childbirth and the neglect of mothers after birth. And after children.

But I must remember that I am living on half a continent, and should correct myself, and follow the paths of this continent, with order and orderliness that lead me to make unspoken, hidden sentiments appropriate to the cold weather and regimen of continents.

Her views are beginning to irritate me, to get under my skin. I wish I was not the man I am.

"I have already chosen the *person?*" she says, with her usual emphasis on the last word.

Not even in that island where flowers bud and blossom all year round, where fruits ripen with golden plentifulness, and things are born and fully grown in record time, and rot sets in equally fast, are fathers selected in this way. They play and shine in the game of cricket; and no woman worth her salt in the wind that blows with equal force and freshness from over the Atlantic Ocean, to become the sea at Gravesend Beach, and then blows over the entire island, no woman worth her salt, getting wet in anticipation of passion, would bring this "trouble" of childbirth upon herself. No woman that I know: not Room, not even the West Indian woman who works in the cleaners – for she's been here too long! – would voice such a desire to carry this burden through life by herself, after having carried it for nine months within herself, then deliver it, and guide it independently, on her own, by herself, from those cricketing men.

She is crawling under my skin. I am waiting to hear what other sentiment she can express to shock my small, islanded looking-out upon the world of continents.

My body is leaning out of the chair, towards her. The chair is hard. I can feel the hotness in the breeze. The stain on my trousers is like faded red ink on the white linen. In that same Scripture class, when we wrote our answers in the exercise book with a blue cover, the ink I used, which came from Canada, from a distant cousin here somewhere, working in the Farm Scheme, was crimson. And the fountain pen leaked. And stained my fingers. Thumb. Index. And second finger.

I can feel the wine making my head light. I can taste the saltiness in the breeze over the sea. I draw myself up, sitting at attention, and feel my chest tighten. July is the time for allergies and asthma. I am in that tension of attentiveness. I paint a picture of her belly, ovalled and lovely, marked by veins and the knife of an earlier Caesarian operation, making her related by this nobility of history to Macduff, "from his mother's womb untimely ripp'd," and therefore untouched by the wand of magic and witchcraft, because the mark of that knife, now stretched like a balloon beyond its capability, has left the new stomach, six months high.

Or I am walking beside her. It is around eight o'clock in the evening. I have planned my walk to match this hour. It is a time when the inhabitants of the tall apartment buildings have come from work, and have locked themselves in for the night, hating work and hating company; when the dishes are put into the machine, after dinner, when few men and women willing to walk their dinners down are available to witness what had been planted surreptitiously when they were not looking, and is public knowledge now, and can be discovered in plain daylight to be reaped. I shall walk beside her when there are no witnesses. And no women to stop and stare, and stoop and hold down and look into the perambulator and tickle the "little fella, coozie-coozie-coo, wadda darling, eh, nice woozie-woozie . . . niiiiice, likkle pickinney dat!"

"It takes after the mother!"

"Me sey, who brown pickney dat, eh, bwoy?"

Whose child is this? With this colour? The women look a second time at the man walking beside the woman with her belly flattened by delivery and the passing of pain and pang and blood and navel-string, and they glance ambivalently, doubtfully at his pride. And then all is forgotten. Put out of the mind. Mother, daddy, baby, cradle and all. But the hidden planter of this seed dropped stealthily in the dead of winter can no longer hide beneath the thick blankets of his lasciviousness.

My seed moves and kicks beneath a maternity dress billowing like a tent, although there is no breeze in winter, when these nightly eight-o'clock constitutionals are taken in the deserted streets, in the St. Clair–Avenue Road–Davisville–Yonge Street area.

And, sure as anything, I meet the West Indian woman working late, coming from her overtime hours with no pay from the cleaners. The space between her teeth, clenched in disapproval, has grown wider now. She knows what that space could have meant for me and her. When she looks at me now, her eyes are arrows baited with poison. I hear the reprimand in them.

"Feh my parrrt, they always running feh white 'oman!"

The bearer of my seed sees nothing amiss in the eyes of this West Indian woman, and says, "Hi! You're working so late?"

The woman smiles with the taste of vinegar.

"When you was picking up your cleaning the last three months," she tells the mother of my pink-black child, in plainer English, "you was carrying pickney, you was pregnant? You was pregnant all that time I seeing you?"

Or I picture myself walking down my dinner and the mother walking off the kicking of this once-hidden seed, every evening along the concrete sidewalk, from Eglinton and Yonge, to Davisville and Yonge, to Merton and Yonge, to Summerhill and Yonge, remembering the significance of Merton Street where the Ex-Toggery store is, just in case things get tight with this growing family, and we have to live in second-hand clothes, in hand-me-downs, and the Summerhill liquor store, which provides solace and forgetfulness when this growing time does get tight. All these Toronto streets, starting out from downtown, near the Eaton Centre, the centre for black men and black boys, who do not know their history and the meaning of Huron Street and Bathurst Street – which are streets they should choose to "lime" on, for they are black streets, back streets – no, these downtown streets are streets I shall avoid with my pink-black child, the fantasy of my loins. Second-hand clothes and cheap Ontario wine. I know I shall take my cleaning in my child's perambulator like a bundle buggy, my bumble-bunny and I, to any other store, and hope and pray that the woman behind the counter is not a woman from the islands, and with no space between her teeth.

"I have this friend? I told him we should have a child. Together."

I can no longer feel the warm peace the wine had given me. The scar on her neck becomes a laceration, ugly and raw and festering. It is a slash received in a fit of hatred. Animosities of wars fought long ago can leave this kind of hatred.

"I told him, straight? I said the child will be my full responsibility only. The caring for the child. And bringing him up?"

"You said you wanted a girl."

"A girl, in a natural situation." She seems flustered. "Boy or girl. What's the difference? I always call a baby a *he*. It's the way we've been socialized in this country."

I measure myself against this unknown father. He is six-foot-six. Brawny and bronzed. He jogs every morning and every evening. In the snow and sleet, along slippery sidewalks. And if he cannot do it before he leaves his apartment for work, he carries the equipment of his obsession with him in a parachute bag, on the subway. He has an exercise bicycle. And wears skin-fitting pants that show his balls and his penis bulging through. And long blond hair, ending down his back in a ponytail. And his penis is the size of the leg of this table that is between us. I must not comment any more on the size; but why do I mention it? I examine the leg of the table again instead.

On the table are bowls of potato salad, platters of barbecue spare ribs and barbecue chicken. Hamburgers look like blackened old dog shit piled against curbs and trees. And the wieners for the hot dogs. And watermelons. They look like striped, green explosives. There was a time when I made sure I sat far, far, far from watermelons. Watermelons and people from the island did not mix. In public. No picnic table with sliced watermelons pulled me to its succulence. And he is younger. And he dresses in clothes picked carefully from men's fashion magazines. *GQ*. And the glossy ones from the Bay and Eaton's. And Holt Renfrew's *Men's View*.

He was not born and raised in an island.

"I told him I'll cover all the expenses. Day *care*? Doctor's appointments? *Diaper* service? For I absolutely hate store-bought diapers. Don't you? And babysitters, and so on? I intend to care for the child. Take time off from work. Not one goddamn thing would my friend be responsible for. Even bringing it up. I will bear all the expense, and my friend won't have to worry about me going after him for child support. Or for the child's university education? Just have the child. With *me*?"

She takes a sip from her glass.

"But men're such bastards!"

She says all this as if she has been rehearsing it for some time, for nine months. And it just came out, naturally, as a birth. She is talking as if she has already conceived, and is now justifying a decision made perhaps under circumstances similar to this one: meeting a man; falling in love with him; disclosing her secrets and fantasies; explaining to him all his frailties and honesty and love, and complete subordination to her; and getting sexual with him after one short social intercourse.

It seems as if all she is waiting for now, all she needs to wait on, is the moment of victory. Birth.

I look at her stomach again. Her dress is too loose for me to tell the age of the imagined child in her belly. She lives, as I do, in clouds of wishful thinking. But the longer I look, the higher her belly seems to rise. It is her assertiveness which makes her even more attractive than she was, when I first sat down beside her hours ago.

I sat beside her hours ago, only to ask her for a light.

Did I ask her? Or did she offer it? I had watched her smoking her cigarette, stubbing it after two pulls, and lighting another, and another; and the way she held her cigarette, with her little finger cocked at an angle, impressed me that she was, well . . . sophisticated. She held the cigarette in her left hand, some distance from her face, as if exhibiting it. She might just have been tense. Or bored.

Now, in her determination to express this independence of spirit to me, a stranger, who is not prepared for it, even now after all this time, during this casual conversation, passing time in drinking wine, she nevertheless becomes attractive in all respects. It is the result of being in the same position, like watching movies an entire afternoon, and becoming part of the fantasy. Time. And sitting in the same position. You get accustomed to time, and to this kind of sedentariness. And you wallow in it. And it becomes your character. And your life. And you feel it is the only chance, the only reality, the only opportunity for your salvation.

Nothing beyond this wooden deck and this woman exists. Nothing beyond this has meaning.

I like her hair. I like her fingernails. I like her legs. I like her size. Size ten, or eleven? I like her mind. Although it makes me uncomfortable. And I look at her, almost staring, almost rude, as I sometimes do on the subway, searching to place a woman's face from the past, searching to catch her eyes, to make a present, thinking of a future, wondering.

"My friend?" Her voice startles me from my reverie. "My friend would only have to help me get the child?"

The wine on her lips is like a smear of saliva. And when she turns her face to get the light from her Dunhill lighter that I am holding to the tip of her cigarette, her lips look as if they are chapped. The wine has now made her lips undesirable.

She takes a puff on the cigarette, and a sip of the wine, and the effect is even more dramatic. If I knew more about movies, I would say that she is now a replica of Greta Garbo. Or Bette Davis. But with the light from the gold Dunhill lighter comes a transformation. Her entire body becomes old and ravaged by children and childbirth. Before my eyes, in this flicker of light, she has changed. She is no longer lithe and athletic, soft and well proportioned. She is taking on another shape.

The sun I know, and grew up with, does this damage to bodies and limbs and meat and figs.

I think of the short shrivelled life of things in the island. The flattened flanks of Rover, disabled by the humidity, unable to walk with the gait she had when she was in heat, after her belly grew, got swollen at the sides, and dropped and almost touched the parched earth. And the cane-field worker dragging his legs and his fork and his crocus bag, and his body, through the last yards of thick, wet soil to reach his home. I think of the last sparrow bird to reach his home in the top of the shack-shack tree, heavy and wobbling because he had stopped to get a last drink of water from the cock of the hosepipe watering a lawn, and the hose had slipped and turned his feathers into grey-black sheets of slate, or aluminum, like those on the roof of our house. I think of the shape her body will assume in pregnancy, when her legs will be thick with blue veins, when her gait will be heavy and lumbering.

She is nearing delivery. She is bearing her fantasy and her avarice in the uncompromising sun.

I do not wish to hear any more. The summer warmth is gone. The day is getting old. It must be seven or eight o'clock by now.

Flies and mosquitoes and large moths, bugs, are invisible in the light. The light has the same opaqueness as their colour. Bugs pass in front of my face. I can hear the noise they make in their travels.

It is getting darker and damp. And things that crawl in these nights, black like those in the island, are coming out, multiplied by the wet slimy darkness of fertility. The mosquitoes are invisible to me. But the dog plays hide-and-seek with them. And I can feel their presence. And imagine where they have passed.

I had not, back then in the island, heard any woman talk about such a choice. And none was raised with so much choice.

67

No woman had ever carried in her slowed-down lumbering gait, throughout our village such liberal views of independence and childbirth. Could not in the language and narrative of rhetoric and custom, heavy as the load she is bearing, consider her own body her own. No woman held such masculine opinion in a body so young, and so feminine. This kind of resignation and reality, this kind of toughness and independence was for older women and grandmothers. And women married to spinsterhood. And women born in continents.

She said that she is twenty-eight. I think that twenty-eight is still too young to be so resigned and broadminded, volunteering her body to this experience, to this experiment. It is also too businesslike. If she were forty-four, it would make more rational sense. For she would have had, by that age, sixteen more years of fertile choice, and would not, as she is acting now, be a woman with only one choice left to deal with. But choice is choice. And choice is woman. And choice is feminine. Still . . . I think she is much older than twenty-eight.

But what, in these times, in 1998, is natural? And is not natural? And normal? And who is?

I am beginning to fall in love with this woman.

The air becomes tinged with a chill, unusual for July. Perhaps, in this night, getting older, with time that passes unnoticed, I am imagining changing moods and light. The red wine in my glass has no warmth. I become restless.

I am not sure now that she considers me a suitable childmaker. So why am I hanging around?

Dismissed and not chosen, I surrender and run, back to the island, to that chapter that spanned years and years of screeling children, and an unspoken fear that all children in the village will die. There was an epidemic of barely spoken words like the epidemic of the sickness itself. There is a panic whispered throughout the neighbourhood, that all the children will die of pneumonia, single or double. It is an affliction. A curse. A blight. And some will die of typhoid fever.

There are not sufficient beds in the public wards of the general hospital. And here, in this cold continent, when the oil in the heating furnace has run out, and the company does not trust your credit, nights of heavy, wet diapers and lasting rain and wet eyes from teething, and gas that does not escape the small bowels of the shivering boy-child, will cause this kind of affliction. This epidemic. This general fear that stalks through the community. It will keep you awake. I am glad she has not chosen me to father the child she intends to bring into this city.

And there, where my brothers and single sister cannot even tell my mother and my father what is the origin of their pain, because they lie in hot and cold shivers on the fevered sheets soaked in their hot perspiration and warm urine, there is no hope they will last beyond the gathering of the dusk. No tomorrow.

"This fever, boy! This fever is a killer."

One brother died two days after he was admitted to the public ward. One brother spent four weeks lying in hot-and-cold shivering silence, reading the Acts of the Apostles. And it was he who told me in my ear two things I shall never forget.

"I saw the nurses take five bodies out," he said in his weakening voice. "All five o' them was dead."

And, when he waited until his disappearing strength came back to him, he whispered, the second time, "I saw the nurse kissing a man, after she came back from taking out the fifth dead. The man was the orderly."

Cold and dead. One brother, no more than two years old, screamed in cantankerous frustration when the round black stopper had been left by mistake in the bottle of brackish miraculous-bush tea, whitened with milk from the sheep tied out in the backyard like a dog. The bush tea and the sheep's milk were better than any medicine measured and poured by the village's apothecary.

The milkish-looking liquid did not pour and flow through the pinpoint hole in the brown nipple, with its natural satisfying flow, into his hungry stomach. And I did not know, until after he had screamed for most of the night, and had eventually screamed himself to sleep, that I should have taken the round black stopper – inserted for safety – out first, before I plunged the nipple into his mouth.

I could have killed him, through neglect.

And another time, when two sisters, the children of my mother's sister, who grew into angels, fell out of their twinned perambulators, I wished that my mother had more than one daughter, and more prams and more accidents. They did not die, from accident or fever.

But sitting here this evening, on this wooden deck, with the large aluminum heads of nails jutting out, I am not sure if I want to be a father. Or the father of this woman's child. Being a brother has been enough preparation for this refusal.

At any rate, I have not been asked, or propositioned, directly, to try my luck.

Perhaps, it is my age. How old am I, really? Too old to cut the mustard any more? Perhaps, it is my birth and breeding in the island that colours my age.

She does not once mention the island. She does not know about the island. She does not know islands. They have not been destinations in her holidaying journeys.

But she could hate the island and love me. Or love the island and hate me. Like white Southerners with black music and black people. Perhaps, with her intuition, she has seen in me, from the very first exchange of greeting and the lighting of my cigarette, and from the few words I have contributed to this conversation, she has seen not one single quality she admires in the unknown, lucky man she has picked to produce the child.

I imagine a scene in the life I may live with her. We are locked in quarrel. The quarrel degenerates into violence. It is a bout of sparring words. Violence is the best man of marriage and relationships in this large city, on this half a continent. The quarrel is engulfing us in the jabbing and punching of words. Our words smash our skin, and leave wemms, bruises that dark glasses and makeup cannot conceal. It is the words themselves that conceived the quarrel. Words that are meant to liberate us and bring us closer. We are drenched in a "dry row." This is my mother's term for these spontaneous, pointless spats that erupt like new fires in a cane field and that feed on themselves and level the entire field and many houses in their conflagration. Fires that have no blood of passion and anger in them. But still they scorch and burn and sear everything in their path.

The quarrel is touched off by no cause. There is nothing between us. And since there is nothing between us, and I am already incensed only by her words, what then can grow out of this relationship? Sexual assault? Violence that is physical? Abuse? The assassination of dignity? Disrespect? Murder? What? And which of these six humours?

And then, afterwards, there is the better, positive picture. We walk out together, side by side, to theatre, grocery store, LCBO, the neighbourhood park, the Island, on the streetcar and subway train, and we hold hands, and in this holding, we grow close and in time, look like one another, like twins. . . .

I imagine in my life with her these scenes of joy and bliss and ecstasy. I am swallowed by the possibility of happiness. I have submerged all the lessons learned in the island beneath the greater sophistication of this half a continent. The blow delivered by her words that stun me, that she has picked *that* man for the father, is absorbed in my new married thinking.

"It takes a man to know when he is beaten," my mother said. But my mother did not, herself, include my own father in this generosity.

It is that first Garden with one man and one woman – and no snake between them – that caused this kind of thinking. We are bound in that equation fixed by the parameters of half a continent and of an island. There are only two unknowns in this simple equation. But they presume too much. They have too great a value that is hidden. They presume too heavy a calculation. Even though it is her body, even though it is her freedom she is tampering with, even though there is nothing between us, even though it is just a conversation, empty talk, there is still too much hidden in this simple equation.

In the island, I was taught a man is defined by his words, whether his words are soaked in strong rum, or in soft tenderness. And a woman, too, is bound by them. And bound to them. Whose words are more golden? Those of an island? Or those of half a continent?

I have no proof of her character, beyond her words on this summer night. Her words are the only truth.

The woman who owns the house joins us on the wooden deck. She is the same build and stature as the woman I have been sitting beside all day. Her hair is cut short round the sides, and there is a kind of muff at the front of her head, and the hair on her head is like fine needles rising upward. It is her summer style.

Her lips are heavy and full, and they make her appear as if she is always smiling. When she smiles, her eyes become smaller. Her mouth is large. I feel kindness and bountifulness when I look at her mouth. And when she smiles for the second quick time, she shows her teeth, strong and white and large.

And I can imagine her eating a thick T-bone steak, gnawing at the sweet flesh in ecstasy, picking at the bone. When she smiles, her entire face becomes round and soft, and her eyes dance. And she smiles often with me. She likes me. And I like her.

Like the woman, she has a habit of licking her top teeth whenever she laughs. They could be family. They could be twins. They could be sisters.

Her eyes are grey. I look at the Siamese cat, and see the same colour of eyes. Her eyes have only two colours: grey and black.

She is standing close to me, and for that moment I see the circles round her pupils, and smell her fragrance. It is like roses soaked in water. I do not know the name of her smell.

"I like him," she tells the woman I am sitting with, about me; and then she smiles.

She speaks with a slight lisp. Her legs are stout, and they go up into her waist, giving it the same strong, wide appearance as her hips. She is more pleasant to look at than the woman I am sitting with. I gauge this from the lightheartedness of her talk.

"You kids having a good time? Been sitting in the same place for a helluva long time, I'd say!"

She talks about the party, about the food, about the amount of booze not drunk and the beer left in bottles, and now to be thrown out – "What am I gonna do with all this shit?" – about the leftovers on paper plates strewn on the lawn, amongst her garden beds of impatiens, and she asks herself, "*Why* do I do it? For what? For who? Why'd I go to all this goddamn trouble? And for what? *Look* at this waste! This mess!" Whenever she speaks, she looks straight into the eyes of the woman I am sitting with, and then at me, and smiles. When she looks at the woman, it is as if she is seeking approval, or as if it is she who she is condemning. The woman says nothing, and lowers her head to the dog.

But I know that the point is made. This worries me. I wonder why, all of a sudden, there is this tinge of insecurity, this show of obedience and weakness in her manner?

Perhaps, it is that they know each other better than the dog and the Siamese cat are friends.

But she is pleasant, this woman who is my hostess, and her personality continues to be bubbly. And she smiles with me, and likes me; and I like her.

"Don't let the champagne get more flat and *waste*," she says. "Why don't you kids have some? Why don't the two o' you come in the house?"

"Great!" the woman I am sitting with says.

"Good," I say, "thank you."

"I like him!" she tells the woman, looking at me as she says this.

But I am ready to leave. The night is uncertain: it is clammy and humid, but I am chilly; I can feel the cool. I can no longer see the impatiens and the roses climbing on the neighbour's fence in such sharp outlines as before. The green hanging plants are deeper greens, almost mauve, are ghosts and ghouls and prehistoric snakes, and goblins, blobs in the night. The dog is sleeping. And the Siamese cat is curled in the belly and the legs of the dog. The dog opens its eyes each time the woman speaks. I marvel at the greater luck the cat has had in pacifying the dog than I did.

This woman who owns the house is wearing a summer dress that looks like a housedress. When she passes between me and the door to the living room, the light points out her nakedness beneath the white cotton dress. I do not see the outline of her panties. But later on, I see that she is wearing skin-coloured hose.

She starts to clear the glasses and the empty bottles from the deck and from the garden. She holds her cigarette in her mouth, and keeps one eye shut. And in the smoke that rises from its tip, she seems able to focus better on the dregs left in the glasses and the bits of uneaten food left on the sagging paper plates and on the edges of the wooden steps leading from the deck down into the garden.

I watch her pick up a piece of chicken leg torn down to its pink bone from the seat of a deck chair and toss it with anger into a garbage pail. In the island, we would have tossed this bone to Rover, or let the neighbour's cats and the neighbour-hood pack of five wild dogs fight her for it.

"Shit!" she says, when the bone misses the pail.

"Great!" the woman says, as she is holding my arm, as she is about to lead me into the house.

But she changes her mind. The woman who owns the house has just thrown a glance in her direction. A glance like a dagger. I do not understand the look. But immediately my arm is released. She goes into the house with the other woman. It is dutifulness, obedience, that I can see in her gait.

The dog and the Siamese cat are left to keep me company. Inside, the two women are laughing.

I can see the screen of the television. And I can hear their voices, but I cannot make out their words. Then, their voices seem to become strained with mild annoyance. A gently flowing tension, like stale gutter water. Something is wrong. I think the time has come to call Room. I think of the time it will take her to drive all the way from Huron Street up into these hickies to get me, and then back down Yonge Street to get home, and kneel beside her when we get to her bedsitter. I am not going home, tonight.

The screen door separates me from them. The dog and the cat are stretching their backs into arches. The cat is almost the size of the dog. Its arch becomes higher and rises, as if its spine has no bones, into a pinnacle. I can see this kind of a cat in those books about Indian temples guarding gods and protecting superstitions.

Inside the house, the women's voices are now raised. Something has happened while I was studying the cat and the dog. And then their voices get lower, as if they have moved away into a farther corner of the living room, away from the screen door, away from the cat and the dog and me, into a room that leads to the kitchen of the house, or into a bedroom. And then, suddenly, they are laughing, and their voices become loud again. I think of the organ in the Anglican church back in the island when the pump I am moving up and down fills the bowels of the organ with fresh power, fills the bellows, and the organ roars louder in a sudden intake of air.

I hear the noise of dishes being put on counters, and see the temper; and then the dishes are placed in the dishwasher. And then there is no sound at all. And then there is more giggling.

Just as I become accustomed to this, relaxed in the long drive back, sitting in silence beside Room driving me south on Yonge, after she has travelled west on the 401, their voices come to me on the wooden deck. Voices. Firecrackers. Up in the enveloping deep blueness of night, there are no sparkles. The Fourth of July was two weeks ago.

The woman who owns the house comes to the screen door and looks out at me, and smiles. Beside her are two more cats. The dog smells the cats and growls. The cats stand their ground and the dog returns to its dozing.

"Coffee?" she says, preventing the cats from escaping.

"Great!" It is the voice of the woman I had been sitting with coming from deep inside the house.

She comes to the door, and stands beside the woman. Her arm is round the woman's waist. Women show this familiarity more easily than men. They look like cousins, standing there. Like sisters.

"Why *don't* we?"

"Don't we what?"

And they laugh, and hold each other more closely.

I feel the warmth in the hostess's invitation. I cannot see her eyes, although she is still standing at the screen door. But I can smell her perfume. I can see that she is a few years older than she seemed earlier, when the sun was sharp, and the creases under her chin blended into her complexion.

I am surprised that in this softer light, the glow it casts on her face makes her face seem cruel, and stern, and old. She is now an older sister.

"I am so pleased to meet you," she says. "I am Eireene. E . . . eye . . . rrr . . . double-ee . . . enn, with an *e*."

"I am very pleased to meet you," I tell her.

"Great!" It is the woman I was sitting with who says this, making Eireene look sharply at her, as she stands beside me. She is saying something to the woman in a kind of whisper, in a kind of code, in a kind of pig Latin that I cannot make out. And every now and then she turns to look away. And when she faces me again, her expression changes, and she smiles. She moves farther from me, and says something to Eireene which I cannot hear.

"Guess I'd better prepare the coffee," the hostess says. She remains at the screen door even after she says this.

The shadows are growing thicker. The hostess flicks a switch beside her and a single naked bulb lights up and just touches the shadows like a kiss, a smack of acquaintance. The bulb is attracting bugs. So she turns it off.

The scar on her neck. It is like an irritation which has to be rubbed, in order to get relief from its itching, before the itch can be quelled. There is barely enough light on the deck. It is dark and quiet. In my mind hours ago, I had taken her summer dress off, and flung it into a bed of red impatiens that was blazing in the sun. I stripped her naked to her underwear. Thongs. Bikini. Strings. Not a string on! Naked. Her belly was not flat. There was a mole beside her navel. She looked as if she were four months' pregnant. I thought of her friend she wants to have the child with.

"I'm going to Weight Watchers? What for, I don't know. Who'm I kidding?"

Her wish of childbirth seems more realistic now than even her words have expressed.

I was satisfying my lust and fantasy. Painting her in outline, with my eyes.

I rest my eyes now on her knee. With the naked bulb

switched off, it is just the right amount of cover for this indulgence. It is the right knee. There is a slash on this knee. It is as if someone has tried to lift the cap from off the bone, with a knife. And has almost succeeded, so deep and painful-looking is the scar. I try to guess how old the scar is. It goes from just beneath the kneecap downward at a slight angle. I imagine that this man, her friend, in some mental torment about not wanting to father the child she wants him to father, has tried to express to her in an obvious manner his disagreement with her proposal and has ripped the flesh from her knee with his bare fingers. She had escaped that violence just in the nick of time. Had slipped out of his grasp. Had fallen. And had damaged her knee on a sharp stone, like those on the edge of these garden beds, which keep the water and the loose soil in.

This scar has a compelling, magnetic effect upon me. It causes me to rest my hand on it, and feel its dead skin. It is cold. The rest of her leg is warm.

Her talk earlier about the child is now out of my mind. But she brings it back.

"The friend I want the child with?" she says. She says it as if it is a complete thought, a sentence, a finished proposal. But she then realizes that she has not said it all, so she says, "He's gay," as if she is asking herself the question, as if she is asking me. She says it as an afterthought. It takes me a while to say anything, to think anything.

"Gay?" I ask her.

"*Gay?*" she says. But it is not a question.

She is asking for my opinion, and at the same time is making a statement of protest, an assertion that does not brook comment.

And I give her none.

Long ago, before either she or I was born, that word, "gay," had a different meaning. It was a word for exuberance. Gaiety. Epicureanism. It carried a meaning of joy, lighthearted-ness, bohemianism, full of naughtiness. I go back in my mind now, back to the island, to that usage and that meaning.

"The friend I want my baby with . . . is gay," she says a third time. There is nothing in her voice. Just the word. With no sentiment in it.

"*Gay*," she says, for the fourth time. "He's just gay, that's all. . . ."

The word comes from her mouth like a bullet, nevertheless. It sends me plunging back over the waves, back over the passage of time to that night when my mother had put me to sit down, in the dim front-house lit by a kerosene lamp, so dim that we could have been sitting in darkness, even though she placed me close to the lamp, which cast a shadow over her face and over my face, and over her confusion.

"*Bullers!*" my mother said.

I had never heard the word. And she made me know, before she uttered one more word, by another death-like silence, that the severity of what she was about to say to me was not going to be pleasant or lighthearted. The silence that fell in the gloomily lit house seemed to have body and a voice, like that silence that falls at home and in the headmaster's office the moment the tamarind rod is lifted to test its pliability.

Her words slow and ponderous and foreboding, spoken one at a time, seemingly individuals, like deadly body punches, or like the single ding of the church bell when tolling, someone is dead; like damnation, purgatory, and Judgment Day, she began to speak.

"Before. I speak. Another word. And tell you. What. I have to tell you. I want the truth. Truth outta you! You hear me?"

"Yes, Ma."

"When I leave you in this house by yourself, anybody does come in here?"

"No, Ma."

"Whilst I at church?"

"No, Ma."

"In Town, shopping?"

"No, Ma."

"*Whenever?* And wherever?"

"No, Ma."

"Nobody, at-all, at-all?"

"No, Ma."

"Not even Sister James from my church?"

"Sister James does come and knock, and when I don't answer the door, she does leave."

"Good!"

And there is silence. That silence that announces victory, a shocking victory, the victory of relief.

"I know I shouldn' leave you alone by yourself. But nobody at-all?"

"No, Ma."

"None o' your teachers?"

"My teachers, Ma?"

"Yes, your teachers."

"No, Ma."

"The Scoutmaster?"

"No, Ma."

"Good!"

The silence at the end of my answer is shorter, and just as deadly.

"I should 'a' left you in the Cubs a li'l more longer, 'cause I did-feel safe with you in the command of the Cub-mistress,

Miss Smythe. Is your father who say that you was getting too big for the Cubs, and that you should be in the Scouts."

"No, Ma."

"No, what?"

"That I not too big . . ."

"The choirmaster?"

"No, Ma."

"Nor the sexton of the church?"

"Nobody don't come here when you isn't here, Ma."

"Good." There is a pause. I can hear the dog in the yard. And a cock crowing. "It suh-hard to bring you up, suh-hard to bring up a child these days without all this evil that swirling 'bout this place touching you, boy. . . ."

"Yes, Ma."

"All these bantu-people with their bantu ways, crawling 'bout the place, all these people acting like real bantus . . ."

I had never heard that word "bantu" before. Not in my schoolbooks, not in the books I borrowed from the public library every Saturday morning, not in the magazines which my mother's women friends, young women who worked in homes as maids and cooks, and who stole copies of the *London Illustrated News*, *Punch*, *Vanity Fair*, and *The Children's Paper* from their English employers, and gave to me – none of these books and magazines held that word, "bantu." It was such a strange word. And it sounded as if it was not born anywhere in the British Empire. For I would know the existence of such a word, if it had.

"Remember what I tell you, boy."

"Yes, Ma."

"Don't tek no sweeties, nor comforts, nor sugar cakes, from *nobody'* hand!"

"No, Ma."

"Not even a' Extra Strong peppermint."

"No, Ma."

"Nor a Kit-Kat chocolate bar."

"No, Ma."

"Nor nothing to eat, to put in your mout'! You hear me, boy?"

"Yes, Ma."

"No sugar cake!"

"No, Ma.

"Not even a slice o' sweetbread!"

"No, Ma."

"And *even* if it is my own-own mother, come back from the grave . . . rest her soul! . . . anybody at-all . . ."

It seems now that her words are tears, cry-water drops hitting the hardwood floor.

I can hear the ratchet of the three-speed bicycle passing in front of our house, *click-click! click-click!* and hear the bell, *kuh-ling-kuh-ling-kuh-ling!* and I know it is Johnnie summoning me to a game of rounders, with the girls, on Highgate Pasture, below our house, and my mother screams, "You not crossing that threshold till I finish with you! Johnnie *could wait!*"

And she began to tell me a story.

"Not long ago, not fifteen minutes ago, whilst I was returning back from down in Town, this big-able, hard-back man . . ."

She stopped talking. Her eyes filled up with water. The rest of the words seemed too heavy for her voice to bear. In the dim light, her tears were crystal sprays of sea water running down her cheeks.

The tears came freely into her eyes and into her voice.

"This big-big man lure . . . *lure* this poor little boy, who hasn't even lost his mother's features yet, a little, little boy. And with a gift of *sweeties!* A blasted lollipop. A lollipop, you hear me? And when you hear the shout! . . . when everything was done . . . and he finish his business with that li'l boy . . . Oh my God in Heaven! . . . Look, boy, go and bring my Bible to me! . . . His *virginity!* You listening to what I am telling you? His virginity! That little boy's virginity!"

She stopped for breath. She allowed the tears to fall on the bodice of her white pleated dress and into her lap.

"That hard-back brute bring his lawlessness to that little boy! Oh Lord Jesus Christ in Heaven, have mercy! My Bible, boy! Bring my Bible to me! . . . His virginity, boy! His virginity!"

I had never heard the word "lure" before that night. But I knew it did not mean silver or gold or frankincense or myrrh, or precious metals that I had read about in magazines about the mysteries and treasures in India. I had never heard the word from her, accustomed to using words in the funeral procession of her lugubrious manner, always in lowered voice, like a whisper, when the subject was my chastisement, or the narration of a ghost story.

But I had heard the bigger boys, talking about the bigger girls, use this word "virginity." On my own, I did not know about "virginity"; and I did not know enough about men and women to know if only women had this thing, this "virginity." The bigger boys told me, the next day, when I mentioned my mother's story to them, "Men don't have nothing like virginity, boy! Because they is men."

From that day in the island, until this night in this half a continent, my lips have never touched a lollipop.

My mother fell asleep that night, with the Bible in her lap, after saying over and over, "That sweet little boy was my god-child. My godchild, my little godchild . . ."

She is tender and fragile. A "flower" is what she calls herself. She tells me the kind of flower it is, all about its fragility and short span of life. And its spectacular beauty. But in the heat of talking, I misunderstand all her words and clues of description, and forget the name of the flower she uses to describe her own delicacy. Years later, however, when she did not provide nor repeat the clue, as it had been laid that summer afternoon, and I asked her the simple question, "What is the name of that flower you told me about, that summer?" she flounced her head and rolled her eyes and walked away. And she turned around, and came back and kissed me flat and full and wet, on my lips. I felt the Pepsodent toothpaste on her tongue, deep inside my mouth. But when I first asked the question, and she did not answer, I behaved like a man and became angry. The clue had been given to me on a platter, that first night. And the moment she used the epithet to describe the flower she said she is, it passed from my mind. "Flower" was powerful enough.

The cats are now inside the house. They are scratching against the mesh at the bottom half of the screen door.

A voice comes to me. It is her voice. Her voice comes to me like a wave that is in that sea which drags up skeletons of crabs, of fish, and of men, drowned in its ancient fury. They have all, fish and skeletons and bodies, crashed against the rusty iron pipe and the breakwater that the sea itself is eating away.

She has been talking, while I am dreaming. "Took a long time. A very long time. Years? For me to remember and be able to admit it to myself . . . that I too, went through . . . molesting? That I too's've been molested?"

In her voice, I hear my mother's voice that turned my blood into something cold, like ice water, when she told me about her godson's loss of virginity.

The woman takes a cigarette from her cigarette case. It is shaped like a lady's purse. It has a silver clasp. The case is red leather. She lights a cigarette for herself, and then offers me one, after it is lit. I refuse it. She drops it on the wooden deck, and crushes it with the heel of her sandal. The cigarette turns into brown dust.

The tip of her cigarette is a light warning me, taking me to that island where danger with the seas is beaconed to me from the lighthouse's whirling eye.

"My parents'd take me down to Michigan, to visit my *uncle?*" she says, putting stress and a raised tone on the last word in her statement. "For years they were taking me there. To leave me with him? Take me there. And leave me? And my uncle always said that I was the darling of his eye? His favourite niece out of all his other nieces and nephews from his brothers and sisters. I never asked my own brother what happened to him. Anyway. So my mother would leave me with him, while she and Dad went off to Las Vegas to play blackjack. Or when they stayed in Arizona, in the winter, for their holidays. For Chrissakes! Leaving me with that maniac? That bantu-bastard . . ."

"Bantu?"

"You never heard that word? Where you from?"

"Bantu?"

"My mother and Dad left me with him. He lived in Michigan, I don't remember the name of the town,

Dearbourne, Dearborn, or something, 'cause . . . I'm sure that I am trying not to remember the name of the place where he lived, 'cause I don't really want to remember it. I try not to remember the name of the town. And they'd drive from Canada in their Volvo station wagon all the way down to Las Vegas, or Arizona. Phoenix, for Chrissakes? And that is when it was happening. I didn't know what was really happening to me at the beginning? I remember my uncle putting me in his lap. His lap was so warm. And then putting me on his knee, and tickling me until tears would come to my eyes, and I would be giggling and laughing and I am screaming and crying and shivering all the time, at the same time. And him, that bantu-bastard, rubbing me here?"

Her words pinned me against the cedar planks of the wooden deck on which we were sitting. And I could feel each individual punch in each of her words as it nailed me further against this deck. I was shaking with anger. Violence had entered my mind with each word. Each word, each punch from her lips, became my own means of attack on this man, on this uncle.

I stood up and went to her, and stood behind her chair, and I put my hands on her shoulders. And feeling that this gesture was not what I had intended to demonstrate to her – and to myself – how she had rocked me with the punches of her words, I touched her hair, fumbling in the first stage of an embrace. The smell of the shampoo she used, and of the fragrance of the perfume round her neck, rose. I held over, and kissed her on her forehead.

"What'd ya do *that* for?"

She held her head up, looking into my eyes from this very close distance. I could see the veins, and the marks on her lips, made clear by the peach-coloured lipstick which the sun had beaten into a more opaque tint, and her eyes with their three colours, and one new colour, the colour of grief. And the beautiful complexion of her skin.

She placed her hands on my hands, now resting on her neck and shoulders. I could feel the warmth in them. And at the same time I had the sensation that they were cold. Cold as a handshake in winter.

"What'd ya do *that* for?"

"I, I . . . I don't know."

"It's all right. You don't have to have a reason, 'cause there's nothing to say. Nothing you can do . . ."

I could feel the first trace of saltiness against my face, as if I were standing too close to the waves at Gravesend Beach, and the wind was high and was sweeping the waves high in the air, to mix with the wind, and then deposit itself against the surface of the sea water, and against my face.

"Sit down. Sit down," she said. Her voice was so soft and kind. "Please, sit down. I'm all right. *Please*," she said.

And I went back to my chair, and sat beside her as I had been doing for such a long time now. It was very little different from any day, back there, when I was a boy, when my mother made a gesture to show me her consideration for my clumsy demonstration of love. Love. Consideration. Respect.

". . . would be laughing and crying and screaming like bloody hell and crying and shivering at the same time. And him rubbing me here!"

She touches the spot. She touches the spot with index and third finger, with the cigarette still in her hand. It is not really a touch. It is more like an act of brushing a speck, a crumb, an insect in the summer from a bowl of fruit, or from a leg. And then she is fed up with the cigarette in her hand, and she stubs it into the glass of red wine, and it seems as if she is ridding herself both of the wine and of that part of her body that she has just touched.

The cigarette makes a fizzing sound against the wine. There is only one half-inch left in the glass. She twists the cigarette into the half-inch of wine until the cigarette loses its shape and its colour, until it is bent, until it dissolves into the wine, and becomes dirty. It is now the colour of old, melting snow at the side of the road in November. Or mud. Not even wet sand.

I watch this through the tears forming in my eyes. And I feel strong to feel this disintegration. I do not know how long my tears shall flow, and in what other time and place. But they feel warm, and I feel useless.

We – she and I – have now become close, in this bond. She is beside me. I can touch her. And feel and know her pain. I hear her words, and memorize her story.

We have now become joined. Me and this woman. And the time passed between us, with the words, is not any longer an afternoon but a life, a life of confidence that makes her reach this depth of a confession. Tears.

I want to fall on my knees beside this woman, and wait on this silent deserted deck, with its two inhabitants, and listen and hear what prayers she is capable of spitting into the face of her experience she has just disclosed to me.

"And do you know? I been trying to tell this to my mother. My own mother? Just to tell her about this, to have somebody to bear this with me for the last fifteen years? And then one day, she starts to believe me. You'd think she would be the bloody *first* to believe me! That bantu-bitch! I'm talking about my own mother. Would've been a *mother*, for Chrissakes, for the first time in her bloody life! You see, my uncle is her favourite brother. Her favourite brother? The more things I told her. Like how I would be sitting. By myself. When she and Dad returned from playing blackjack. And from Vegas or Arizona. The more she started to try to remember. One thing brought out the other. One detail. Led to another memory. Including all those times. When she'd come back from Vegas broke. As usual? And the one time she found me on the curb by the front gate. In the cold. Crying? Without my mittens on? Or my coat? Then, she finally decided to listen. To the whole story? And me calling up the past? She finally decided to listen. And I was giving her details and pointing and drawing with my finger so she'd see that what I was telling her was the truth? I was giving her details about her own brother, for Chrissakes! The truth, the whole truth, and nothing but the bloody truth, for Chrissakes!"

I try to look at her closely, when she is not aware of it, to see if I can see what is in her heart, what is in her mind, what she is capable of hiding, of holding back – if anything. What could there be left to withhold, after what she has just told me? And I can see nothing. Nothing but a woman who is very beautiful. And strong. A blessed woman. A woman I have sat beside on this wooden deck, from when the sun was a zenith of heat, to this moment of falling darkness, in this evening, not so dark as dusk can be back there in the island, but nevertheless the same theatre of sudden sunset and mosquitoes and fireflies and crickets and night bats, the scenery that presages the bringing out of tales and emptying of cupboards and skeletons that can break your heart.

She takes another cigarette from her leather case. She holds it for a long time before lighting it.

I am remembering that Friday afternoon, when the tide changed its mind and held me by my waist and legs and threw me into the mountain of the wave, and I died once, in the belly of the wave. And it was only the brightness of the sun that kept the total darkness out.

She is still holding the cigarette, unlit. Finally, she lights it, and immediately afterward throws it into the bed of impatiens. These impatiens have now been eaten up in the darkness.

"She was madder'n hell! I thought she was going to get up right outta her chair, and fly down there to Dearborn, Michigan, and shoot the bantu-bastard, *him*!" She pulls another cigarette from her case. "Before she could believe what I'd been telling her, she had to believe her own brother was capable . . . The bastard! Prick! She told me this herself, a year later."

"When?"

"What d'you mean, when?"

"When she told you?"

"What does it matter?"

"It's not what I mean . . ."

"I was twenty-three or -four . . . something. When I told her. Fifteen years after it happened. It happened many times. She told me some crap, last year. Shit about first having to believe it was her own brother before she dare accept the heavy weight of accusing him, before she could bring herself to believe me, and believe that I was telling the truth. Her goddamn brother!"

"What did he do?"

"Why? Is there a difference?"

She takes another, her third, cigarette from her case. I saw this as her way of occupying her hands, of controlling them from shaking, which I could see. And she lights the cigarette. In the long white stream that she shoots from her lips and through her nostrils, she says, "Why're men such pricks, eh?" and laughs. She extinguishes the cigarette on the floorboards of the deck. She does not crush it with her shoe this time. "Now why would what he does . . . *did*, be important? And you don't even know him!"

She shoots another stream from a new cigarette, through her nostrils only.

"Dick."

"That's his name?"

"Dick."

"Dick?"

"Rhymes with prick! That's what I said his name was. Dick. Prick. Ricky, Ricardo. Rick Ricardo the Prick."

"Ricardo Who?"

"If I had the child, if my friend wasn't so chicken, Ricardo's the name I would call my son. It's a lovely name! I don't mind saying so. It's all right to mention his name, now. I've forgiven. He's my uncle, after all. I don't like many skeletons to be in our family's closet! That kinda man, some women feel, don't deserve to have balls. Or a prick. Some women have used knives. Cut it the fuck *off*! Not worth living, some women would tell you. He's a fucking animal. But not me. I can't bring myself to call my own uncle an animal. What would that leave me? An animal too? An animal-ette? A bantu-lette? So it's not a matter of Ricardo Who. He's my uncle. He has my family's name. That's probably what my mother was trying to say. But she couldn't say it, because she couldn't find the right words, and didn't have the insight to put her feelings into the words she wanted. So, you know the name. You know who it is. What difference is it? Is it life? Is it fate? Or our individual experience? But if you want to know the truth, Ricardo is not his real name."

She leans over and whispers a name into my ear. In my present state, with the wine, with fatigue and with drowsiness, I do not hear it.

"I could not keep . . . just could not, did not want to hang on to his real name, walking around with it, taking it to bed every night with me, this burden. . . . And you could understand why now, can't you?"

"I am sorry," I say.

"Few men would say that. But then again, few men would know what to say, would not know the correct thing to say to a woman. Thanks."

"I am really sorry."

"You're sweet. I know you are sorry. I don't know why, but the moment you came around that corner there . . ."

YEARS HAVE PASSED. I AM now living with the woman. I sold my house and moved in with her. My friend, the Judge and priest, told me when I told him what I had done, "You frigging fool!" I laughed.

"You sure?" he said.

"Sure I'm sure!"

"I should hear your confession, one of these days."

"My confession?"

"Seriously."

I have not yet met her friend whom she said she had chosen for fatherhood. Perhaps he never existed. I am coming to believe that some of the things she told me about, on that summer afternoon in July on the wooden deck, never took place.

Perhaps it was her sense of humour, her sense of the dramatic, her cynicism, her way of making me feel at home, something. Some of it was the guile she used to jolt me, and to test my sincerity and my broadmindedness. Or my endurance. Perhaps, it was simply the wine.

Between us now, there is less conversation. Less need for that kind of protracted conversation. Not a fraction of the words that passed between us on that afternoon. We talk and laugh, and listen to music, but not to our hearts, and not with the passion for communication that we once knew. Our verbal exchanges are mainly about meals, the food we eat, the food that we should not eat, about cholesterol, about why we do not talk to each other more often, about arriving at the apartment and departing, and arguments about going to Tafelmusic concerts, and arguments about spending week-ends in hotels when our apartment is comfortable and large and well furnished and has four large windows and a wide balcony and a solarium. And about bills. And about not paying them – on time.

"Why should we give them the opportunity to make interest on our money?"

The best pills for my sinus and allergies is one of the things we talk about a lot. We talk about foods that contain low fat, or no fat at all. With her, as we discuss these health matters, usually after dinner, I am attentive and co-operative. But at lunch with my friend the priest, he and I order T-bone steak and rib steak and pork chops, lamb chops and hunks of ham, and lots of bread with butter, and we eat and laugh at the regimen for protecting health and for ensuring long life that is imposed upon us by the women in our lives. At the apartment, I dutifully eat whatever she suggests, and cooks and places before me: fish, three times a week, with two vegetables, broccoli and string beans; chicken without the skin, two nights a week, and boiled carrots, and with no gravy or sauce. On Fridays and Saturdays, spaghetti. And every Sunday, forty-eight Sundays of each year, roast beef and Yorkshire pudding. She is an excellent cook, as she is an excellent lover, whirling and laughing and screaming in bed and then crying.

"I'm gonna kill you one o' these days!" she threatened me, and dearly wanted to carry it out.

I am suffering from the healthy meals she cooks.

And when we have exhausted all these important topics of conversation, important and frivolous, which define the boundaries of our living together, and when she thinks of it, usually three times a month, on a Friday night, when we eat spaghetti, and when it is she who wants it to happen, we have sex.

"Should we have sex?" she says, making it sound like an inquiry. But already in her mind, settled. And as plain as that.

"Put your cards on the table," is the phrase that comes into my mind whenever she says, "Should we have sex?"

I am living in a different world from the one with flowers in a garden, with dew and water from the hose, and bugs and flies and green worms on the plants and flowers, cut off from the passion of that summer afternoon that seems so long ago.

Late on cold sleepless nights, when her body beside mine is warm, and she is breathing through her mouth, I lie quiet, pretending to be asleep. And my thoughts leave all this wealth and luxury in this large apartment, and escape through the large picture window to the north, ooze out like a genie from a bottle, and circle above, always this, circling above that small, clean basement bedsitter on Huron Street, with the linoleum, and the single bed with the iron springs, and the devout Filipino woman who lives in it, Room. It is because I did not end our relationship properly, did not return to the scene of the crime, a dog to its vomit, that I am suffering the sorrow I have caused. . . .

The last time I saw Room was on that July afternoon, when she drove me to the party. She was wearing brown Crimplene slacks, brown leather sandals, and an orange T-shirt, 20-per-cent cotton, 80-per-cent polyester . . . thinking of that last phone call, and thinking of that last time and not seeing her since.

In all these years this woman and I have been together, two . . . it could be three, or four. Three years are long and do not really measure time, they measure days and long nights of a sentence. I have forgotten to count . . . she has never mentioned her uncle, and seldom her mother.

We have no children.

I really do not know how hard we have tried. Three times a month, for two years; or is it three years? Twelve months in one year; multiply twelve by two, or three . . .

Her friend Eireene, the owner of the house, who built the wooden deck where we met, began by hovering on the horizon of our lives, and has now become part of our lives. She visits us often as a sister would, more often than this woman's mother. As often as a social worker, or a godmother.

She still laughs with me when she comes to the apartment, and says, "You're one of the family."

Eireene is part of the household now, just like a pet, just like our pet, just like a sister. At Christmas and Easter and Thanksgiving and Canada Day, and for my wife's birthday, her chair and place at the table are set.

Whenever Eireene is at the apartment, I feel safe and protected, and I laugh a lot, but I suffer very badly from allergies. It is then that I go into the bathroom, lock the door, and turn on the hot-water tap full blast. And light a stick of Himalayan Healing Incense. And without my urging, see Room in the mist and vapour that rise like clouds.

Eireene passes messages to my wife, in my presence, on small yellow pieces of sticky paper that secretaries use, notes written of the things I might have said to the woman I am living with; and the woman I am living with agrees with her more often than she agrees with me.

When Eireene is not at the apartment, there are no words of animosity that pass between the woman I am living with and me. No words pass at all: we exist peacefully, in this created silence.

At first, when we were still making love, often as a whim and a wish, she insisted on precautions. And then she said she cannot have children, should not have children – putting it as a question and an answer – and cannot bear them. She told me so again, only one week ago, when Eireene was at the apartment.

"Do you think I am goddamn crazy to bring a child into this home?"

"Do you think she's crazy to bring children into this world?" Eireene said.

And then the woman I am living with said, as if to smooth what her anger had inflicted, "You *know* I . . . that we cannot have children! Tell him Eireene!"

Eireene did not tell me; but I wondered how she would know. But I, a man from a custom and place of asking no questions – "Ask no questions; hear no lies!" – schooled in this catechism, I knew that I should not ask the reason.

So, we have no child. Only the dog.

But before this stiffening of her attitude, she did say later on the wooden deck when we were still able to talk that, if her male friend did not agree to have the child with her, there was another way. "I could adopt." I did not answer her, then.

The dog and Eireene are our children. My wife talks to Eireene and to the dog more easily and with more affection than she seems able to do with me.

"I can't communicate with you any more," she says.

The dog sleeps in the large queen-size bed with us. In the middle. Between me and her. Every morning I find him snoring between her legs. When I am asleep at last, after counting sheep in endless fields, I do not know in which trough of comfort the dog lies. He knows he cannot cuddle up to me, or kiss me, when I am awake.

When I was about to leave Eireene's house that night, I went to the telephone in the kitchen to call Room, to ask her to come and get me. I dialled her number. But the line was busy. It was about that time of night when Room usually talked on the telephone with her mother and father in Thunder Bay.

The second time I entered the kitchen to call Room, the woman rested her middle finger, which had a silver ring with a turquoise stone, on the cradle of the telephone, and cut me off. I did not protest. I did not condone the impulse. The hour was still daring and naughty. And there was still seductiveness in the evening. And also, because the wine had implanted this daring and adventure into my mind, I was not thinking clearly. But I did nothing about it. I sometimes wonder, in new fantasies which are too painful now to draw, even in the brightness of daylight, how life would have turned out had she not touched the telephone.

"You're going with me," she said. Eireene shot her a glance, like a long, fat icicle. "In a taxi," she added.

Eireene continued to look at her in a sharp, cutting, and questioning reproach. She then saw me looking at her, and she averted her eyes, and smiled with me. But the glance of dis-approval had spoken words of rejection and caution.

"You're taking him home?" Eireene said, a bit later, back in the kitchen, too loudly, louder than she had intended.

"We're sharing a cab."

"*Call* me when you get home."

She sounded like a protective friend, or sister.

Eireene's attitude now rested upon the woman standing silently beside me, as disapproval, as we prepared to leave. I felt a sudden, cold sensation from the way Eireene had looked at her. But I did not put more meaning to it, other than that Eireene did not think it safe. Besides, as she had said more than once, "I like him," meaning me. "I like him." I was a stranger, someone she had met for the first time, at her party, someone she smiled with, and said she liked.

The coffee was eventually prepared, and we looked at photographs taken in Spain the previous winter. I saw Eireene in a white bikini.

There was another photograph, this one of Eireene with a woman. It is out of focus. I could see Eireene kneeling in front of the woman. Her right hand is placed on the woman's back. The woman lying on her right side, getting the lotion rubbed into her back, that woman is now the woman I am living with.

There was no strap round her back, just the mark where the strap had covered the skin. There was a mark, the colour of natural skin, where the brassiere had been taken off. The scar on her left kneebone had reddened in the tropical sun. Eireene was lying on her left side.

I wondered who the photographer was.

But my viewing of the photographs was interrupted by the serving of coffee and homemade cookies. They were delicious.

The woman I was with put a tape in the stereo, and we listened to music, especially the song about strange fruit, which was played over and over during the party. And we had more coffee, this time the woman I was with making espresso for herself and for Eireene. And we looked at more photographs, which Eireene selected for me to look at. She showed me each photograph with a laughing running commentary. "There's me! There's her!" The woman I was sitting beside took each photo from my hand and said, "Great!" And after coffee, as if the party were about to begin afresh, we had the champagne from the bottles already opened, and then liqueurs. And then the taxi came.

The driver rang the doorbell five times, in quick succession, as if playing the notes in a song. I went to the door, on their suggestion.

"Because it's late," Eireene said, "and it could be unsafe for a woman to answer the door at this time of night." And she added, "Not knowing."

"Not knowing," the woman with whom I had been sitting said. "What son of a bitch could be out there ringing the goddamn doorbell!"

I saw the driver, a man from either Africa or the West Indies, and I waved to him.

"Right!" he said. And when I heard his accent, I knew he was not from the West Indies. "I been driving round this neighbourhood for fifteen minutes now. Trying to find this address."

She came after me, along the hallway, walking beside Eireene. I looked back when I heard the front door close and then their footsteps on the gravel path. Eireene dropped her left hand from her waist. She and Eireene then stopped at the top of the steps leading into another garden at the front, and then they walked on down a little distance from each other, and beside the garden beds which seemed to be growing out of the concrete pathway. They kissed each other goodnight, as women kiss, saying goodbye. Their backs were turned towards me.

"Goodnight, dear," Eireene said. She looked at me and said, "I like him." And smiled.

I was at the opened rear door of the taxi, listening to the driver saying over and over, "Fifteen to twenty minutes I driving through this neighbourhood . . ."

"Goodnight, dear," Eireene said again. "I hope you had a good birthday party."

"Goodnight, Eireene," the other woman said. "Great! Was a great time! I had a great time!"

"I like him," Eireene said, and smiled. "*Call* when you get home."

And it was when she moved away from Eireene's embrace that I noticed the long string of leather which got longer as the small, ugly dog scampered into the garden beds, sniffing and raising a hind leg; and the leash got shorter when he was pulled into some reluctant obedience. This dog that had been licking my ankles and smelling my crotch all afternoon and night belonged to the woman who was taking me home.

The dog was placed between us by her. For the long drive during which no word was spoken, either by me or by her, the dog jumped from me to her. I could not show my true attitude to dogs. In the taxi with the three of us was the shrill loud voice of the taxi driver, asking for directions from his dispatcher, and the voice of the dispatcher screeching his advice with turned-up volume into the small speaker. "*You better, I think . . . you better take a turn at the next lights . . .*"

And the noise of the dog sniffing the seat, sniffing her lap, and snorting and wagging its tail, and sniffing me between my legs accompanied us south along Yonge Street.

"He just *loves* taxis!" she said. "Don't you, doggy-woggy?"

The driver said he did not understand why it was so difficult to find places in Toronto, when it was so easy to find any street in Mombassa, where he came from.

We did not speak to him, after that declaration.

We live in this large two-bedroom apartment with a solarium and a large balcony, in the same area as the cleaners where the West Indian with the space between her teeth works.

One month after we started living together, the cleaners lost the pair of white linen trousers I had worn to the birth-day party, in July.

"Man, these people always lossing your clothes!" she said.

"What can I do?" I told her.

"Sue them! That's what I would do. You want to write in a complaint? I would witness it!"

"It's an old pair of trousers."

"You sure?"

The following afternoon, the woman I live with in this apartment came home in tears. The cleaners where the West Indian woman works had lost her favourite cream silk blouse. It was a gift from Eireene for her last birthday, she said.

"I hate them?" she said, with her usual emphasis. And nothing more.

I thought of gifts and birthdays and favourite silk blouses and West Indian women who work in cleaners.

The dog is left alone, to himself, during the day, while we are at work. She takes the subway to College, goes into College Park, walks south past the post office, a coffee shop, a clean-ers, Black's Photography, W.H. Smith, and then through a passageway with large glass panels, westwards past Kentucky Fried, a coffee shop, and then north, to enter the elevator across the indoor plaza from Grand & Toy, to her job on the eighth floor, in the provincial civil service. She is the manager of her department. And I walk and retrace those landmarks with her almost every night, in the form of little things, gifts, when she picks up a memento from almost each store and shop. An Italic pen, a plastic bag of day-old muffins, a box of Kentucky Fried Chicken on "Tooney Tuesdays," a popular novel, a set of stamps for local postage, and a lottery ticket every Wednesday and Friday. And I continue on the subway, southbound to Front Street to the court for refugees, where I sit with my friend the priest, who is also a Judge. She and I do not always leave the apartment at the same time.

The dog refuses to be induced onto the middle pages of the *Toronto Sun* newspaper.

"That's all it's worth!" she says.

She would rip the middle pages from the previous day's edition of the *Sun* and lay them on the hardwood floor, every morning at seven-fifteen, and straighten them out with the heel and tip of her high-heeled suede shoes, just before she left for work. And then she would guide the dog over to these middle pages, on a practice run, holding its collar, coaxing it, pressing its pooch to the pages, praising it, telling it, "Nice doggy. Be a nice doggy-woggy today? You a nice dog, ain't ya, nice doggy? Mama's nice doggy-woggy?"

And the dog would lie on the middle pages on its back, roll from side to side, and wag its tail, until she moved to the door to leave for work.

She tried the middle pages of another daily newspaper, the *Toronto Star*. The dog was not impressed, and was not coaxed to obedience.

Do dogs take on the preferences of their owners? She herself did not read the *Toronto Star*.

"It's big and still empty. Nothing in it to read."

She tried the middle pages of the *Globe and Mail* next. The *Globe and Mail* is our national intellectual newspaper. I do not read its editorials, nor follow the arguments in its political commentaries. But I cannot live a day without studying its horoscopes. I believe they interpret and forecast my life. The last horoscope said, in the words of Sally Brompton, "You don't have to be perfect but you do have to be honest and you have to tell partners and colleagues if you cannot deliver what you promised."

This was a nice one. I clip the nice ones and stick them on the door of the fridge, along with her yellow sticky pieces of paper, fastened by magnets in the shape of a shoe, of the head of a bear, and of the stylized body of a ladybird. She is a Cancer. "Your Daily Horoscope" does not like Cancers. Theirs are usually grim. "You have rivals who would like to see you take an embarrassing tumble."

I pinned that one above my own, and giggled all afternoon till she arrived from work.

"Fuck!" she shouted. I heard her from the bathroom although the door was shut. When I came out, wiping my hands clean, she had ripped her horoscope from the door of the fridge. Mine lay in a ball on the kitchen floor. Did it miss the garbage pail?

But the dog rejected all four pieces of the city's journalism, including the new *National Post*, and did not use them for the intended purpose.

Only once, in all the time of trial, did the dog adapt to the middle pages. These were from the Sunday *New York Times*. These middle pages from the travel section I had myself laid out, one Monday morning after she had left for work. I spread them on the floor, and secured them with thick, strong masking tape.

It was as if the dog understood vengeance. Or better journalism.

One afternoon, at five, she came through the door, after announcing "I'm home!" outside the door, as she usually did. The first thing her eyes rested on was the mound the dog had left. She saw the size of it. And smelled its scent. And its pungency. And she shrieked.

"*Shit!*"

She went to the telephone immediately, and called Eireene. She sat and talked about dogs and about work and about her supervisor, and in lowered tones and in pig Latin some comment on me, and about her supervisor again. Whenever I had to pass close to her, she lowered her voice and switched from speaking English to talking loud and audibly in pig Latin; and when I moved away, about dogs, again in plain English. The dog held his head in her lap, on the dress she had worn to work, while she chatted with Eireene. It was the blouse, detached from the skirt, which she always wore with this outfit, that the cleaners for whom the West Indian woman worked had lost.

At seven o'clock, two hours later, with the mound still on the hardwood floor, she got up from her conversation, most of which had been conducted in a whisper. Her cheeks were almost the colour of rosé wine. Her face was fresh. And she seemed relieved of some heavy weight.

Eventually, she used yards and yards of toilet paper to remove the mound. And then she ran a mop dipped in detergent and Dutch cleanser and furniture polish over the hardwood floor, and added pine-scented fluids, to purify the air. All the time hugging the dog and kissing it and saying, "You mama's doggy? You mama's good doggy-woggy, ain't ya?"

The dog is drawn to the floor in the living room, near the television. The dog watches television with us. This part of the floor is made of hardwood. And this, arranged in small rectangles varying in colour, flows into the kitchen and the dining room. When we return from work, at two different times, usually I have to hold my breath when I enter the apartment, itself breathing with the smell of piss and dog shit. I am amazed that a dog so small that it can be carried in a handbag is capable of leaving so large a load. "Doggy-woggy, I want to drown you. Daddy's doggy-woggy. Daddy want to kill you!"

We burn incense in the bedroom, in the bathroom, in the rest of the spacious apartment, and outside the door, in the hallway. Ordinary, powerful incense. I burn my Himalayan Healing Incense in the bathroom with the door locked.

She is conscious of the comments of the neighbours. Dogs are not allowed.

We burn incense, and its fragrance changes from musk to sandalwood to cherry to other exotic smells, as the dog's system changes and neutralizes the nose-burning pungency of the incense.

But I love incense. It reminds me of church, especially the cathedral church where my colleague the Judge officiates at Communion and preaches sometimes, and of choirboys and altars and high ceilings and windows that bring in the sun in colours of the rainbow, in stained glass, with the faces of angels and of Christ on the cross, stained glass made stronger with lead.

There is no relief from the dog in spite of the incense we burn. Dots and other shapes, pieces of evidence along the hardwood floor, mark out the frolicking, fun-loving nature of the dog who roams throughout the apartment like an uncaged little beast in our absence.

The dots and smeared dashes, like exclamation marks, sometimes, like Morse code, this excrement on the floor tells me that the dog is sending a message. If only this dog could talk!

But as my mother used to say, "Dogs amongst doctors."

I think of Room's bedsitter with its patterned linoleum, which she waxes with an old towel wrapped round a broom, sparkling and clean.

And I think of the quiet, the absence of words which used to bring us closer in our communion. And I think of her daily prayers, in the morning and again in the evening, and of the small Bible that she keeps on her night table, which once served for dealing cards in poker games, and of the small enamel sink in which there was never a spoon used more than one minute before, to measure the cough syrup she used to clear her voice, and her chest, and prevent colds.

"Fall on your knees, friend," my friend the priest said, through the soft, polished wooden panel of the confessional, he hidden from me behind this thick gleaming wood, and I in this box, unsafe, unprotected from the words that shall issue from *his* hidden lips. "My son, I shall hear your confession . . ." Before I can find the strength and the voice to utter a word, before I can find the strength and the legs to slip out of this heavenly presence, his voice is reading from the Collects of Good Friday. It is a Friday after work that we are in the empty church. But it is not really a Friday. It is any day after work. The hollowness of the cathedral church makes this uncertainty about the day possible, this hollowness which sends his voice bouncing back to me, from off the thick stone and the stained-glass windows. "Have mercy upon all Jews, Turks, Infidels and Hereticks, and take from them all ignorance, hardness of heart, and contempt of Thy Word . . ."

On another evening, she lost her temper with the dog, and threatened to throw it over the balcony, cursing and shouting and bloody-helling as she tiptoed and skipped from square to square, from spot to spot, trying to evade the dog's shit and vomit, as if she were playing a game of hopscotch. She did this for almost the whole hour it took her to clean the dots and dashes from the hardwood floor.

I could taste her anger. Shame for the dog's disobedience made her angrier still.

But I have never seen her train the dog. Just kiss it. And love it. And let it eat the leavings of her ice cream from her dessert dish. And call it, "Nice dog, nice little doggy. Mama's nice doggy-woggy!"

The dog is small enough to be carried in her handbag, hidden from sight and from the eyes of her bordering neighbours. And sometimes she did carry it like this. One Saturday afternoon, as we were leaving to shop in the Kensington Market, the neighbour on our left came to her door, and saw us, and slammed the door, and used a word I would not repeat. As we got near the elevator, her husband pushed his head out their door. He did not use that word, did not say anything. I know they can hear our business, the barking of the dog and her cries of ecstasy, through the thin walls that join us together as neighbours. They do not speak to us. They have never said "Good morning" in the elevator, or "Merry Christmas!" along the garlanded hall.

She was not sure of their attitude to dogs. But the dog always barked its pleasure at being transported in this manner, and exposed her.

Day after day, I watched as the hardwood floor lost its sheen, and the two colours of the rich wood became one colour, blotched, and looked more like sandpaper.

Eireene told her what she should do to bring the sheen back.

"A good brush with varnish. And lemon oil. In two twos!"

But she was too tired and frustrated, and ashamed. I was witnessing all this.

The polish did not work. The ammonia did not work. It was too strong for the finish of the hardwood.

Only one other occasion, or incident, shall I mention. Only because it irritates me and the repetition of it irritates me also.

She had ignored, or had tried to ignore, the mess left by the dog on the floor of the dining room. She had spent a long time talking to Eireene about work that day, and about dogs, and about her supervisor who had left her husband and was now living with a member of her staff.

"That is shit!" she said. And then she started to prepare our dinner. In this, as in other matters about our life together, I never seemed to have the courage, or the balls, or the outrage to tell her, "Aren't you going to clean up the mess before we sit down to dinner?" It was a Friday; and it was spaghetti she was making.

I could have cleaned it myself. But the dog was her dog.

I once tried to stop the dog from running out into the hallway, and expose her to the two neighbours on the left who we feared would report our breach of the apartment's regulations, when she screamed, "*Don't!* Ever! Again! Lay your goddamn hand on my dog! Don't have anything to do with it! Goddammit! *It's my dog!*"

In secret delight, and after her reprimand had worn off, I watched the dog use the apartment, one Saturday, room by room, as its toilet; and in my heart, I was glad to see her have to clean it. I spent all that time in the bathroom, with the door locked, to keep in the smell of my Himalayan Healing Incense.

That Saturday night the dinner she cooked was excellent. She made spaghetti better than any Italian restaurant in Little Italy, on St. Clair Avenue West. But that night I did not touch one creamy strand of the wriggling worms of pasta.

So the dog continued its happy carefree life with us. And in a way, it made me happy to see it play and roll on its back. And seeing this, and she seeing me see this, brought a respite of love and warmth into the large apartment. Her face showed me the love that was hidden inside her body. The dog had done this for me. This dog, which could be mistaken for a sausage, or a wiener, left a little too long on the barbecue spit. It would wrap its small body round my feet while I was asleep before the television set or in bed.

It was always cold in the bed. And I would drift off, after sheep and flowers by the hundreds and thousands had passed and bleated across the floral sheets, into sleep; and the bedroom would turn warm, and the dog would be comfortable in the warmth it had helped create.

In the morning, when it lay flat on its stomach on my feet, I would hate it and would want to send it flying with a kick, through the glass window, down the eight floors to its flopped, splattered end, on the iron railway tracks where the subway trains stopped in the Davisville station. The dog was not a mongrel. Not a salmon-tot retriever, like my Rover.

This small, helpless animal, endearing in its ugliness, became one cause in a line of disagreements we were to have.

Eireene continued to telephone at six every morning, to wake her up, and wake me up in the bargain – even though she sets the alarm on the hand-wound clock, and the alarm on the clock radio – and to call again at eleven each night of the week, even on those evenings when she ate dinner with us, to chat, to revisit the day, to plan, to console and advise, to deepen the sisterhood of their love for each other, to close each day with the woman I am living with.

I got to know Eireene through these whispered conversations she conducted with her friend, who would be lying on the bed, on her stomach; then change to her left side; tired on her left, change to her right; and in the heat of their words, tied in their bond, she would lie on her back and spread her legs. The dog was always with her, imitating every turn she made, and she had four large pillows propped behind her back, and the puny dog between her thighs. I got to know half of Eireene's personality, the half my wife provided me with, in those long telephone conversations conducted in screams and laughter, loud and in whispers, and in pig Latin. I got to know her as I got to know about dogs. I continued to like Eireene; and she continued to say, "I like him," as if she was calling my name.

My woman begins her mornings, even Saturdays and Sundays, with a vigorous brushing of her teeth. All this time, the first bubbles in the coffee machine are rumbling. The smell of winter and of love in the apartment is the smell of Pepsodent and Blue Mountain coffee. All this time, she moves in silence, as if in a meditation, as if angry with me, not talking, as if deeply in love – but not talking, for the radio is playing classical music – sending me a kiss and flinging it whenever I pass near her, with her kissed fingers, while she has to keep her mouth closed, because of the toothpaste – no talking by her – as she then moves throughout the apartment, banging into chairs and slamming doors of cupboards, in this daily ritual of personal cleanliness.

Her mornings follow this routine as strictly as a religious ceremony.

Eireene gave the woman I am living with the coffee machine last Christmas. It has a clock and a timer and it plays a tune, like an aria in Italian, when the espresso is ready. Eireene buys her coffee from Jamaica at international duty-free counters in America, and coffee from Kenya that is already ground. Eireene buys her nightgowns and silk panties, as gifts. Very expensive gifts. And cigarettes, plastic cigarette lighters, and cigarette cases on every vacation trip, from souvenir shops at train stations and bus terminals, and from duty-free counters. And at every celebrating anniversary. And Eireene does this, she explains, because "Eireene is my best friend. Like a sister! For Chrissakes!" And I have no difficulty, or feel no jealousy, with Eireene's generosity.

In the two and a half years, maybe three or four, that I have known her, Eireene has bought me *one* present. It is a plastic statuette of a black American woman wearing a long blue dress. She resembles a singer I have seen, a singer I heard years ago at the old Towne Tavern on Queen Street East.

The statuette wears this rich, blue dress, long and formal, with white flowers and a necklace of white pearls, every day of her life. Her hair is black, and looks like real hair, taken either from another woman who is dead, or from a pig. And I would wonder which dead person, which slaughtered animal, pig or sheep or horse, had been robbed of its natural hair to have it placed on my statuette. The head of this black American woman, this statue, turns like a real head. When I turned its head one time, as I was lying in thick bubbles, it came off, in a clean, complete decapitation, as if a guillotine had come down with vengeance upon it. And then, the rich brown oil came out.

The statuette was filled with bubble bath.

The bubble bath was made in America. The head of hair on this statuette reminded me of the long, black silken hair on the head of the Filipino woman I loved so much, Room. Where is Room now? My former Filipino lover. My former lover, my Filipino lover. Room would wash her hair in the bathroom sink, and let it hang long and wet and silky, and cover it with a large white towel, and make herself look like an Indian or an Arab or a sheikh, and walk around her damp basement apartment until her hair was dried in the humidity and the wind. And then she would sit on the edge of the narrow, single bed and run the comb gently through it in such slow fastidiousness that I thought I could count every strand of hair. And this would take hours to complete; and I would feast my eyes on her hair and her legs, eating in greater freedom all this sweet Filipino body than the imagined bodies drawn in the dark room.

In this basement, with the same dimness of lighting, there was no need to hear "Someday My Prince Will Come," no need to have faith in fantasy.

And when I touched Room's hair, it seemed like cold conger eels dripping fresh and virulent out of the sea.

Once, in playful rolling over the bed, Room tied her hair round my face, and I could feel the pulse of those thousands and thousands of women from the southern island of the Philippines, Mindanao, where she was born, an island washed by three seas and the Pacific Ocean, and smell the perfume and the incense of their breaths and the oils they put in their hair, and on their skin. And then Room tied her hair round my penis, and pulled it into a tight reef knot. The pleasure of that moment exploded like an egg whose water had boiled out, leaving only the shell. The yolk was smashed.

The statuette of the black American singer-woman was made in China. For months, I wondered which Chinese model the Chinese manufacturer had used to produce this startling Afro-American likeness?

I thanked Eireene that night for her gift. And for months, I kept the statuette on the top shelf of glass in the medicine cabinet in the bathroom. The head had been put back on, and the statuette became a woman once again.

Sometime afterwards, when the woman I am living with had used up the remaining bubbles from the statuette, before she had remembered to buy her own expensive choice from the Body Shop at Church and Wellesley, I would see the dog playing with this black American woman, nuzzling it over the unused middle pages of newspapers, chewing her hips and her head, and biting her breasts, in such ecstasy. He would sniff her natural hair, and make a noise like sneezing.

She could not run away and escape the assault on her body by this dog, because she has no legs. Her long blue dress sweeps the floor, and serves as a pedestal on which she stands. She stands in a posture of grace and contentment and feminine power and great womanly strength, just as how I have seen Room stand in a line at the cash register in the supermarket, waiting her turn, quiet and arrogant at the noise and informality around her, her right hand resting on her left, and crossed, and held in the middle of her thighs, as if she is protecting something there. I have also seen women at the Communion rail in the cathedral church stand like this, in this posture of patience as they wait to receive the body of Christ.

My lover from the Philippines has the same complexion, the same build as my statuette from Afro-America.

So, I am surrounded by Eireene's gifts to her best friend, the woman I am living with. They are the statues and monuments that define my life in this apartment, in this half a continent. They remind me of nothing in my life back in the island. Eireene's gifts and articles of remembrance include bouquets of roses, now dead and dried; a creased and folded program from an opera; ticket stubs from the Tafelmusic concerts at St. Paul's Church across the street from Loblaw on Bloor and Spadina, from Roy Thomson Hall, and from the Hummingbird Centre, where they saw *Guys and Dolls* and Harry Belafonte; an unused subway transfer, with the name of a restaurant written on it; books on weight reduction and on furniture and interior decoration; and one large, autographed book dealing with men.

These mementos are like a culture: markers and milestones, signs that give direction to their long friendship. Her friendship and mine has no such signposts.

She washes dishes in warm water, with suds billowing high as the bubbles she sometimes puts into my bath. Since we have been living together, I have never had to touch a tap to draw a regular bath for myself. Before work and before bed. The baths I take in the locked bathroom with the statuette and the Himalayan Healing Incense are special baths, baths of meditation and for fantasy. The attention she gives to me is so religious. She worships me, in this way. But when she is not looking, when she is engaged in her long conversations with Eireene, I splash about in the large deep bathtub to my heart's content, with the statue of the black American woman as my companion. My wife does not always show that she loves me. And when this happens, I spend my time taking baths, with the door locked.

And she is clean and beautiful. Strong-willed and explosive in temperament. She smokes all the time she is standing on her feet, all day long, and never empties an ashtray until it is full to overflowing.

My wife cooks all our meals. Candlelight blooms on the white tablecloth, making it rich as alabaster, with the ironed napkins of the same colour and material, and folded sometimes in the shape of pyramids, sometimes flat like thin steps of marble. But whether pyramids or steps, they look like slabs of gravestones and sacred marble. And this candlelight is there as often as she remembers to restock the candles, which she buys at discount prices from the Indian bargain stores along Yonge Street, stores stretching from the Eaton Centre all the way north to College Park and as far as Wellesley Street.

I would stand beside her, on those shopping binges, and watch her rummage through bins of goods damaged by smoke and fire and by indifferent handling and import, turning each item over, examining it, and buying it only after she has compared the price in this bin with those in other bins in other stores along Yonge Street, satisfied that she has struck the best deal. She also buys lipsticks from these stores, and pantyhose – for work – by the dozen.

On all occasions when dinner is like a romantic eating adventure, we are joined by Eireene. And we become like a family: one husband and two wives. Or two women and one man. But a family, nevertheless. And immediately after we have eaten, after I have outlasted Eireene's visit, and watched her suddenly catch herself and feel self-conscious that she has been lingering and chatting too long, and seen her about to doze off, nod, then catch herself, she would put her coffee cup down, take up her purse as if to go, take a cigarette from her cigarette case, similar to my wife's except for its colour, light the cigarette, and then say, "My God! Look at the time! I have work in the morning!" And she would remain to smoke another cigarette.

"My God!" she would say a second time, and then she would leave. And the moment she got home, she would call to say that she got home. And she and my wife would talk for one hour more. Whispers and laughter and pig Latin. I would take the opportunity to think of Room, and my friend the priest; and recently I have been conducting my own conversations with the black American statuette and addressing monologues to Room. There is no one else I have to think about, no one I know. No friends. Except Cliff and Jack and Olli, with whom I play poker on Friday nights.

I would watch the woman I am living with, with her back turned towards me, as she was buried in the four large pillows which helped to smother her words on the telephone to Eireene.

"What do you talk about?"

"Things!" she says, smiling. "Women things. Things that women talk about."

"Oh."

Or sometimes, with Eireene gone, she would lie on the couch and fall ponderously to sleep, snoring a little, for she was always tired from working hard at the office. And her voice, which I could faintly distinguish between her snores, would revisit and remember ghosts in her sleep, ghosts brought back from the past, taking her into the farther darkness of her dreams. She looked so beautiful when she lay like this.

She slept with her arms between her legs. Room slept on her back, not moving, not making a noise, the sleep of the innocent. The sleep of the sepulchre, the sleep of the dead.

I would sit in the almost total silence, and listen to the dog trying to imitate the sleeping sounds of this woman, her restlessness and her snores, and wish that I could penetrate her dreams. To find some answer to my growing unhappiness. And to understand what Eireene means to her.

Watching my wife sleep and snore in her peace and beauty and safety, I would wish I could talk to the dog, and that the dog could talk to me. If he could, I feel he would have deliberately not spoken to me, not have told me the whole truth, since speech is not feeling.

And later on, when she was roused from her nap, she and the dog and the plastic black American statuette would play. The dog would get a ball of newspaper and run after it, until the eleven-o'clock television news went off.

Now, it would be as if she too had missed an appointment.

"Look at the goddamn time, for Chrissakes!"

When the weatherman came on to tell us about more snow, the day was over for her. The newspaper ball and the black American doll would be discarded on the floor. And the dog would sit beside them, guarding them with snarls, begin to doze, and wake up again in its cat-napping slumber, to nuzzle again at the ball and the black American doll.

I would wait for the sound of water draining from her bath. For the sound of doors being shut, and of things being turned off. Life and function would be switched to silence, in an exact reversal of the order she had taken when she awoke that morning.

When she had completed her bath, she would whistle, and the dog, all ears and wagging tail, would dart into the bedroom after her.

"Come!"

And he would jump on my side of the bed, although I would not be in bed. The night was over. I was left alone . . . to read the files for tomorrow's cases, and reread "Your Daily Horoscope." Today it told me, "Stop panicking and trust your instincts." I did not pin this advice to the door of the fridge.

But when I am lying in the bathtub, the suds come up to my neck. And I think of books I read in high school, back in the island, and at university here, about women buried alive in water, with flowers strewn on the water of their graves. Ophelia and the murdered wives of Roman senators. And I think of that woman seeking to be a refugee who sat in front of me, in tears, knitting her fingers in her anxiety. I sit from the elevation of the Bench, and look down upon her, and see the gold flashes as she moves her wrists, and imagine that these golden bracelets are bells, ringing, like the bells that ring, *ting-ting!* at the start of the Holy Communion liturgy, a bell that welcomes more than it warns; and from that distance in the airless court that I am from her, the curve in her body under the sari is like the undulation of sand in a desert. . . .

One evening, during our first winter together, in this apartment, I am in the water, buried almost completely in a bank of fragrant clouds, inhaling the smell of soap and the smell of Himalayan Healing Incense, and I go over in my mind all the things that puzzle me.

There are never any answers good enough to plug the hole of insecurity and doubt. Nor fit the hole in the bathtub to keep the bathwater in until the bath is over.

But always there is the dog who continues to be my foot-warmer in the cold bed. He has not yet been trained not to paint the stained hardwood floor with his dots and dashes that demonstrate his moods, and which wash away the sheen. The dog wipes away the sheen with his own recalcitrant discipline, which is ordered as that of the subway trains that leave the station beside the apartment, on the dot of time, every day of the year.

In dog time, this dog is thirty-five years old. He has been with her in a longer relationship than the three-year journey we are travelling through.

When I am awake, the dog walks in large circles around me

and then away from me. And she, knowing the ways of dogs, and what is in my heart, lifts the dog into her arms, and kisses it, and places it between her thighs where its body is warmed by the silk of her nightgown, and the skin of her body.

It is the affection which she cannot give to me.

The corrosion of the sheen on the parqueted hardwood floor increases day by day.

One cold Friday morning in November, the clouds were heavy. They were the colour of lead. At exactly eleven o'clock, I slipped the thin, expensive gold ring on her finger.

We stood frightened and cold but full of private, speechless joy in a judge's chambers, in the small room in the Old City Hall. Courtroom Number 3. There were no witnesses. From that cold November morning, on Wednesdays, Fridays, and Saturdays, I have included the number 3 in all my lottery tickets, and not *once* has my number come up.

In this small room that smelled of soap and Javex, and with no one sitting in the chairs that lined the walls, with a few tables made of spruce and unpainted, the judge dressed in civilian clothes came to administer our vows and our sentences. We did not know his name.

"Till death do us part." He said it; and told us to say it, too.

"Till death do us part," I said.

I had heard this vow so many times when I was a choirboy. This cold Friday morning at the Old City Hall was the first time I was called upon to say it. My heart rejoiced. She was smiling all the time, and shaking as I held her. Rosewater came to my lips as I kissed her on the ear, and the cold stab of feeling from the earring in that left ear, like a drop of gold blood.

"Till death do us *part*," my wife said, making her vow sound like a question. She seemed to put the most stress on the word "part." But the room was stuffy and my allergies were violent, and I could have misunderstood her. I was also nervous. But I do think, and I am adamant about this, that when the judge said, "Till death do us part," and told us to repeat it after him, in his tone of voice, he could have said, "Death is the only sentence that can end this joy."

Queen Elizabeth the Second stared at me from her photograph near the ceiling. She was the only witness. The ceremony lasted ten minutes. We were all three, wife, judge, and me, on our lunch hour. The gold wedding ring took up a little more than one centimetre of the skin of the third finger on her left hand.

"If ever we get married," she had said to me many times, "I want it to be quick. In. And out. Just like that! Bang-bang!" And she snapped her fingers to illustrate the celerity of the ceremony she would agree to in matrimony, in holy matrimony.

One minute later, we were standing on the cold front steps of the Old City Hall. And laughing. Wondering if we should return to work. Or have a drink at the Sheraton Hotel across the street. Or, after work, at her favourite bar in the Park Plaza Hotel. Or, wait until we got home.

I had read "Your Daily Horoscope" before I left my office. It said, "Someone who is envious of your success will look for ways to make life tough for you today but they won't do it openly."

We stand on the cold steps, and people pass and look at us, and do not recognize us as newlyweds. No cheers go up. No felicitations and wishes.

And I go back in this quiet cold to that small island, to the weddings of persons I did not even know back there, and hear the shouts of approval and of admiration for the style worn

by the bride, and the cries of criticism for the way the bridesmaids look in their homemade frocks, and the laughter and
the throwing of rice by those not attending the wedding. The
laughter. "For better and for worse."

Here, in the bigger space of this half a continent, she and I
stand alone.

"Thank you," she says to me. "I really love you so *much*.
For Chrissakes, I'm your *wife*?"

And she laughs loudly, recklessly, at the sudden turn of this
dramatic event.

"In sickness, and in death . . ."

It is a cold, scary thing to say. Back there, there would be
shouts of joy.

"Good! Good! Yuh look good!"

"Treat she nice. You hear?"

"Where the two o' wunnuh spenning the honeymoon?"

"Look, child, don't mind this malicious girl! Enjoy yuh
honeymoon. You spenning the honeymoon at the Crane
Beach Hotel?"

"God bless the two o' wunnuh . . . go 'long in the name of
the Lord. . . ."

"Thank you for making me the happiest woman in the
world, today," my wife says.

When my wife says this, the magic lantern of recollections
stops suddenly, becomes faded, and the picture that was
moving is a white, static blur. I have just begun to live. This
afternoon brings a new birth.

But it is a cold, scary day.

And we are going down the concrete steps now, and I am
walking beside her, as if I am a tourist with no interest in
taking photographs of old buildings; and she is walking beside
me as if we had just met each other on the bus that tours

Toronto's landmarks. No one passing can guess what we have just done. We are going down the sturdy, dirty steps hard as granite in the numbing cold, and we are two steps from the bottom, from the level of the streetcar tracks, and there before us is Eireene. She appears before us, like a dream.

How did she know? It was a decision we had made the same morning, by telephone, from her office to my office. Secrecy . . .

Eireene runs up to my bride, whose face is flushed both by the shock of matrimony and by the biting, cold wind, and she holds her and kisses her. Eireene's lips wipe off some of the beautiful shining lipstick from my wife's mouth, and replaces it on her cheeks, and on her forehead. I am happy to see it. It is a wedding. And this love makes the day less cold.

"*Con*-gratulations!" Eireene tells her. She says this four times, each time louder. She says nothing to me. This is probably the love that only women know and can express, and know how to show and how to give to one another.

Eireene leads us to a cream-coloured stretch limousine that blocks one lane of crawling streetcars and taxis, and is almost as long as a city block. And in a flash, we are buried in its deep, rich leather, behind tinted glass. There is no one on the uncaring street witnessing us in this sweet-smelling darkness. Loud music, rock music, fills the luxurious body of the limousine. And as I sit, and settle myself in the new luxury, the music is changed to classical.

We are laughing and shouting and laughing and talking, all at the same time.

"You did it! You did it!" Eireene screams, holding my wife round her waist. "You did it! When you told me you would do it, I was on my coffee break . . ."

We sit back in the rear seat, which is as large as our sitting room back at the apartment, and we drink champagne and listen to Mendelssohn's *Midsummer Night's Dream* coming through the upholstery, eating lobster tails and shrimp. The limousine takes us south, at a snail's pace, along Bay Street, into the financial district; turns left along Front for the one short block which is the site of the court for refugees and my office, where, one hour before, I was listening to a woman tell me of the tortures she suffered at the hands of her husband, and that for ten hours a day she was held by the soldiers who seized power. When I could not bear to listen any longer or to imagine the pain of her fingernails being extracted by a pair of rusty pliers, she said that she had escaped through a toilet.

"Through a toilet?" I asked her. I asked her the question four times.

"Through a toilet," she said, in plain English, forgetting that she had told her story, for the first hour and forty minutes, through an interpreter, in a native African language.

"Through a toilet?" I asked her a fifth time.

I did not ask her to describe the toilets that she knew. A toilet was a toilet. It was at that point in the evidence when the priest my colleague beside me passed me a note that said, "Do you find this credible?" . . .

The traffic is thick on Front Street, and we have just reached the front of the Hummingbird Centre, where my wife and Eireene have tickets to attend *Swan Lake* by the National Ballet of Canada; and the limousine slows down and blocks the other cars in order to turn left, to make the turn north along Yonge Street, where I can see some of the discount stores my wife shops in for candles and lipstick and pantyhose, and the men's store for men who are the size of giants; then onto the Yonge Street strip, empty now, since all the kids are up in Scarborough and the surrounding suburbs attending school. There is no homeless person lying on the cold cement; and we move in and out of triumphal, unknown streets, until I can no longer see the skies or the people walking on the sidewalk deep in snow and slush.

Midsummer Night's Dream plays over and over. I see red and pink impatiens in the music, and hear water rolling over stones. No one but me is listening. And then there is "Both Sides Now" coming through the speakers. The music my wife and Eireene listen to, for hours and hours. But I like it, too . . . when they eat designer popcorn.

It is my favourite. How did Eireene know?

And when it ends, the music and the drive, after a lifetime of eating shrimp and lobster tails and drinking Dom Perignon, I remember that the three of us stumble out of the limousine, and walk, and stumble a little more, collect our balance, and walk up the slippery front steps of the apartment building, shouting and screaming in the elevator, right up to the eighth floor, eventually. For we had gone back down to the lobby three times before anyone remembered to press the button marked 8.

I remember the man on our left opened his door, looked the wrong way, and then looked to his right, and when he saw the three of us, tottering along the hallway, he slammed his door. Before he shut his door, he uttered a word I shall not repeat.

And I remember now being laid out across the queen-size bed, with the four large pillows propping my head up. And the clouds outside the window turned grey, and then black. For late afternoon had caught the three of us flopped on the bed, with the four large pillows on the floor. And then, there was only blackness and silence surrounding me.

REENS AND ME'VE GRABBED A CAB BACK TO WORK.
YOUR WIFE.

The note was in my wife's handwriting. In green capital letters made by her Sheaffer fountain pen. The time recorded on the note was 4:30 p.m. The time I saw on the red-eyed alarm clock was 7:30 p.m.

I was completely naked.

From that day, my wife has called her best friend by this new name: Reens. And I learned to call her that, too.

The sheen on the parqueted, hardwood floor was eventually erased. In its place was a different patina, with an acrid smell. It seared the skin of enjoyment from my happiness.

Christmas was coming. Before any of us noticed, or could prepare for it, it was around the corner. It would be bringing the smells of new wrapping paper and Hawes Lemon Oil, and chocolates and oranges from Israel and tangerines in small quaint boxes and wrapped in soft reddish paper. There would be colour in the shops, red and green and silver. Little gold. And we would walk with our shoulders hunched, our heads farther into our collars and scarves, to hide from the wind and the cold that numbs you at the corner of Davisville and Yonge.

The West Indian woman at the cleaners took loads and loads of our laundry, promised to get it back in time, and smiled showing the space between her teeth.

"Happy Christmas!" she told me.

My wife told her, "You, too."

But the ringing of bells on donation boxes and in jingles in store windows, the loud music of the Salvation Army groups of musicians, and "Jingle Bells," carried me back to the island where we used to sing Bing Crosby songs and imitate the crooning of Nat the-king-of-them-all Cole, in "O Little Town of Bethlehem"; and I was happy, as if I were still there.

I was happy, though I was cold. Christmas is so sad. . . .

She bought tickets to a Handel concert at Roy Thomson Hall. Three of them. The third ticket was for her mother, who would be driving up on the twenty-first, from Kingston, where she had lived with her brother from Michigan since her husband died. She was now nursing her brother, who was dying of cancer in the penis area.

"Fucker!" my wife said, when she told me the news.

"Prostrate cancer?" I said.

"Pros-*tate*," she said, and laughed. "I hope it prostrates the fucker!"

She said, the day before she bought the tickets, that her mother was returning from Las Vegas on Christmas Eve, three days *after* the concert, which was to be held on the twenty-first. I ignored the slip in her words, as she had no memory for dates. She wrote all important and unimportant dates in her pocket diary, and forgot to look them up. Or wrote them on yellow stickers and slapped them on the fridge, and took them off the door – by mistake – before the date she wanted to remember.

We had just finished dinner. Reens had taken the dishes to the kitchen. As she washed them, she sang "We Three Kings of Orient Are." And my wife joined her in the singing. It was happy in the apartment. The Christmas tree stood beside the piano, propped in a corner, naked of decorations, but sturdy and deep green, waiting to be trimmed. Its only clothes, for the time being, was a long ribbon, hanging from the uppermost branch, that my wife had taken from the two gifts her mother had sent to her and the dog by Federal Express.

I remained at the table, sipping a Grand Marnier, listening, singing silently, wishing I could join more openly in the merriment, seeing my own happiness ebb from me into these two women's more expressionable, easy enjoyment, watching my place being taken, taken care of, and being taken away from me.

But I was imagining Room in the large church, far, far north on Yonge Street from where I am now, standing straight, hands folded, right hand on left hand, on the polished wood of the pew in front of her, mouth wide open in confidence and memorization of the Christmas carols . . . "I See Three Ships Come Sailing In."

"Don't you just love religious music? Classics?" Reens said. She had just put the three damask napkins that had been shaped into white Egyptian pyramids back into their silver rings, and had placed them on the table beside me.

Before I could answer, she removed the three napkins and put them in a drawer. And she lit a cigarette.

"Want one?"

"Great!" my wife said, taking the cigarette.

My wife, with cigarette in hand – Balkan Sobranies, with gold tips, in various colours, for Christmas – said, "Let's stay at the Park Plaza Hotel the Friday and Saturday before Christmas . . . the three of us. As a family . . . the twenty-first and twenty-second. . . . Why don't we, for Chrissakes? It's Christmas!"

"Why?" I asked.

"Why not?" Reens asked. "Let's."

"Why not, indeed?" my wife said.

"Why the hell not?" Reens said.

The water was running over the plates in the sink. The kitchen was filled with steam. The mirror over the dining table was fogged up.

"Great!" my wife said. She shot the smoke through her nostrils, and took a sip of her wine. Reens had contributed the bottle of Beau Rivage to dinner.

"Why?" I asked.

"And why not?" Reens asked. "Let's. We're one happy family!"

My wife put her glass down, and rested her cigarette in an ashtray. The ashtray was already full. The new cigarette caught the filters of others, and the smoke mixed with the steam. A sickening smell rose from the embers. And in the time of this interval, she softened her words.

"Let's have a little gaiety in our life? For a change? Eh? We can afford it. It's only money, for Chrissakes!"

Eireene stopped washing the dishes, wiped her hands on a blue-trimmed dishtowel, went to her handbag, took out her Royal Bank Gold Visa card, threw it on the white damask tablecloth, and said, "It's on me!"

My wife picked up the cigarette, and her glass, took a long sip, and walked up to me and passed her hand gently across my face, and then placed the same hand plumb on my penis, and grabbed it in her hand, firm but just as gently as I had seen her handle dough when making banana cake.

"Eh?" she said. "Eh? Eh?" she said, smiling.

"Yes," I said, and smiled; and then she joined Reens in the kitchen at the sink. From the kitchen, she shouted, "We'll have a good time! With lots of food! And gifts! And books! And red roses and cut flowers and books and wine, champagne, and pheasant for Christmas."

I remember how I had touched my jacket on the side of my heart, and then touched the other pocket, to check if my wallet was still there. But when I did that, years ago, we were just sitting on a wooden deck, talking.

"Why?" she said. "'Why, why?' Why're you always asking 'why'?"

"Because he works as a judge," Reens said.

"You would think . . . ," my wife said.

"You should do it," Reens said.

She had come from the kitchen, and was standing behind the chair my wife was sitting in. Her hand was on the back of the chair. She was talking in the singular. She went back to the kitchen, and I could hear the water running over the knives and forks. A sudden urge welled up in me, and I wanted to be invisible. And I imagined that I was not in this room, and that there were only these two women having a conversation, but that I could hear the words they were using.

The dog was gnawing at the head of the black American statuette. I saw strands of her long black silk hair in his teeth. And he shook his head frantically to get them out. My mind went back to the narrow laneway between the two large three-storey houses, off the little street that came east from Spadina Avenue into Huron Street, a short walk from the St. George subway station; and I was walking in that laneway, and I stopped at the red-painted door with the aluminum screen, and the brass doorknob that was almost falling off; and I could see, by standing on the tip of my toes, the wooden steps, worn down in the middle of each stair by the passage of time and of feet, leading down into the small bedsitter, to the linoleum on the floor, and the single bed, narrow as a nun's cot, and the white sheet covering it, and a white blanket, and its two white pillows. The sheets were folded neatly, and the pillows beaten fluffy. There was no body on the bed. I thought I saw, in a far corner of the squeezed space, the marks where her knees had eaten into the linoleum from constant and successive kneeling, to pray, perhaps, that my love for her would have lasted, and to wonder in whispers to God, what was the cause of the sudden silence; and I could feel the grains of dust and escaped grains of rice from the plastic bag in the larder or from my unwiped feet move under my knees, even though I was wearing thick trousers, and was not half-naked like that last time, when beside her I pretended I was communicating to the same God as she. My focus on this picture, on this tableau like the ones I drew before in the room with Miles Davis, became fuzzy, and I was, in the next moment, listening to Reens and my wife as they began to sing "Silent Night." I wished I was not so far away from these two women; that I hated them less, and did not dislike them; that I appreciated their company, on this white, snowing night. It was only that, at this moment of the jubilation of birth and conviction, I wanted to be in a different place, a humble place, a place where smells were more natural, and high, where the feet touch and disperse the dust and the grains of rice, and where the space available for living is small like the area of a stable.

And then, my wish frightened me. Suppose I should be granted my wish. My wish for invisibility might turn into the reality of death, or of fulfilment. And I saw the miracle come true. The miracle of invisibility.

These two women began to talk about me, as if I were dead. And I was dead. And when they were finished with me, they went on to talk about fun, and work, and food, and hotel rooms, and classical and religious music, the *Messiah* and Mendelssohn. And in all this time, Reens never once called me by my name.

In my invisibility, I heard my wife tell Reens, "I intend to make this the best Christmas I have ever had, if I have to spend every penny he has and every penny I have, as if it's the last Christmas we'll ever have!"

"Let's!" Reens said.

A few days after the discussion about hotel rooms, I bought three tickets for the Handel concert we had talked about. And the next day, I returned them. It was the day the refugee woman who had escaped her torture by slipping through a toilet, probably also slipping into what in that country is known as "night soil," the day this woman told me the names of her torturers. I did not tell my wife about the tortured woman; and I did not tell her about the tickets.

The day after that, she said, "I was not asking you to buy the tickets, dear."

I remained silent. She showed me her envelope with her three tickets.

"If you don't want to come with us, I'll give your ticket to my mother. I mean, I'll give it to Reens. If my mother can't come, if she can't get a flight from Vegas, and can't be with us for Christmas, and if Reens can't make it, I'll throw the goddamn tickets in the garbage! Would you like that?"

Her voice grew wild and high and tremulous; and her last words were drowned out by her own crying. Her tears rendered me useless, as if I had been overcome by ennui, unable to move or speak. And I wanted to be able to go up to her, and put my arms round her, and hold her close to me, as I had done that first July night, when we arrived at her apartment from the summer party.

But the power of her reprimand was too strong and indelible for physical effort to erase.

We postponed Christmas shopping. Shopping for our annual party she had planned was postponed, too. Her mother, her two brothers and three sisters, Reens, and other friends from her office were to have been invited. And I was going to meet her whole family for the first time. I had already met her mother the first year we lived together.

"You sure there's *passion* in this relationship?" her mother asked me. She talked like her daughter, putting extraordinary stress on her words.

Her friends from work had already been invited by word of mouth, and then their invitations were formally written. She had bought the cards at one of the city's best-known stationers, and had written the notes and their addresses in her own handwriting, in green ink, in capital letters. Each note had an individual, personal greeting, along with the invitation.

She held the shoebox in which she kept the invitations and other greeting cards over the garbage can, pressed her foot on the pedal, and pushed the invitations into the already cluttered can.

At times when I am bored, I try to make head and tail of her calligraphy. I try to read the hidden message, find the interpretation buried in her handwriting, penetrate the mystery of her characters, and understand her hand. And understand her. And her character. I do this to see if can know her better. It could make our life together better, and "passionate," this breaking of the puzzle that clothes her fascinating handwriting.

So I bought a book, *Handwriting Analysis: What Your Handwriting Reveals About Your Personality, Health & Emotions*. The long title of this book encouraged me that I would indeed discover everything that lay buried in her calligraphy. But after browsing through it one night, when she was in her bath, the things the book told me about her handwriting did not describe my wife. The book made her an even greater stranger to me.

I knew already that I did not know her. So I threw the book away. And decided to face her intractability by myself.

With her handwriting, as with her friendship with Reens, all I needed to know would have to come from her.

Why do you write your letters the way you do?

The book had told me about the dots on her *i*'s, made like circles, like small eyes, small like the dog's.

But I could never bring myself to ask her about her handwriting.

There were a few occasions when I felt brave enough to ask. But the question lodged in my mind, like a bone caught in the throat. On those occasions, it seemed as if she had read my mind, and dismissed the question before it was asked, and dismissed me, by saying, "Do we have to discuss this?"

"Do we have to discuss this?" was her favourite parry. And so it was left at that. The bone of contention remained, lodged perilously, and perhaps mortally, in the same spot, in my craw.

Then one Sunday morning, without notice, she turned her attention to the Christmas party again. It took my mind off asking questions. She started all over to write the invitations. No one I knew was on the list. "It's a family affair," she said.

I have no family living in this half a continent.

My father is dead. He died the day after I arrived in this country from the island. My mother is dead. She died the year before I left the island.

I have no brothers or sisters in this country.

My family, including father and mother, are in the memory of tombstones, beneath the grey sun-scorched mould in the graveyard of St. Matthias Anglican Church, back in that island, where, at this Christmas-time, there would be the smell of varnish and new paint to make the day and the house smell sweet and fresh as birth, and new for guests and friends, whose names are never placed on invitation cards. People, not all of them friends and family, arrive at your door in democratic, licentious spirit on the ravenous day of Christmas, for Christian food and rum. I cannot say that the few friends I have in this half a continent, my colleague on the Bench and Room, would be acceptable. But there is Cliff; and there is Jack; and there is Olli, the Ukrainian. They too would not be acceptable. But they sit with me round the poker table every other Friday night, some of them matching the Fridays my wife has designated for having sex.

"Well, should we have sex?" she says on those Friday nights; and I have to decide which activity, poker or fooping, would result in the greater loss.

We play poker, Cliff, Jack, Olli, and I, every other Friday night. Sometimes, I am left with only one Friday night "to have sex in." And once, it shocked me to discover that in one month there were five sex-Fridays!

But I do not complain, nor regret the absence of family. I live now in this half a continent, and friends are sometimes hidden in snowbanks, concealed in the driving cold winds and the darkness. Going to the court for refugees five days a week, in the dark mornings, and tied to stories of horror and torture and rape till evening, and coming back to this apartment from the narration of horrors, like reading novels of horror, in the same darkness, have all contributed to hide many friends from me. And even the man and his wife, whose life I hear next door coming through the thin walls, in the squeak of their springs, rapid and violent every Saturday night, while we sit and eat spaghetti next door, neither he nor she has ever told me,

"Good morning." They keep their lives and their neighbourliness hidden under the fold of their sheets. But I am sure they take notes on our activities.

I gave her the impression, after she started writing the invitations a second time, that she is the only family I have. She will be my mother and my sister.

And soon after this, Reens began to be addressed as Auntie Reens.

On the twentieth of December, Auntie Reens was at the apartment to dinner. She was removing the dinner dishes from the table to the dishwater when the quarrel erupted.

"Well, you tell me!" my wife said. "Do you have any family? Give me their names, then! Give me their names! Do you have sisters and brothers here in Toronto? Well, do you?"

Her eyes became large, and her voice was raised.

"It's a family affair, dear," she added.

"I like him very much, but can't *he* understand it's a family affair?" Auntie Reens said.

"And you? Are *you* part of this family?"

When I said it, I could not believe that the words had come from my lips. Auntie Reens received the shock. I heard a glass fall and shatter.

"I thought I was . . . ," she said. I could imagine her entire body shaking.

"Now see what you've done?" my wife said.

"Wouldn't you at least . . . ?" My habit and my training in conciliation were beginning to betray me.

"She's goddamn bloody family!" my wife said. Her voice was now a shriek. "Remember that! One of us! Remember that!"

"I can see that," I said.

"And what the fuck do you mean by that remark?" my wife said.

"I shall leave," Reens said.

"Like *hell*!" my wife screamed.

I went to Reens, and put my arms round her soft bounteous body, and I smelled the fragrance in her bosom and the scent of musk in her hair, and her breath the same sweet comforting sensation as that first night in July. I said nothing to her. She said nothing to me. We just held each other. It took my wife longer to seek reconciliation. I went back to sit at the table.

"Well, bloody well invite your mother!" my wife said. "And your father! And, and . . . are there any brothers and sisters, stepchildren, hidden away on the islands that you haven't told us about? We could invite them all! One big bloody family!"

Her voice was now uncontrollable. Hysterical. She understood the wound she had inflicted. She put the serving dish with the spaghetti back down on the counter in the kitchen, moved from standing beside Auntie Reens, wiped her hands on the soiled dishcloth, put it back on the door handle of the stove, and came towards me, still seated at the dinner table. She stood a few inches from me. She looked me straight in the eye. I saw her eyes, and I saw the three colours of her eyes. The candlelight was reflected in her pupils. She remained standing a few inches from me. Then she passed her hands over the skin-fitting ski pants she had changed into. I saw the tears begin to well in her eyes. She moved her hands over her hips, as if making sure the pants fitted her correctly. And then she passed her hands through her short hair. She had cut her hair in the same style as Auntie Reens's. Tears were in her eyes.

"*I'm sorry, I'm sorry,*" she said. She emphasized each word. "Why do you feel I don't love you? Can't you see . . . ?"

Auntie Reens wiped her hands on the same damp, blue-bordered, soiled dishcloth. She passed her hands through her hair, and the next noise I was aware of was the apartment door closing behind her. She did not say goodnight.

And then, the smell of Chanel No. 5, sweet and sensual, and the touch of her body, and the rosewater in which she bathed her hair, sensations like the softness of her hair pressed against my head, and her hands round my shoulders and my neck; and the comforting heaviness of her weight on my legs as she sat on me, still at the table. And the fuzzy noise of insects coming out of the dark night through the screen door. The screen door was ajar. The fireflies twinkled like sparklers in their short, luminous span of life; and I can hear the waves licking against the old, black, rusted pipe, and I see deep down through the aquamarine water into the sand the colour of coral to the bottom of the water; and I see the small dead sea animals and the fish and the sea horses that choose the sea for safety and for home.

The teacup at her place setting trembled. It fell out of its matching saucer. And we watched it roll to the edge of the dining table, and fall off. And neither of us did anything to stop its breaking. The dog heard the noise, and came scampering out of the bedroom, and looked up and saw us, and hung his head, and returned to the bedroom.

"We are one family. Why can't you understand that we are, dear?"

I am sometimes shocked at the language that I use. All these swear words.

From the time I met her, and we have become man and wife, I notice that the way I swear when playing poker with my three friends shocks them. But they are too nice to tell me.

I am imitating my wife's language. I also hear this language whenever I pass a construction site where men are building things out of wood and concrete and glass. And I hear these obscenities in the general washroom for men at the court for refugees. From the mouths of men in steel helmets and safety boots. With them, it has now become a natural means of punctuating frustration and of colouring boasts.

At this time of year, all round Davisville and Yonge, and west of the building where the court for refugees is, on the Bay Street side, there is a lot of this kind of construction, men tearing down things with obscenities and ripping-irons, pneumatic drills and large iron wrecking balls.

Sometimes, when I walk the street, the street shakes and trembles from the vibrating pneumatic drills. Obscenities drown out the loud jabbings of the drills made of iron. They are harder.

On the bus, I hear young men and young women speak this new, liberating language.

"I went to this *fucking* party, Friday? *Fuck*, man! I took the *fucking* subway at *fucking* eight o'clock so's I won't be *fucking* late? And guess what the *fuck* happened to me, man? I *fucking* forgot my *fucking* student pass in my *fucking* jeans that I had *fucking* worn to school, the *fucking* day . . ."

His friends listen, and one of them says, "*Fucking* right, man! Here's our *fucking* stop. Let's get the *fuck* off this *fucking* bus, man!"

And I listen, and I say nothing. I dare not chastise the young of this city.

I worked with a gang of men who fixed sewers in Scarborough, dug into the land that once was planted with corn and wheat, on which cows grazed, land that is now a development, with bungalows and stores and schools and police stations. And jails and detention centres for immigrants from the island.

This suburban land was slipping. Many pipes burst before we could fix them stronger in the shifting ground. Many men slipped. Some were buried alive. Some were drowned in the reckless mud. And whenever this happened, all the Italians learning to speak English said was "*Whadda fuck?*"

I am really very close to her, in spite of the fact that Auntie Reens has plopped herself upon our privacy, and has ploughed into the landscape of our matrimony. Her presence in the apartment is sometimes like asthma that constricts my breathing.

I am close to my wife. I know she has got into my blood. And neither reason nor thought of separation can erase this infection. It is the dermatology of the thing. She is in my blood. Though not of my blood.

Nevertheless, I can feel her running through my veins in such a way that it will cause death, or murder, or suicide, some passionate extremity, to end this affliction of my blood, to end this love. When I get the chance, and take the priest at his word, and have him hear my confession, I shall remember to include this. . . .

And so, I carry all these things in my mind, like an indigestible craw, deep within me, in the same way as I carry all the other masculine resentments that have been hammered into my personality in that island, resentments which said that a man should not expose or talk in public about the stake that pierces his heart. Never in public. The hate and the resentment, the unanswered questions, Reen's shadow, and the fear that my time with my wife might someday end in disaster, with violence and in sorrow, must never be discussed.

How then will I conduct my confession?

I have never been able to face or see the picture of my future. That is too frightening a face to gaze upon.

One afternoon, a Friday, after court, I walked along the sidewalks of Yorkville Village by the fashionable district couturiers, stationery shops, and shops that sell candles and expensive cigars, dragging my feet in the deep snow, soft as powder, and shoulder to shoulder with women in furs who came and went with beautifully painted bags from shops with French names, and Italian names . . . meandering and released from the hard narratives I listened to of persecution taking place in the People's Republic of China, I measured my pace, and stopped once or twice to admire the women and the shops and the luxurious bags they held in their leather-gloved hands. I was going to see a psychiatrist. But I was postponing my appointment. My wife had made the suggestion. "Look at it as two men in a high-class bar, like the Roof Bar at the Park Plaza, shooting the shit!"

I moved on and came to a large door made of glass and marked with gold lettering, in formal Italian script – or Old English? – with a name and three academic and professional degrees behind the name. My wife had told me that he was "bloody well qualified, the best bloody psychiatrist" for my problem in the whole of Toronto; and my friend the Judge had told me that his fees would be as high as the prices of trinkets in the bags I saw the women carrying from the shops of French and Italian designers.

Psychiatrist?

On the way back down from his office door, in the elevator, I was alone with the janitor. We travelled in silence. He, with his mind filled with mops and cleaning and the end of his shift; and I, frightened even now that I had saved myself thousands of dollars to expose my weaknesses and manias and phobias to a complete stranger.

"Never in public, boy. Your linen I'm referring to. Your dirty linen," my mother said.

To bare them to a stranger, and spill the beans, which the island had taught me to withhold even on pain of death, on pain of ridicule and whispers? On pain of being labelled mad, and sent to the madhouse at 999 Queen Street West? That insane asylum, now made respectable with a new name, the Toronto Hospital, "but inhabited by the same nuts, the same crazy bastards," so my wife, knowing Toronto better than I, said. A psychiatrist? That would be the end of any future serious consideration of an opinion I might subsequently offer from the Bench to a refugee.

I had tried to get help. She always talked about getting help. For weight, and for her eating problem. I would get help. For sleepless nights, I would get help. For smoking cigarettes, I should get help. For this life with this man, meaning me, I should get help. This was her reasoning. She always talked about getting help.

I was brought up in an island, and disciplined to hide things that hurt, or that embarrass; I was schooled not to ask for help, not to raise the hand, to offer answers, because that was being a braggart and pushy; I was advised not to talk to psychologists, the need for which is the first sign of mental collapse.

Why then would I seek help for my problems? Not to talk about them, not to accept them, is to feel that they do not exist. And if they do not exist . . .

"*Your dirty linen!*"

But I still cannot bring myself to disclose my feelings to a psychiatrist, to a friend, to a psychologist, to a counsellor, or to a woman. And I know that sometimes a man needs to bounce things off another man, if only to ensure that his own suspicions about work, or woman or wife, or a situation with his profession might have no ground and no substance, and no truth.

Some men cannot as easily bounce these doubts off another woman, and remain her friend.

I can feel my own personal injury. But I ignore the pain and the blood, and endure the slow tightening of the skin, as the wound heals in its own slow, painful time.

"I sit beside you five days a week, Monday to Friday," my friend the Judge was saying, "and in a way, I still do not know you at all."

It was a Friday afternoon. I was going to the poker game afterwards. The wine bar, Vines, was full. Chatter was rising, and the smoke of cigarettes and cigars rose above and around us, and remained like a large raincloud over our heads. Men with women sat at the small tables that ran up and down the room, cozy, warm, holding hands below the red-and-white chequered tablecloths. And men, unaccompanied by women, were by themselves, standing at the bar – as I was with my colleague – twisting their cigars inside their mouths, puffing on them, sipping their wine, and twisting their cigars in their mouths again.

We were drinking Pommard. We were on our second glass, each.

"As I was saying, brother. Having spent all the years I have in the ministry, for which I don't think I was psychologically ordained, if you would pardon the pun . . ."

He paused to sip his wine.

"I won't ask if you need my professional help. I'll just say that, any time you need to talk, if you need me to hear what's troubling you, not to hear your confession, all I have to do is put on my black surplice . . . as your friend!"

"Yeah."

"I understand," he said. And he began to play with my box of wooden matches. He opened my cigarettes, French Gauloises, plain; put it to his nostrils, and inhaled, deeply. "Nice! The times I enjoyed smoking! But mind you, I'm not prying. It's just the priest in me . . ."

"Fine."

A draught of cold air struck our backs each time a customer entered. We would each gauge the descent of this new customer from the road above, which we could not see, by counting mentally the number of steps his flopping rubbers took to reach the floor of the warm basement bar.

"You are right to think," he said, "of the delicacy of talking to me about these things, and you and me are sitting in judgment, that's what it really is, sitting in judgment on all these refugees, while you – how can we put it? – when you are in need of advice and counselling yourself. To be blunt and candid. But think about it."

"Yeah."

He ordered an imported beer from France.

"To cleanse the palate," he said.

"To cleanse the palate," I said.

He drank his beer off, in two draughts. I sipped mine.

"How do you spend your weekends? I know how you spend Sundays. You don't come to church!"

"Reading the *New York Times* on Sundays. And reading 'Your Daily Horoscope' in the *Globe and Mail* on Saturdays.

And shopping in Chinatown, Spadina and Baldwin. We buy the same things, and eat the same things, every Saturday, for lunch. I feel there is some Chinese in the two of us."

"I read the *Sunday Sun*."

"The dog loves the *New York Times*, as I've told you!"

"What breed of dog?"

"It's a fancy breed. But to me it's a salmon-tot retriever. Do you know what a salmon-tot retriever is?"

"It's self-explanatory enough."

Distractedly, he opens my Gauloises cigarette box, closes it, opens it again, and places it to his nostrils and inhales deeply. "Ah!" he says, exhaling, "the pleasures of sin!"

"We go to bed, after dinner, but we don't talk much. We would talk about a new dress she saw, about deals in hotel rooms, and cheap airplane tickets. That sort of stuff. We have learned how to quarrel without even speaking a word. You enter an environment and you just know that it will remain tense. Silence and speechlessness. You know that something is going to happen. A word, an action, even a look. And then, there will be the explosion. You know this, before it happens."

"But you love her, don't you?"

"You know what my best times are? You're going to think I am weird . . ."

"Not more weird than anybody else."

"When she is putting on her pantyhose . . . the way she rolls the silk like an extra skin, unravelling it, smooth, the same colour as her skin. . . . Just watching her. Just watching . . ."

I notice the change of colour that comes to his face. He takes matches out of the box and lines them up like railroad ties.

"You are talking about sexual pleasure, sexual satisfaction, aren't you?"

"Yeah."

I begin to realize that this man standing beside me at this bar is analysing me, this man with whom I travel the world of degradation and depression, terror and rape and torture, with whom I share a common existence through translations and documents and personal files, files that vomit up the lives of wretched persons who come before us; he and I, Judges, with the power to give these strangers new fortunes in their new lives in this country. And here I am, this Friday afternoon, with this same colleague listening to my evidence of personal disaster.

He who would rest his hand on mine, or pass his legal-sized page of notes, with a red circle at the bottom, in which would be his advice, "We don't need to know that."

Yes, we don't need to know the most horrible detail in every horrible story. No. The pen does not have to travel to the end of the line to complete the sentence of compassion.

"She is very beautiful, a very beautiful woman. A good woman."

"Who?"

"My wife."

For a while, we just stood beside two high barstools which had become vacant, and watched the men beside us inhale their deep, pungent smoke from their Cuban cigars; and we glanced at the young lovers, with their hands locked on the small, square tables, and at those whose hands were hidden under the red-and-white chequered tablecloths.

"That night in July, three or four years ago, at the birthday party you invited me to, the night . . ."

"You know, I never apologized for my bad manners! Cripes!"

"You told me about the party."

"That Saturday afternoon, I had to do a funeral. A dear friend from divinity school with me. But how did it go?"

"You set me up."

"And look what it has done for you! You met your wife at that party! Cripes! Now, I can tell you that it is her friend, Eireene, who is my parishioner. Or, parishioneress!"

"You knew my hostess, and my wife-to-be, to-have-been? They were your parishioners?"

"Lovely women! Lovely women who used to be devout Christians."

"But in three-and-something years, my wife she has never gone to church!"

"In the Lord's house there are many mansions."

"I wish I could talk to you, and forget you're a priest."

The Pommard is beginning to make me mellow and prolix. "I have experienced something like what you would call a kind of annunciation? I call it a state of bliss. And joy. And I live in these plain scenes of joy. Yes! Now I remember! It was "Strange Fruit," the song that was played at the birthday party. They played it over and over again. Was it played at the party? Or at her apartment when she took me there, after the party? Anyhow. I asked her the name, and she said it was her favourite song. I think she brought all the music played at the party. Yes. When we left together, she took a handful of tapes and CDs. It was a good party. I didn't meet many people . . ."

"What're you doing this weekend? Church in your itinerary? You want to come around for matins? Or even after church? At twelve-thirty?" He is fumbling again with my matches. "We are in Portugal on Monday, are we? The Portuguese are now Jehovah's Witnesses! Claiming religious persecution . . ."

"I read the files."

"Jehovah's Witnesses?" he says, with no insinuation. "We're going to the cottage, first thing tomorrow morning." He puts the matches back into the box, lays it beside the empty glass that held his beer, and lines up the cardboard beer mats, just a I have seen him tidy up the space before him when sitting on the Bench: his fountain pen, his notepad, his box of paper clips, and his pocket watch, all in a line of tidiness and order. "We are going to the cottage this weekend. I said that already, didn't I . . . ?"

"We are going to Chinatown, Spadina and Baldwin. And Vietnam, for sweet and sour soup, and roast pork with crackling, and noodles."

"Should we have another one, before I push off?"

In the island, I had frequently been told by mothers and schoolteachers and at Sunday school that a man is defined by the words he uses. I have used words in this half a continent with a different, more creative lawlessness. With a vengeance, as if I had no confidence in the words themselves. In the words I use now, to express how I feel, I am not sure that they are the words that come from the heart. Words that have no possibility of being interpreted in more than one way. But they are my words. I have only my words.

So, I can tell you that I can see her, Room, the woman from the southern Philippine island, taking her clothes off to step into the narrow, tin-lined shower stall, which is colder in winter, and an oven in July, because of the tin. And I can see her putting on her flannel nightgown, to cover her body before she steps out of the tall, cell-like shower.

I am really thinking of something else while I use these words. I am thinking of having the words describe my lust, at the same time as they are meant to describe the woman, the picture, the portrait, and the painting of this lust.

It would be better, stronger, more realistic if I were a poet or a painter, and not a Judge for refugees.

My mind is wandering, and into it comes strange things, like the song I listened to on that July night sitting on the wooden deck. And for some reason, I think of Room every time I remember the words in the song about strange fruit, the blues song I came to know about, the song that Billie Holiday sings. I should be finding another person to associate this song with: I should be thinking about my wife, who played it for me first.

And Room does not even listen to this kind of music. Nor to ukuleles, guitars, or Filipino music. No leis. Room listens to hymns. The hymns that Room sings, at home, and at the Congregational church north on Yonge Street, are songs of redemption, songs of praise.

This is a song, this "Strange Fruit," also about redemption and about blood. Blood on the leaves, and blood at the roots, as if it is painting a picture of slaughter. Like "Guernica." Or Breughel's scenes of human depravity and gluttony. I am face to face, five days a week, for fifty hours, with moral and social slaughter, even though it is presented orally.

Some of the victims are women, like the one whose sari I fell in love with; and some are from the Far East, women like Room. None of them reminds me of my wife. She, and her life, have escaped, are purified, are superior even to that fantasy.

But why didn't she have the presence of mind, that night in summer, when the impatiens were blooming, to tell me why she loved this song, "Strange Fruit," the song of lamentation that I was listening to? It was played over and over, as if the CD had had a bad groove, and had to repeat itself for the whole evening. Its playing dug a groove in my memory. And still I hardly listened to what the words were saying to me.

The first time I listened to this song, I thought it was a romantic ballad or a torch tune about some of the fruits that were at the birthday party, in a large platter made of wicker material. Pears that were all green, and apples also green, and bananas, also green, and green grapes. These green fruits are strange to me, coming from an island where everything gets ripe and turns yellow with black speckles, before its time.

I had looked at this wicker basket, but there was nothing red in it to suggest blood. And none of the fruits there, untouched the whole afternoon, except for the occasional, casual fingering of a grape from its stem, to plop into the mouth, had stems, not to mention roots.

And another thing from that July afternoon. I did not ask her her name. The first thing a man does when he meets a woman, whether his intentions are temporary or long-lasting, is to get the name of the woman he is facing.

But it was not a courtship and not a "move." So, even that tactic was neglected.

I did not know her name even when we sat, later that night, in her apartment. I did not ask her her name.

But even though it took me some time to realize that Billie Holiday's song was not about the picked fruits in the wicker basket, the words she sang, with tears of blood in her voice, and the story itself about dripping blood, took me back to another story about blood.

Polyphemus the giant and Odysseus. That was about ancient times, when violence is magnified through reporting the distance that the past is from the present.

The story came back to me then, with the same graphic urgency, as Billie's song, as Room's exposure to my cruelty of silence, and my sudden disappearance, as my unmannerly absence, my rude neglect; all these played upon my mind. And with Room, I am beginning to admit that something is wrong with my eyes.

"Polyphemus drove his sheep and goats into the cave," the story goes, "shut up the doorway with a large stone. Then he milked the ewes and the goats, and lit his fire; and the fire burned so brightly that the giant spied the strangers. 'Who are you?' he asked. 'And what are you doing here?' Odysseus said that they had been driven to the island by a storm; and the giant did not answer Odysseus, but leapt up, took hold of two of the sailors by their legs, and dashed their heads to the ground. Then he cut them into pieces, and ate them; after which he stretched himself on the floor, and went to sleep. . . ."; I see Room sleeping soundly in her flannel, with its long sleeves, in the cool basement with all the lights turned off, making her bedsitter into a cave.

She shall dwell in this cave, and it is her loneliness born of the way I have abandoned her, her loneliness shall grow into the size of a giant of cruelty and violence.

But had I not abandoned Room, in her cave of peace and safety, I would be getting into the cold bed with her, beside her cold body, and with our prayers said, our relationship shall be left balancing, until the dramatic coming of God's words and intervention. Hearing them, His words, will be the only thing that can place the benediction upon the same small bed with the noisy iron springs, and give me the clearance to touch the hair between those legs and enter her, and rejoice that, at last, the blessing and the permission have been vouchsafed from above.

But I cannot even patch that fantasy onto the fabric of that July afternoon, and afternoons since then, for the dream goes back to that afternoon, when even the fantasy was interrupted by the talking of the woman sitting beside me, the woman who is now my wife.

"This friend," she was saying, in the midst of my imaginary journey to the subway station at St. George and then the walk to Huron Street, "this friend, this person that I told you about? Remember him? The one who I wanted to have the child with? I didn't tell you something else about him. . . ."

But, at this hour, my mind tells me, travelling fast on the last train I am on, going west and then south – south where the Island is! – in my postponed haste, this train shall arrive after my woman from the southern Philippine island of Kiambo, Room, has crawled under the thin, imitation-wool blanket that is cold; and the sheets with no pattern, sheets that are white and with no flowers on them, plain as her flannel nightgown, shall give her slow comfort and warm her body.

But she is already comforted by the thick, black Bible which is always beside her. It was taken from a hotel room, and it bears the name of the society that leaves Bibles in hotel rooms. "This Bible has been placed here by the Gideons with the earnest hope that it will prove a joy and comfort to the one who now reads it." There is a vase, like those buried in dumps and ruins in Rome, in a circle. I think of this vase in a circle as the symbol of me and Room. She took the Bible, "placed here by the Gideons," from the room she rented, for safety from the driving snow, in a whiteout one Saturday night, when she drove north to visit her mother and father, and to bring back the three plastic containers of curried prawns and jumbo butterfly shrimps.

When I am in her bed, there in the basement of the house on Huron Street, she reads it to me, as I lie on my left side close to her lying on her left side, like two sardines.

"Move a little closer to me. I am cold."

I am thinking this, wishing that it would happen, as I am going down the three cement steps to the red-painted door, after I have passed the two cars that are parked two car-lengths from the door. And I walk along the path which is not so bright, even at nine o'clock in the summer. Imagine how dark it will be in the winter, at this last-train hour.

I have to calculate whether she is in her first sleep. Her first sleep is lighter. Or if she is buried already in her second sleep, which is deeper. And I have to calculate the heaviness of my knocking on the red door, so that her landlady, who is from another island in the Islands, does not open her window on the floor above, and hold her body out, exposing her breasts in the pink silk nightgown that I have seen her wear, and rain abuse and stale pee from her po on my head. But I remember that we are not still back in the Islands and that there are no pos, no chamber pots that can be emptied on intruding heads. . . .

One December, when the landlady saw my shadow, she screamed, "Thief! Thief! Thief!" I had just knocked on the door. And Room had pushed her head through the blinds of the single window in her basement apartment, and she had seen me, and she had pulled the blind so hard to close it, it was ripped from its metal bar.

She saw me. And she did not come back to the window.

This was five months from that July afternoon when everything changed. I could not pound on the red door. I could not call out to her. So, that night, I waited in the shadows under the window, and saw the landlady put her left breast back into the thin, loose-fitting silk nightgown, as she remained leaning out over the windowsill; and I waited in the shadows for her to control her loud temper as I trembled at the chance that she might raise for the second time that night the venom in her three-pronged alarm.

When she was satisfied that the thief was only a shadow, and had faded into the darkness of the laneway, and had departed, she was still grumbling. "I don't know why that bastard is coming 'bout here, bothering out that poor girl. I don't know what she see in that bastard!"

The upstairs bedroom window is closed and I, unknown to her landlady, am still cowering in a cave her alarm has created out of the darkness, waiting to see if Room would come to the window.

But she did not.

But I am like Rover, that dog of mine, dragged by another dog around the screaming paling, in agony and in love, relishing in the suffering of my pleasure, my lust.

Sitting around in a small circle on the beach, in that island, at five o'clock near sunset, when the colour of the day is richest, when the smells from cooking in the surrounding houses is strongest, like the quick rotting death of crabs and fruits and fish, we used to talk about Odysseus and about giants which did not live in our island, but only in the islands of books we read together in the reading room for juveniles, at the public library.

We would exhaust all the things in these books, and retell stories of the sexton and the vicar drinking Wincarnis wine, the tonic for strong bones and sinews and for Christian straightforwardness, and for Communion, in the changing room of the choir, up in the belfry. We would tell one another what we wanted to become. What we wanted life to provide. Life that seemed so fragile and so easily to be "turned," to be "tetched," to get rotten, and become inferior in the power of the sun and the strength of the waves whose currents were stronger than these boyhood smells of ambition.

And as soon as we were big enough and thought about girls, and what we liked about them and did not like about them, because girls were made of "sugar and spice and all things nice," whilst we boys were made of "snips and snails and puppy-dog tails" and things so terrible that we ourselves did not eat them, things we kicked in the street, as we kicked empty cans that contained Fray Bentos corned beef, and salmon tots, and milk tots, and soft unripe breadfruits as if they were soccer balls. We kicked anything that was not buried under the melting black tar of the macadamed streets. And we raged about the streets in gangs, with this catechism: girls were not to be liked, because they were made of "sugar and spice."

We even kicked the loose rocks from the streets, and rehearsed amongst ourselves these commandments regulating girls and women, and women who would become our wives.

The night when we sat so long, talking so long on the wooden deck, I remember my wife-to-be saying, "Took me a long time, years now, for me to come to terms with the fact I'd been molested. You don't call it that, by that name, when you are facing yourself and trying to remember it. You call it by a dirtier name. And you accuse yourself of being dirty."

I remember the interpreted words of the young woman wearing the sari and rubbing her palms; and I remember her sudden silence before she testified about the peacekeeping soldiers.

"Years now since it happened, and still I find that word difficult to say, even to myself. Easier to say to a complete stranger, like yourself. But this is years after it happened."

She told me that on the long drive from the Victorian mansion in Kingston, she and her brother and sisters would sit in the back seat of the Volvo station wagon and play, and sit up, and lie down, do anything in that car that was so big and so quiet. They would play cards and paint in picture books, whose colours were easy to do because they were numbered, as the wagon made its way along the snow-covered highways to Michigan, on its way to Las Vegas, with mother and father, and with the children, she and them, dropped off at the stately house of her uncle in suburban Dearborn.

"I remember my uncle patting me, placing me on his knee, and his knee was my horsey, and he was my own big horsey, 'Giddy-up, giddy-up, giddy-up, horsey!'; and I can still smell the smell of his thick woollen trousers, always with a crease in them, and I would ask him not to place me on his creases, so's I would not mess up his pants and his creases, but I wanted off for another reason. The obvious reason. I can still smell the smell of his thick woollen trousers, with a crease that you could peel an apple with or slice the butter on the breakfast table with. And the smell of his tobacco, that sweet, seductive smell that I grew to like and that made me want to smoke a pipe when I grew up. I tried smoking a pipe, his pipe, when I was nine. *Aiieeeekkk!* I remember him putting me on his knee, my giddy-up horsey, and tickling me and saying all the time, 'Giddy-up, horsey! Giddy-up, horsey! Nice horsey!' and tickling me until the tears would come to my eyes and make my face warm, and I would break out in laughter, laughing and crying at the same time. I would then feel his hand, the same hand he holds his pipe in, moving, and moving up my legs until it stopped. And then the pain and the pleasure started. My uncle was rubbing me *here*? On my pussy."

She passed her hand that held the burning cigarette, ever so gently, like a suggestion, over the front of her loose-fitting summer dress, and left it on the spot. It seemed that her hand had always been placed there. It was a long moment. But I knew it was only for a second, because the woman who owned the house, her friend Eireene, had not moved more than one step from the screen door leading to the wooden deck, towards the kitchen, before the hand had been removed.

"It was years before I had the nerve, and the feeling of innocence, to tell my mother. But I told her," she said. "I told the bantu-bitch about her favourite brother?

"'Dear, you always had such a fertile imagination!' my mother said.

"'My dear mother, Mommy Dear!' I told her. 'Time after time,' I told my mother, Mommy Dear, 'and always at Christmas, during the Christmas holidays.' That is why I have this thing, my depression about Christmas. And then one day, when she brought the trunk of the Volvo packed with presents, I gave it to her. It was a Christmas, too, when I told her. I told her in the only way I knew. To get it off my chest. Off my conscience. Off my innocence. 'Was I the fucking abuser?' I asked my mother.

"'From the time you were little,' my Mommy Dear told me, 'from the time you were just six or seven, you always had a vivid imagination.'

"'Fuck you, Mother!' I told her.

"She was taking the wrapping off the gifts she had brought, the red ribbon, easing the Scotch tape off, saving the wrapping as she always did, to put it in her handbag and take it back to Kingston, for the next time, or the next person.

"'Mommy Dear,' I told her, 'don't you want to know that your favourite brother, my uncle, has been fucking me since I was five or six years old? Do you know that, Mother? Can you fucking handle this?'

"All I remember is that the room became quiet after that.

She drank another cup of coffee, and forgot to add cream. By mistake, she poured the cognac into her coffee. She loves her cognac.

" 'If you still don't believe me,' I told Mommy Dear, 'call him. Aren't you brave enough to call your own brother? Call your fucking brother. Why don't you call your brother?' "

She told me she was a grown woman when this conversation took place. A grown woman, and she thought she had grown out of the hurt and the memory, but it came back with a firmer grip, the older she became.

One Friday afternoon, I was numbed by the stories of Bulgarians who told me and my colleague, the priest, that they were being persecuted by the Bulgarian government officer in charge of giving apartments and singing jobs and cars to the leading artists of the country (the Bulgarian before us now was a woman, an opera singer), and who, because she did not go to bed with him (she did not say this explicitly: but after all, me and my colleague put two and two together!), was given a hole in the wall to live in, and was demoted from being the lead singer, the prima donna with the heroine's role, to being a member of the chorus.

It was snowing, and I was tired; and I did not want to join the priest at Vines Bar, so I decided to take a taxi to Room's basement apartment. My wife would be with Auntie Reens, watching the Maple Leafs play a hockey game on television, after coming back from their Weight Watchers class.

I hailed the first taxi. It came to a sudden stop. The slush left the street, and travelled for the short time it took to stop the taxi onto my shoes and trousers and winter coat.

I opened the door with the words of reproof already fashioned on my lips. I sat down, and before I had pulled the tail of my coat inside the door, the taxi roared off again.

"Hey! Hey!" the driver said, laughing, and looking at me in his rear-view mirror. "I know you! I know you!"

The words of my reproof melted in his loud enthusiasm. I recognized the accent and the intonation.

"I know Toronto like the back of my hand, now!" he said. "I remember you! You and the lady with the dog! How is the little dog? I know Toronto good these days! Last two Fridays ago, I take the same lady to her house far far up Yonge Street to the place where I drop you off that time in the summer. I know Toronto. I love living here, now. You tell the lady with the dog that I send my regards."

I tell him the address I am going to, and he smiles at me in the rear-view mirror. For a while, we drive along Yonge Street, just north of Front Street, clogged with the other taxis cutting in and out of lanes, and the offending drivers blasting their horns, and the offended motorists honking their horns in response; and the driver of my cab turns around, ignoring the cars in front of him, and says, "They cannot drive well in this city, sir. They probably got their licents from the grocery stores!"

We exchange banter like this until he drops me in front of the three-storey brown brick building on Huron Street, with the two cars parked in the driveway. The snow shows me how long the two cars have been parked. The marks I leave, they too will be measured by the peeping landlady, for her to guess at their hour of arrival and departure, by the depth of the imprint.

The front garden is now white, as if a workman has thrown a bucket of white satin latex paint out of the skies. I see one line of footprints going towards the door I am about to knock on. I get out of the taxi, and he asks me, "Is this where you live now, sir?"

"Yes," I tell him.

"The lady with the dog she live here, too?" he says. He says it more like a statement of knowledge. "But I take her to your other home many times."

"This is where I live," I tell him again, and immediately regret I am giving him so much information.

"I am Canadian citizen, now, you know. I pass my refugee hearing last year."

"Congratulations," I tell him. And I wonder if he was before me, to hear his claim? But I would remember him: and he would make sure I did. Still, there are so many faces that I see, so many names, so many different stories, that I have difficulty remembering them, even after two days. I want to ask him if I was his judge. And I am tempted by a wicked streak in me to ask him if he ever escaped torture through a hole in a toilet. But I apologize to myself for thinking that. He is a happy man now, and he is a Canadian, like me.

The two-dollar tip, I hope, will win his confidence, and keep his mouth shut.

Three inches deep, in snow that is deeper than that, the foot-prints lead me, in single file, to the red door where they stop. And the determination of the person whose prints they are is not diverted by the thickness of the snow. It did not make this person waver, nor stray from the destination intended. Something about these footprints tells me that they were made by a self-assured single-mindedness. The person will not be coming back out tonight.

There is a storm brewing. The weather reports must have verified that. I know only one person who takes this route.

A tightness comes into my chest, like the pain of near-exhaustion. But I know that these footprints are hers. They belong to a woman. Mine completely wipe them out, in the same way as I wiped away any chance her prayers, said in my presence, would have to endure.

The pain of jealousy made my chest stiff; and the thought that I might not see her ever again was like the pain itself, excruciating and deep. I was seeing the result, the realization of the thought even before I had fully faced, in my mind, the absolute vacuum that the thought of not seeing her would bring on.

Now these thoughts return and I recognize them. I can do nothing about them. They are like the deadly words dealt when you learn that some ordinary illness that you have has become terminal, like cancer.

Room will never open the window blind and let me in, even to see her in her basement room. These thoughts have a way of making a man vulnerable, and making sure he thinks kind thoughts even of strangers, and being compassionate, and looking at the world in a Christian cleanliness of thought. And honesty.

But my egoism is too strong for this moralizing. It contradicts the thoughts of charity, and disregards the obvious consequences of this godliness. I begin to think like a man.

These footprints in the laneway that I am following to her red-painted door could belong to another man. There is always this man, this other man, real or imagined, lurking on the horizon.

It began with *that* other man. My jealousy. I had to imagine *him* with blond hair tied at the back of his head, in an exercise sweatsuit, with athletic bag and sneakers. And now *this* other, new man?

If these footsteps belong to a man, then someone is reaping my harvest. I had tilled the soil, had experienced the sharp jarring pain in my arms, in my entire body, when the fork struck the unexpected stone in the soft, moist earth; I had moved the boulder out of my way, and somehow still had energy left to till the land.

After she closed the window blind in my face, and after I had lurked in the darkness a little longer, hoping to outlast her landlady's patience in catching the thief that came to rob her tenant's virtue, I called her from a pay phone. The moment she heard my voice, she slammed the phone down. I held the telephone in my right hand, at my right ear, listening to the monotonous sound of the dial tone.

But now, the reaper is not the sower. He did not plant anything.

I must once again hide as I try again to take up this planting occupation. Just as I had imagined it years ago, walking out with the child in my fantasy of fatherhood, matching my wife's fantasy for wanting the seed planted in her womb by the gay man . . . I must build a new fantasy to compete against hers.

My misfortunes have a habit of striking deadly blows, two times in the same solar plexus. The first with Room, after the party in July, on the deck, caught in the tragedy of avaricious curiosity, and in lust that engulfed me, caught deeper on that wave, far far out, out of reach of the shore. I saw Room standing at the edge of the water, waiting. I never saw her after that. I never saw how she moved away from the wave that was heading in her direction . . . the wave. . . . The second time is just as startling as the first, and in my case, more deadly. I am not prepared for it even by the experience of the first blow. The second time is always more dramatic, more hurtful. And fatal. And instructive.

The second time I visited Room, her car was parked in the driveway. I pressed her buzzer. I listened. I thought I heard her feet moving, just as they used to move when she would prepare for her shower; just as I would see her move, after her shower, when she would then prepare to kneel, to say her prayers with me beside her. But a transport truck sped by, and killed the picture I was painting. I pressed the buzzer again. Held my finger on it a long time. No one came to the upstairs window that overlooks her basement door. The landlady was not at home. Was Room at home? She did not answer.

I can see my footprints following hers right up to the red-painted side door. I can see my footprints veering off beyond the door, taking the passage of escape, taking me into the snow-filled garden, over the wooden fence, down the wider lane to the broader road that is Spadina Avenue, which becomes Spadina Road north of Bloor, and then straight onto the subway lines. Perhaps the train will miss me, if I stand on the tracks . . .

I could take this train, if it did not run over me, and go farther north, and transfer, criss-cross my straight direction, and find myself back in front of the apartment building in which I live, with its frozen fountain and circular garden beds that are now, in winter, irredeemably white with death. No red and pink impatiens grow at this time of year.

I am standing now in front of the red door. I can hear everything happening inside. Each silent non-activity. Because she was never a woman who made normal household noises when she was at home, her home was always like the dark cave of Polyphemus. Quiet. Powerful. And sovereign. Not needing the casual and contemporary sounds of the electric vacuum cleaner, the washing machine, or the dryer, either for her hair or for her plates. Always quiet, and foreboding. And filled with whispers.

I stand and listen. And try to decide if I should ring the

buzzer or knock. I stand and listen, and wonder how much longer I can stand in this shuddering cold.

Perhaps the footprints do not belong to her. But there is no other one who takes this route. The footprints had stopped on the first steps, and had banged themselves against the threshold, to knock off the evidence of the kind of weather they had travelled through to reach this destination, to reach this decision.

There is decisiveness in the way the foot hits the path of this alleyway. One after the other.

All my energy and curiosity about things I used to think about are outside this apartment in which I live with my wife. I take up reading the Bible. And I read only from the Book of Proverbs.

And I go into the bathroom and have long conversations with myself, and between these two women, Room and the black American statuette. I sit on the toilet bowl with the lid on. Sometimes, to prevent detection, I sit on the bowl with the lid not on, and my trousers pulled down, as if I am really in the toilet for the normal purpose.

My trousers cover my shoes, and I see the shape of my legs, and think of exercising. I cannot see my knees.

I take the small black bound book, no larger than a brocaded pillbox we bought in a Chinese store on Spadina Avenue, out of my pocket, and I open it at the page marked by a used Canadian postage stamp, when local postage was twenty cents. This stamp marks the spot.

"Happy is the man that findeth wisdom, and the man that getteth understanding."

And my mind breaks the chains that are holding me to this toilet seat, in this half a continent. I flip through the small book, over the pages I read in elementary school in the small island, over the walks along the shores with a woman whose hair is red, whose family is a family of friends and fishermen, and who, like me, live in an island.

Some of the stories, I now know, are not from the pages of this little book: they are from a book of *Stories for Children*, and from *Biblical Stories for Young Christians*.

I like the sound of the sea in some of them, the sound of the sea in the words of the stories, and the sound of the girl's voice, calling her sheep home; and this takes me over oceans to another island, far, far away to Greece, where Odysseus and his sailors escaped from the cave, tied under the bellies of the sheep that belonged to the one-eyed Cyclops, the giant Polyphemus.

"O, Mary, go and call the cattle home,
And call the cattle home,
And call the cattle home . . ."

Three times Mary is told this. Just like my mother, who had to tell me things and give me instructions three times before I understood their seriousness. Before I learned to understand that the fourth time was her "last time," and that I would feel the weight of her heavy hand upon any part of my body that the blow was lucky enough to find.

I would remain in the safe bathroom, protected from the whispers and conversations my wife carried on with Auntie Reens, and would, amidst the smells of incense and bath oils, and the dog's box, recite, "O, Mary, go and call the cattle home, And call the cattle home, And call the cattle home," as if it were a chorus of the island's popular calypso.

I have a strange love for this little girl with the red hair. She reminds me of that little boy who had lost his "virginity," my mother's godchild. Mary lost something more. She lost her life. We were told so, in plain words, plain as the sands along the River Dee, in Aberdeenshire in Scotland – the nearest association we had to the name of that place was Aberdeen, a big black man who owned a rum shop and played the tenor saxophone in a band – plain as the sands on Gravesend Beach, in the island.

There was once a river in the small island. Now, there is only a street, called River Road. But I imagined rivers. My rivers were big and broad as the River Dee or the Ganges, which we read about in little picture books of adventure and mysteries of India. And tigers and elephants; but not sheep.

But still the little Scottish girl with the red flowing hair, walking along the edge of the brown Scottish river, lived amongst us, every day of the week, except on Saturday and Sunday, when our own girls with short black hair, which did not flow and was not red, walked on River Road on their way to the sea.

When I'm about to take a bath and I raise my left leg and place it into the tub, and then with my hand correct my balance, and then raise my right leg, and sit, the suds come right up to my neck. Sometimes, when I get into the bath in the wrong mood, I think of lowering my head beneath the thick clouds of oily beads and bubbles, and not holding my breath.

When I am inside this sweet-smelling, warm, misty room, I talk with my black American statuette.

I ask her questions about my wife's friend, the gay prospective father. I ask about his address, and whether he really lived in Toronto. I ask her if Room was home that Thursday evening when I walked to her door, and had to leave because her landlady poured a bucket of warm water on my head and on my clothes.

The only answer I hear is that Room still wears her nightgown of light-coloured flannel at night. I ask if Room was alone that night. But the only answer I get, over and over again, is, "She puts a cardigan over her nightgown because it is cold in the basement. It is cold in her basement. It is cold in the basement. She still reads the same, single sentence from the Books of Proverbs: 'She is more precious than rubies. She is more precious than rubies. She is more precious than rubies.' Over and over again."

And then, as if it is a miracle or a fantasy, clearer than a dream, I am no longer talking with my black American doll. I am hearing the voice of Room, answering me.

She is in this bathroom with me, somewhere in the clouds and the mists and the waves in the bathtub.

She has just told me that the woman who sat beside me on the wooden deck, who told me about the man she wanted to have the child with, was saying this to make me jealous, and to have me declare my hand. She says the man does not exist. I had never seen the situation like this.

"She did it deliberately," she says.

"No."

"I read the Book of Proverbs that night," she says.

The day of the concert at Roy Thomson Hall arrived. The snow came also, thin and light and like powder. It was cold. I could not tell the difference between the smoke exhaled from her cigarette and the vapour from her mouth.

She had changed from her regular mentholated cigarettes to multicoloured Balkan Sobranies.

"It's Christmas!" she chimed.

The vapour or the smoke that came from her mouth as she breathed, as she talked, as we waited at the front of the apartment building for the taxi to take us to the concert, swirled round my head.

I prayed that it would not be the African driver who had taken us that night in summer from Auntie Reens's house, and who a few Thursdays ago had taken me to the house near the St. George station, where Room lives in the basement on Huron Street.

I am in formal wear. It is rented from Custom Rentals of Formal Wear of the Tuxedo Junction store. An imposing name. It is not made to my measurements. The suit I wear is not my size. The sleeves of the jacket are two inches above my wrists.

"Roll the French cuffs down and cover the two inches of skin," my wife had said.

And I did that. I am now monkey-suited, formal and stiff in the tight-fitting suit, and obedient. I can feel my testicles rub against the stiff black serge. The crease in the trousers, and the crease in my behind, are cold. I am wearing a suit made to measure with a younger, smaller man in mind.

In this cold wind which slaps me all over my body, face, chest, and legs, I stand and think of undertakers back in that island. We called them "duppy-agents." They could stand in the afternoon sun when days are over one hundred degrees, on sticky Friday and Saturday afternoons, always at four o'clock, when funerals usually are held, in tropical heat, and they do not sweat.

In this wind, I think of planes scampering to the island in the escaping month of March. It is the collar that is causing me this discomfiture. Once again, I am seeing the undertakers of the island, in wonder at their ease in wearing thick black and starched white in that sweltering island sun. I wonder how they were able to breathe long enough to complete the slow walk behind the bloated, heavy-bodied coffin, made heavier by the deadness of the weight and the humidity, and the ornaments and the luxurious wreaths.

In this taxi now, no word passes between us. We sit and listen to the taxi driver. It is similar to our first taxi journey together. But this taxi driver, knowing the city like the palm of his hand, better than the African, a new Canadian now, moves in and out of traffic without losing his nerve or his concentration, without missing a word in his unanswered monologue about how cold it is this Christmas, and about his certainty and fear that we will not have snow on Christmas day.

We are now at the subway station which has the same name as the liquor store. Summerhill. Passing the special meat store where a steak can cost you the price of a concert ticket in the orchestra at Roy Thomson Hall. Canadian Tire, and Christmas trees, and the outstretched fingers of the intersection of three roads, Yonge, Dupont, and Davenport, are bare and cold and greyish white at this hour.

She bought the Christmas tree at Canadian Tire for five dollars, "for a steal," weeks ago. She brought it to the apartment in a taxi that cost her ten dollars, with the tip. The tree still stands in the corner, beside the piano, undressed.

At the corner of Yonge and Bloor are more people walking in the bright Sunday sun. A small band of shivering soldier-men and soldier-women of the Salvation Army stands around their collection cup hanging from a stand, like the cage of a bird. A trumpet, a fife, and a drum. I can hear their music, even with the windows closed.

"Away in a Manger."

Leaves of advertising broadsheets and pages from news-papers, plastic cups, and the plates that held wedges of pizza and are now like discarded, battered Frisbees are in the street. The green bins for garbage are stuffed and overflowing.

Last night, Saturday night, was certainly not the loneliest night. No word passes between us. The taxi driver has not stopped talking. He understands his job is to drive and talk.

The taxi driver is now telling us about bargains he got in his Christmas shopping.

Turkeys thighs: "No point getting a whole bird, not for myself alone!"; a pair of warm slippers for his mother: "She's in a home!"; and a twenty-inch TV for himself: "Just love those American football games on television, during the holidays!" And we are in front of Roy Thomson Hall.

She gets out the curbside door, shivers a little, leaving the door open, thinking I will use that door; but I pay the driver, then leave from the door on the street side. Absent-mindedly, she comes back to the taxi. I do not know what she has forgotten. Then, the slam of her door shakes the taxi. She smiles and says, "Merry Christmas!"

"Have a happy Christmas! Happy Christmas to the two o' you!" the driver says.

My wife is already at the large glass door of the entrance and does not look back. It is very cold on the sidewalk.

An usher is standing beside me. She touches me on the thick woollen jacket sleeve, getting my attention. I compare her manner of greeting and welcome to a gesture of brushing off a dead moth.

The usher is still touching my sleeve, soft and light as a moth itself. But she is only about to lead us to our seats. I move off, expecting my wife to be behind me; and as I walk, I admire the women standing in the lobby bright as fluorescent lights, like models, and I compare my rented suit against the custom-made ones of the men, and the designer finery of the women, and all through this I suddenly realize that she is not behind me. She is still standing near the entrance. Smoking a cigarette, smiling at the men and women she does not know. The surroundings make her beautiful. My heart flutters. She is my wife. I like her in these surroundings. I like her in the distance she is from me now.

I am glad that she is not close to me. The dress she is wearing is too revealing, now that I see it in these fluorescent surroundings. I wish she would walk off and make it hard to tell that we are together.

She is wearing a frilly dress. It is short. If I look, I can see with no difficulty where the panties of her tights, which sparkle with specks of silver, begin. Her shoes are red. Her favourite colour is red. She is standing, looking around at the other women also in expensive dresses, and is comparing the length of her own dress with theirs. Theirs reach below the calf or below the knee. Some sweep the carpet and the floor. They have bodies that are tanned, and faces that are tanned and arms that are tanned. Some of these women, with their new complexions made in Florida and the Bahamas, have the bronzed faces of coloured women, like my American statuette. I can read their itinerary just by looking at their tans. Their complexions contrast sharply, beneath the fluorescent lights and the cold, pale, biting temperature of this evening, with my wife's white skin.

She is inspecting them, as if she is counting them, subtracting from them, and selecting the right one to emulate. I go back with the usher to get her.

"We're together," she tells me, making sure the usher hears her tone.

There is a smile on her face. On the usher's face, too. So, I decide to smile.

"This is my husband," she tells the usher.

I am not about to answer her.

"Tell her, dear."

"This is my wife," I tell the usher.

The usher has not had a chance to speak a word yet in her defence; but something about her posture tells me she could be from the Islands, and I know that that could cause a riot in this lobby. I become very uncomfortable. A tight, burning pain comes into my chest. I want to tell this young woman something to make her think kindly of my wife and of me, but I cannot think of what to say. I know that this usher, no more than nineteen or twenty years old, has seen something in my wife's attitude. And I think too that there is something, a dis-position, a temperament, in this usher that matches Room's loss of temper, which begins with complete, cold silence, and then can erupt in the strongest language, much of which is spoken in Filipino Spanish. In the strong, fierce juxtaposition, usher and Room, and usher and my wife, I do not know if tenderness is what is required to make this Sunday evening in this brightly lit lobby a night to remember.

"I am very sorry," I tell the usher.

I see the usher's face change colour back to its natural soft, brown smoothness; and her long black hair gets blacker and shinier against the red woollen blazer of her uniform. The change of colour makes her fragile, and I get the urge to put my arm round her body, and draw her close to me.

"Prick!" my wife says.

But the usher does not react to this, if she hears it. She is looking into my eyes. I think she sees warmth and confusion in my eyes. But more than anything else, she sees allegiance and consolation. And then, she leads us into the hall.

Men and women are moving slowly, like waves of water strewn with the debris of the leaves of autumn, some of them yellow and brown. But gold and red are the predominant colours this Christmas. It is as if this auditorium is decorated with tuxedos and gowns that sweep the thick carpeted aisles, shimmering with trims that have been dipped in precious jewels of gold and silver and ruby. And this makes me feel that the dresses and the jewellery and the tuxedos will be strung on the tree as decoration the moment they get back home.

"I've been coming to these concerts for years!" she says. "Since I must've been in my teens. From the first time my uncle brought me to one. The first time he came up from Michigan to babysit me. And I tell you . . ." I am seeing my reflection in a panel of glass as I am moving from the huge lobby to a door that leads into the hall. And I see my wife's too. And I can understand now why the usher does not think we are together. My wife looks so young and coquettish, yet fragile, like a flower; like a "petite" flower, as she told me that first July afternoon, is what she is. And in the fluorescent light where she has been standing admiring the women, she could pass for my daughter.

The makeup she wears is thick on her cheeks, under her eyes, on her lips, making them appear flushed and thick and like the first signs of pubescence.

She looks like an adolescent.

"Do you believe that?" she says, as we creep behind the wall of waves, bodies ebbing through the doors, into the auditorium. "You believe that? That my *uncle*, the son of a bitch . . ."

She is whispering now, for the press of people touches us and we can touch them as we crawl to our seats. "The same uncle I told you about, that afternoon? It was he who brought me first to these concerts?"

We cannot move too fast now. The crowd is funnelling itself into our aisle. So we stand. The couples ahead of us stop and wave to friends they see, and know, and smile with us. My wife smiles. We are now, at last, inside the auditorium.

I am overcome by the size of the audience, and by the splendour of the occasion. It is the first time I am in Roy Thomson Hall. I look at this huge, comfortable, fortunate gathering; and not one person, man or woman, have I ever seen on any street in this city. None of them resembles any of the men and women who come before me seeking to be refugees.

This is a different branch of the Canadian tree in the forests of this vast half a continent. I know that most of these women wearing their small firmaments of stars and other constellations of jewellery have left maids and nannies and servants dressed in starched blue and in white aprons and muslin dresses, in uniforms with caps, at home in mansions, to keep the children quiet, to put the finishing touches to the after-concert dinner, to plan the soirée of pâté and champagne and white wine. I can see their tables and sideboards laden for the feasts to follow this performance.

"That son of a bitch came here. In this very hall. Brought me here!"

I have the sensation of being cowed, of just entering a church. The aisles are full. The tide is slowed for one moment, by a gesture, a glance, a wave of recognition. There is a look of surprise to find the neighbour already seated in the congregation. And then, a second glance. This is the glance of recognition and envy and hostility. Her dress looks too much like

175

that the neighbour is wearing . . . and she did not have the decency to say she was attending the *Messiah* . . .

". . . to this sacred concert, and to hear Handel. Would you believe the gall of it?" And she laughs, a high, girlish giggle of short sarcasm. "My mother put me to sit beside him, on the other side from her. I didn't hear one goddamn note of the concert. He didn't give me a chance to listen to one goddamn chorus the choir sung that evening. You want to know why?"

We must appear to all these happy people as if we have not come from the same bedroom, from the same bathroom, from the same apartment, from the same taxi.

You can tell just by looking that some men and women you pass on the street are coupled, can judge and conclude that they belong to one another. I could be a man she picked up off the street, and brought out of the cold. She looks as if she is coming from a corner of a schoolyard, or the stage of a beauty pageant for women not quite women, or from the rehearsal rooms of the National Ballet of Canada. She is too young and too beautiful to be in the same photograph as I in this scarecrow outfit. She is like a painted, precocious nineteen-year-old.

In times like this, a man should be proud that the woman beside him is beautiful and alluring. . . .

We have to stop and stand in our row before we can get to our seats. She fills this pause with the memories the hall is coughing up.

"Four Christmases ago, I think it was four, yes, only four years ago . . . or maybe three . . . but four Christmases ago, I came with Auntie Reens, and . . ."

I am looking at her brown hair, made red by things she washed it in. It sticks to the sides of her head, and sticks up from the scalp, and then becomes plastered again along her temples by the use of a stiffening, plastering agent. Or hair-spray. Looking at my wife now shows me how hairdos can transform an older woman and make her appear to be nine-teen, like a kid who screams and jumps in the crowd that jams itself against a stage when her love of rock and roll music gets the upper hand of her body and emotions, who wears boots with leggings and short black ballerina dresses, and silver in her ears and nose and lips.

I am in moth-eaten black. There is a whiff of camphor retained in the smell and age of this black armour. Black makes me look old, like something taken out of the cupboard or the dresser where once old and priceless things that have now lost their value are taken out for the sake of a glimpse of nostalgia. And when that moment for memories passes, it will be put back up, zipped in a plastic bag, and quieted like a wayward child. It will be forgotten until the next visit of aunts, and Christmas when it comes around.

In the large telling panels of this Roy Thomson Hall, I see the true picture of my wife. The way I see my wife is the fortunate glance in the apartment, in the bedroom, in the bed, any-where, is the fortunate glance that brings home the shock that we are man and wife, "till death do us part."

Yes. She does look unattached from me. She has probably seen this too, and wants to make amends. For as she talks about her uncle and concerts, she still clutches my arm as other couples do. And we move in the same slow joined wave as they do.

The moment she presses her tight-fitting dress against my black cloth, I can smell incense and fresh wrapping paper for gifts, and the smell of Grand Marnier with its bottle uncorked. And rosewater. And I smell oranges from the East packed in tissue paper in a box. One of the poets of this country once sang a song about tea and oranges that came from as far away as China.

Her smile as she talks is the handmade silver star, the Star of Bethlehem, that she will put at the top of the green tree. It will be I who will attach it to its tallest branch. And I can smell Chanel No. 5. We shall kiss, as we have done for three straight years now, under the Christmas tree when the lights are plugged in.

"Happy Christmas, dear," I say.

"Merry Christmas, dear," she says.

There is a postcard of a ballerina which she has framed. It hangs over the washbasin in our bathroom. The ballerina wears red shoes. Shoes for dancing. My wife loves red shoes. I have seen her sitting on the side of the bed, on the side where I sleep with the dog on my feet, the side that gets the full blast of the cold wind from the north, and apply her makeup and nail polish, and press her lips on a white Kleenex, after the small cosmetic brush had travelled too thick and too slow over her lips. And she would leave a perfect duplicate of her lips and sensuality on the delicate, receptive piece of paper.

I carry in my wallet the tissue with her lips on it. I transfer it in the hidden pocket of my robe when I sit on the Bench. I am carrying it now, in this sombre black suit I am wearing. It is folded into four.

I fall in love with her always and again, in that powerful and dramatic womanly moment of correcting colour and tint.

In the same way as she corrected the application of makeup, the stained Kleenex she used on her lips had disintegrated the moment she tossed it into the toilet bowl in the swirling green water. She had not even aimed for the bowl. Did not even look. She just flicked her wrist. Careless but sure, like a basket-ball player, and it was gone. *Slammmdunked!*

Before we left the apartment, she had drunk two glasses of red wine. "To put the right spirit in this old body!" she'd said. And she walked around the apartment as she dressed, all the while talking to Auntie Reens on the telephone, selecting one piece of clothing and jewellery, the colour of bras and panties and pantyhose, and rejecting them, as the long extension cord trailed behind her, leaving the rejected items on the bed.

"There's an extra ticket," she had said, days before.

Part of this moving conversation she had had with Auntie Reens I could not hear. She spoke in single, bullet-like words, shot and pronounced in something like a code, in a lowered voice. In their pig Latin language. All this time, I had been struggling with the button at the neck of the starched white dress shirt.

She has been drinking just a little more heavily as the days draw close to Christmas, as the temperature drops. Slowness and a slight loss of balance have come into her gait. When she drinks like this, an expression of satisfaction, complete con-tentment, the face of someone who is smug or hiding a deep secret, replaces her own face. Tonight, she has this wiped, drugged countenance. The smugness that comes to the face after smoking a marijuana joint. But she does not smoke pot. The auditorium is warm, overheated to neutralize the cold outside, and this could be affecting the way her face looks.

Perhaps, it is the anticipation of excitement and the joy in the large auditorium. For this music we are about to hear, and with Christmas on our breaths, she is as excitable as a child. A happy woman. And I join her in this reflection.

This is one of the things I love her for. Small things. Things that move her. And make her passionate. Things like the dead smoke that rises from a snuffed-out candle. And she can shout for joy and shake her body in laughter and raise her voice, and lose her voice in her high-pitched laughing. At the sight of a green leaf on the stem of a geranium plant, in a pot on the balcony. Or when colour blossoms on the leaf. And when she sees the red and the pink of its first flowers, it is a celebration and victory, and she yells, "*Awright!*" And throws her arms high into the air, as a baseball player does at the crack of a home run. Or when her favourite hockey player, Tie Domi, scores a goal for the Leafs.

I have seen her taste the first cup of coffee brewed in the coffee-making machine, and which she has to drink first thing every morning to settle her nerves and help her face "those bitches I have to work with," as she calls her colleagues and her boss. She is the second in command in her department.

As the first thick mouthful touches her empty stomach, I hear the exclamation of her delight. And where I am in the bedroom or the bathroom, I picture her in a Blue Jays uniform, trotting in a dance of high-fiving fingers and hands round the three other bases with her arms raised in victory, pointing and pumping and hot-dogging.

"Oh *shit*!" she screamed, one morning.

She was late. The alarm did not wake her. Auntie Reens had forgotten to call. It was a morning of frayed nerves and tempers.

I thought she had cut her leg and bloodied it while shaving. She worships her legs. And I do, too. Or that the coffee had soiled her silk dress. She dresses with the same fastidiousness of style to go to work as to go to concerts, the ballet and plays, bars and restaurants with Auntie Reens. Thinking about this now, I realize I do not have her culture. I do not go with her.

That morning, I did not move immediately. Why didn't I move and run to her rescue?

"You all right?" I asked, without moving.

For a while, there was no answer. I began to feel guilty. I imagined her bleeding to death. Having lost blood and consciousness. Was this a wish? Then her voice exploded.

"*Holy shit!*"

She was not dead. My terror wound down like a balloon with escaping air. I was not guilty. Laziness or disinterest? My wish for her disappearance had not been granted. She had not sliced her finger off as she was slathering her toast with thick butter and orange marmalade from Jamaica. She was not bleeding slowly to death. Had not died.

"Are you all right?" I asked.

When I did enter the kitchen, she was standing before the sink. She was calm. She had the same look of complete composure that she has now, in the auditorium when she was telling me about her sitting beside her uncle to hear the *Messiah*. She kept her back towards me.

"*Taste* this goddamn coffee!" She still did not turn to face me. "Isn't this the fucking *greatest*?"

I went back into the bedroom and continued dressing. Nothing had happened. It was the coffee. The coffee from Kenya.

And soon afterwards, when she was leaving for work, her lips were printed on two places on the white demitasse, in red. The cup was full to the brim. Her lips were also stamped on the discarded Kleenex tissue, which she had left on the counter beside the mug. She had left back all the coffee, made strong like espresso, after that first taste.

She does this often. Tasting things and discarding them afterwards.

"I told you, didn't I, that there's an extra ticket?" she says.

"Yes, dear. You did."

I am falling in love with her again. In this formal environment.

"I wonder if I have it with me?" she adds. "'Course I have it!"

Her lips are full and red. I feel I want to kiss them, and ignore the music. She is a "petite" flower.

"Perhaps I already gave the ticket to her."

"To whom?"

She does not answer.

"To your mother? It was hers, wasn't it?"

She does not answer.

And I do not care.

She had been referring to herself as a flower, this flower, this "petite" flower. I have been trying to find a flower of that smallness, that fragility, in the English Flower Shoppe in College Park where, for the first anniversary of our meeting, on her birthday, I bought her a dozen long-stemmed red roses. Red is her colour for all things precious. The florist strengthened the stems with green wire. I placed the flowers into her hand. I did not write a note on the card the florist gave me. I placed the roses into her hand, and kissed her cheek; and she thanked me.

"I prefer yellow," she said.

She laid them out on the counter.

"But these are very lovely, too," she added minutes later.

This is the first time that we have dressed in such formality and gone out together. But why couldn't she have kindled this excitement before, and made it take over the apartment, and, and, and . . . and overwhelm the dog and Auntie Reens and warm us with its singular purpose? Consume us, even she and me, with its love?

There is a black mole at the right side of her mouth. It looks larger and artificial tonight. At this time of dressing up, women put things on their faces to make them become a deeper, surer object for seduction.

Her mole is no aspect of this seasonal fashion. It is real. It is natural. A blemish from the womb. She used to try to hide it, under cosmetics, but a photograph in a fashion magazine made her begin to cherish it.

"The times I've been coming to this bloody place! And the conditions under which . . ."

In this magnificent hall named after a man who came to this vast half a continent, and from an insignificant beginning became, in short time, a billionaire, it is Christmas, and privilege. Roy Thomson Hall.

The instruments are brass and silver, and glistening. Some are of polished wood. The men and women who hold them are setting them to the correct pitch, with trial outbursts of shortened scales and trial notes. The women in the choir file on stage holding music sheets at their hearts and breasts. There are one hundred, or one thousand of them. They walk in solemn, creaking step to suit the buzzing, whispering anxiousness in the hall. The men in the choir are more robust and less reverent. They have had more practice; and they hold their music sheets as if they are about to toss them at the audience. All of them are dressed in the same stiffness. They look like penguins, and the blood in their faces, or the tans they have collected down South or from the liquor bottle, brings out the features of their freshly cut short hair with distinction.

They enter in much more disarray, and settle with greater noise into their seats than the women.

The austerity and the stiffness of the evening grips me in some awe.

She has introduced me to this kind of company and music, telling me it is good for me, it is a civilizing influence to my life on the hard Bench where I listen to nothing but desolation and terror.

"What the hell? It is Christmas!"

I do not know how I will listen to two hours of this sacred music. One thousand voices singing the *Messiah* is the population of misery of any island in the chain where I was born. Or is it one hundred?

But years ago, in a church that is two hundred and fifty years old, older than the political declaration of independence of this piece of continent itself, and which looked its age because of the crumbling belfry that was made of limestone quarried locally, I sang in the choir of this Anglican village church. And I fell off tune each time during my soprano years, from the thick richness of cooing so many hosannas and hallelujahs at Easter time. And we sang some Handel, a little of the *Messiah*, and knew the *Passion*, at Easter.

Afterwards, I slumped on the soft cushions, which the Mothers' Union group had made, on which we knelt when the organ, which breathed like a whale, stopped abruptly in its deflated anger. And the choir stopped, too. And the vicar's eyes turned grey as the blade of a sword of steel.

Now, facing this stage, I see that my loneliness then and now is deep as the note struck from the bow against the shining dark-stained instrument, larger than a violin, tucked under a man's chin.

I wish that I had read more of the program notes about the

Messiah. I wish that, in this audience of sparkling dresses and formal suits and nervous clearing of the throat, I knew precisely at which moment to begin my clapping applause. I hope that I am able and bold enough to go to the bathroom at the right moment after waiting all this time for the music to begin.

There is something about being in a strange place, a place above your means, and wearing a suit that is not your own, and that is too small, that brings on, without reprieve, the urge to pee.

I wish that I was back in the apartment, watching a woman on public television make recipes and dishes that come from France.

I move in my seat. And I seem to be sitting heavily on my bladder. It is the tight-fitting trousers. My testicles are being squeezed. I ease the pressure. The seat is becoming hard, and too small for my squirming body. I put one leg over the other. I then change to the other leg. And go back to the original position.

"Would you like to *leave?*" she whispers, too loudly. She does not mean it. But is she reading my mind? She moves in her seat too; and I wonder if she too wants to pee. She looks behind, and then up in the balcony, as if she is searching for someone.

The lights are being lowered now. She has not found the person she has been looking for.

The first few notes of the *Messiah* come into my mind, and I realize that I did sing this song, a song of acknowledgement of sorrow and resurrection, all my life back in that island. The names of Caiaphas and Josephus come back to me. But I did not sing the *Messiah* with one hundred competing voices. "You can, you know." It is her whisper in my ear.

It takes me a while to realize that it is her voice. And that she is not talking about numbers. Her manner is so calm. This makes me uneasy.

"Reens! I see her! Behind. Look!"

And I turn and look into thousands of faces, and do not pick out Reens's.

"She could have your seat, if you . . ."

I lose the last words in the rustle of the skirts of a woman who adjusts her weight and balance to move along the aisle in front of us. My wife is peeved at this interruption that cuts off her words.

"*Leave!* If you want to." Her voice is calm, as if she is not really ordering me. It is a whisper. And this frightens me. "In all the years I've been coming to the *Messiah*, I've never come with anyone who wants to get up and leave the minute the curtain rises! Not *even* my uncle, who . . ." She is hissing this into my ear, for me alone to hear. But the woman next to her can hear, too.

"*Would* you please . . . ?" the woman whispers back.

I see the usher at the end of the long aisle, standing between the velour drapes, beneath the red exit sign. And I see the Filipino woman from the southern island of Kiambo putting her hand between the plastic curtain, parting it, to let her body through its division, to enter the hot steaming shower. I see the usher, and I see the smile of contentment on her face. I see the smile that comes over Room's face, her eyes closed, as the water of warm holiness comes out of the fifteen holes in the round galvanized spout above her closed eyes.

"Bathroom," I whisper.

"At a *time* like this?"

"Bathroom," I say. "And a drink of water," I add, to soften the accusation of being uncivilized.

"You want to have a drink of water? Are you gonna *miss* the opening of the *Messiah* for a bloody drink of water?"

Her voice is no longer subdued. The woman beside her shoots a glance in my direction. Disapproval.

"Go *now*, then," she whispers, as if telling me the coast is clear.

She is no longer angry. She seems too happy, relieved by my insistence. I become suspicious. But there is really no reason. She is an understanding wife who understands a husband's eccentricities, even if they suggest a lack of civilization.

Yes. I used to sing in choirs, and I carried solos, too; and it was during the festivals of Easter and Good Friday, and I would sing with a heart filled with the glorious light of the daytime, and feel as holy as the days were consecrated. I would follow the melodious voice of Vicar Gomez, born in St. Vincent, reading the Scriptures in an English upper-class accent, in tones reciting the names of horror and brutality and flagellation and bodies lined in blood. All this remained with me all through my solo.

And at night especially, after the church was shut, when the cush-cush grass in the mattress rustled and made me think there were boots of soldiers coming to carry me to that hill named after skull and bones, the hill of Golgotha, I would dream of gardens with flowers whose names I did not know. But I knew the name of that garden: the Garden of Gethsemane. And I would dream of trials. And once in a trial, I would know the word to set my liberty at peace, and not taunt my superiors and my betters and any high priest who belonged inside the Sanhedrin.

Oh, those nights after the singing of the solo! Those nights when it seemed that nights were the cruellest things that could happen to a little boy! For even at my choirboy age, I had been exposed in the narratives of my mother to this nature of nights that were reserved for trials of love and of fidelity, of infidelity and fornication, and the smashing of virginities. With sicknesses bordering on death that seemed to come only at night. Anger at night. Murder at night . . .

"*Go!*" This is another whisper.

"Would you mind if . . . ," I begin to say, "and I don't want to leave you sitting alone while I . . ."

"I *am* alone."

". . . visit the bathroom. My collar is too tight."

"Go!"

The National Anthem starts. She is not moved by this summons to national pride. But she stands with the rest of us. And while "O Canada" is being sung, I am squeezing my body between knees and thighs and legs, walking out in this narrow aisle of men and women, passing and smelling their perfume and their resentment, and the alcohol on a man's breath, so close is his resentment to me, as I bend and twist my body, and almost lose my balance and fall into a woman's lap. A woman beside her smiles as I squeeze past and accidentally rub against her breast.

"Get-to-fuck down, man! *Move!* Man, move! Move! Jesus Christ, look how I miss that last right cross, because of this fucking . . . !" I was entering the pit of the Olympic Theatre back in the island, years and years ago, to see the movie *Death at Tuxedo Junction*, and I blocked a man's vision, for one second, when he said this to me.

I am brought back to the present now, saying, "Excuse me, excuse me . . . I am so sorry," after each inch that I creep along the aisle.

The thousand voices on stage have reached ". . . *our home and native land.*"

And soon, my escape will be made. I am almost below the red exit sign. And then, face to face, in this same aisle, in this narrow space and coming towards me, against the flow of my escape, is Auntie Reens. She does not look me in the eye . . . and I do not hate her for doing this, for the space we share is narrow and restricted and the light is dim and we are blocking the vision of others; and I am going and she is coming . . .

It is behind me now. That choice. But in the hard sense of unhappiness, like the ice I am travelling over on the sidewalk, the choice is still with me, in this present, in this cutting-off from the auditorium of Roy Thomson Hall.

Behind me now is the entire building washed in exterior lights. The applause inside it I am now too far to join.

But I can imagine the one hundred or one thousand voices and the orchestra in the packed hall, happy and loud, settling down in black serge and sparkle, to the long rejoicing hosannas with the *Messiah*.

Yes. I was in choirs, too, in the hot island where on a certain Friday night, choir-practice night, I walked with the other choirboys, including the three who had sat with me on the drenched beach when we talked about bigger girls during the long journey from the top of Clapham Hill down into the lower bowels of the neighbourhood, through Dayrells Road, to reach the dark church in St. Matthias Gap, now a silhouette against the purple skies.

There was no moon as I was going to choir practice on that Friday night before the Sunday, the Sunday before Easter, when I was to stand in the polished mahogany stalls with the silver crucifix round my neck, and sing the solos in the *Messiah*. The bishop would carry his crosier in his hand, holding it like that giant from the times of myth and legends who roared anger and desire because he had sired too many sons in his circular walk round and round a pole, grinding and grinding corn and women alike, to populate his captors' streets. That man who roared with anger and with desire, and the walls came tumbling down. That man who, with the one eye they left him, saw more with one than I did with two.

Sitting in the stalls on that and other Friday nights, with the rest of the church in total darkness and in silence, except for the voice of the sexton sitting in the very last pew, drinking rum from a bottle, at the back of the black church, I was in a different world, although I was in the same place as the darkness.

But it was the darkness of the church, on these Friday nights, that taught me about nights and darkness.

In the stalls, with the other voices, with the faces of my gang, group, bunch, my posse.

Yes. It is behind me now, all that singing.

I am walking down a darkened street away from Roy Thomson Hall, on this sidewalk of hardened ice. It gives no reflection of my movement because it is dirty and old. Not like fresh snow and thin ice, which sparkle and in their monotonous expanse can take away all sense of direction.

There is no light on this street. And there is no signpost to tell the name I shall call it by. It is like a field of snow scratched by three parallel lines made by a child's tricycle that has no tires.

I can see butts of discarded cigarettes and empty matchfolders and garbage bags that are green, and red-and-white supermarket bags, frozen into the glistening ice that I am walking on. Pieces of chicken, plastic bottles, empty cans that had beans and peas and cartons once filled with skim-milk leak from these tossed and discarded bags as in the slow motion of time in the frozen ice.

Where I am now, on this street that has no name, the debris is everywhere. This is not the city that tourists hear about.

I think of this dying time, the hour of the night, and the month of the year, and this time of death, and of flowers and of other fields like those that were once part of Scarborough's farms, but which are now frozen beneath the heavy blows of winter.

I hope I will see a man to break this heavy monotony, one of those who lives and spends his nights on round iron man-holes, which let in water in summer, and give off heat in winter, and that at least he has a hole to himself on a night like this.

I see a man in the tricky, uncertain light. He is sleeping on a sleeping bag, many layers thick. His possessions are crammed into plastic shopping bags, whose number and assortment tells me the scope of his journeys through the arteries of this city, and the success of his rummaging in garbage bins and the amount of spare change dropped into his cardboard tray.

There is a bundle buggy, which looks like a shopping cart from a supermarket, filled with his possessions. It looks like a small, well-made piece of machinery of war. And the closer I get to it, and can see its shining metal, it looks like a peram-bulator for a child.

A perambulator of that substance and model would not be found in front yards in Rosedale, whose mothers and fathers are in the audience I have left behind, in Roy Thomson Hall.

I can see this man pushing his buggy through streets that are no warmer during the day when the sun is shining than they are tonight. But he is as careful as if he were pushing his offspring on his daily rummaging and constitutional. And he must carry it, buggy and offspring, with him everywhere he goes to find food and shelter and spare change.

There are other homeless men who would steal his bed, and his makeshift perambulator, and his offspring, at the drop of a quarter.

I wish him success in his rummaging and in his requests for spare change. And I hope that if he endures the coldness of this evening, that he will live to see Christmas.

I am going down this street dark enough for loiterers and murderers and thieves to hide in, dark enough and neglected enough for the poor people of this city and those with no roofs, and who live on welfare, to be lost in, dark enough for a policeman to beat a loiterer to within an inch of death and then claim self-protection: "I feared for my life!" These streets belong to this beautiful cold city.

But these iron grates, manholes, which are the bedrooms of these men and women, leak steam and comfort and heat. They still make their dwellers safe from the thunderous, murky, cold waters that rage below in the sanitary sewers they cover. These covers are beautiful pieces of metal sculpture.

I walk on, looking right and left, as if I am anticipating thieves and murderers and loiterers, and the police. I am really searching for a neon sign that announces the name of a bar to enter, to get warm in, to get a drink.

Tonight is Sunday night. This Sunday is too close to Christmas for this cheer of liberality to be spread at so late an hour. At this time of night and season, people in this city are with their families and friends, are in hospital beds unconscious from interrupted holiday attempts to slice their wrists, or cut their throats, to kill the anxious coming-on of Christmas.

I walk on, trying to forget the past, and recount the good things I have done, the things with my wife, the good things we have done even after the arrival of Auntie Reens to congest the apartment, to take up residence, to take my place and take my seat.

I see a mound on the other side of this dark street, and it gets larger, and remains motionless as my steps echo on the cold, hard sidewalk. The sidewalk is made with cobblestones. I am walking on the memory of grandness and civility that once ruled this city.

And then I see in the distance getting shorter something that frightens me, steam rising above the object and the crammed shopping cart. This buggy has no rubber wheels. I see the plastic shopping bags. I see the red of a cigarette stub. It appears and disappears, like a message sent by lights, from a ship at sea, or on the lake.

It is a man. A tramp. A victim of the city's wars fought over the cost of welfare and the cost of borrowing money to pay for welfare. A war veteran. A homeless man. "A fucking disgrace to this beautiful city," a city councillor said, off the record, to the *Toronto Sun*, on the steps of Metro Hall last week, seven days before Christmas. "The hardworking people must be embarrassed. Only God knows what tourists will think about us, and this god-awful city, now!"

"Merry Christmas!"

It is a voice from the pavement that speaks to me. It is a man's voice. It takes me by surprise. It is too cheerful a voice for the cold in which he lives. It is sprightly, as if he has summoned up all his courage and cheerfulness to keep himself warm by talking.

I am beside him now. Standing over him. I can smell that scent that comes from cold nights like these, that inexplicable smell of coldness. Perhaps what I am smelling is the smell of human flesh that is frozen, or that is rotting. It could be the smell of the sewer leaking through the holes in the manhole.

"Happy Christmas!"

I tell him this, and he greets me one more time; and his greeting follows me as I turn into another street. And as I change direction, I realize that I have not pushed my hand into the right side pocket of my tight-fitting black serge trousers, to pull out a loonie, or a two-dollar coin, and drop it into his palm.

I turn into another street. It is a street that has a name. It is a street in repair. The buildings are in repair. Dust, which can still rise in the cold, strikes my nostrils; and the silenced, frozen construction boardings and an engine much larger than the shopping carts I have left behind tell me the street is waiting for the gentry. It is quiet as Sunday always is in Toronto.

The season's greeting of that man behind remains with me. Certainly, in his down and present state, he must know and remember a time when he would be under the tree, giving wrong instructions, as some men do, to his wife and son and daughter, about the clipping on of decorations, imitation icicles, chairs, toboggans, elves, Father Christmases, and animals that are in children's picture books, and that are made in Lilliputian size. And if he was one of those fathers back there, dressed like me in a rented suit from Tuxedo Junction, he would certainly be in his basement in the suburbs where basements are bigger, or in his den, sitting before a fire that rages more than the heat from this man's present iron grate. He would be drinking Canadian Club whisky from a large crystal decanter with lead in it from Holt Renfrew or Ashley, and not from the twisted mouth of a brown LCBO paper bag.

I carry his greeting with me, as I know I must, as I know its significance. As if I know it will be significant. And I walk on in greater loneliness and unexplained anxiety. For as I go alone now, I remember that she has always said that this habit of doing things alone, this walking alone, will be my fate and my future.

"You are such a miserable son of a bitch, you're gonna die alone, if you're not careful!"

I go, feeling stiff in this killing cold, hardly able to bend my legs to make the proper, normal steps.

I go. With no companion, with no one to exchange greeting. I am not much warmer than any man who lives on grates and manholes during the night.

I do not know what to do now. Or which other street to take. If I were still sitting beside her, before she saw Auntie Reens, I would feel her leg touching mine, even by accident. Even that would make me know she is still there. And I would feel the silent, untalking love, the love of a man and a woman who live together and hate to speak to each other. I would feel less lost than I am now.

Even into the harshness of her voice is brought a sense of belonging. A sense of affection that is not cancelled out by animosity. A sense that I belong to someone. Belonged to her. Belonging is belonging.

And I remember how calm and confident Auntie Reens looked, as we passed each other, going in opposite directions in the narrow aisle.

You see me now, as a man who has walked out on his life.

Because of what? What for? Ego? Anger? For what? I have no answer. Sometimes, there are no answers. I have just walked out . . .

I see my ego and my anger even before they are brought to my attention, even before I took the first few training steps to reach where I am now, along the aisle out of the growing darkness as the lights were lowered in the auditorium.

It is late. Now, after all the distance I am travelling on these streets that I know only in the gaiety of daytime, during the bottle of Pommard at the wine bar just around the corner on Wellington, walking with my colleague the priest and talking about God, and if there is one, purchasing a carton of Gauloises cigarettes, depositing a cheque at my bank; on these streets whose names and bumps and manholes and addresses I know, I am left free and with no rudder and no compass to force direction and destination with which to take my new journey in hand.

Time between her and me was not always wrong, was not always right. The spring had been wound too tight by the clockmaker. He was in a hurry to reach another appointment. In all this time, as always, the questions were set aside like peaches that have gathered bruises through age, and are not fit for the dinner table. Or like an avocado pear that is touched too often, is felt for ripeness too often, and then has to be discarded at the time of appetite and of serving. It can only be looked at now, and watched with disappointment, as it is replaced in the dish.

There is no patience great enough to quell the desire for eating green fruit or new love, even though it will be ripened in the morning. And then devoured, without notice.

Or else the fruit and the love are left with an impatient, testing bite into its green skin. Forgotten and green, or rotten. And spared the further marks of ravenous teeth.

I remember the Book of Proverbs just as I leave this street whose name I cannot see, and turn the corner in further darkness.

"Happy is the man that findeth wisdom, and the man that getteth understanding."

I can see the flannel nightgown that covers her body. When she passes under the ceiling light that is only a naked bulb with flies attached to it, the light plays tricks on the flannel, and I can see the outline of her legs.

I carry in my frozen footsteps along this street of cobblestones, St. Nicholas, the name I see below the light stand, a picture of the red basement door on Huron Street, and the dislocation and loss that that picture brings one more time in my life. I can say something about dislocation and loss. l can do nothing now about the circumstance which tore me irrevocably from that connection to her.

"You know I do not like crowds, nor wearing bright Polynesian colours," I remember was one of the last things she ever said to me.

The apartment smells now only of incense and her cooking. The Christmas tree leans green, with the single red silk ribbon, like a river of blood, frozen in one place, now that the dog is not here to play with it and turn the tree into a carousel with one swinging seat.

The dog is in Kingston, kept by her mother. It is the dog's Christmas present. Three years now she has wrapped gifts for the dog: designer dog food, designer coats like waistcoats for the dog, boxes of bones in the shape of hearts, made to look like chocolates, and a coupon to take the dog to a spa to have its paws brushed, its coat brushed and shampooed, and its nails clipped. The dog will be out of my sight all this cold, snowy Christmas-seasoned weekend.

I am sitting on the chaise longue, and passing my hand over its silk, cream upholstery, and I drift off into a doze, but I am going over the events of the day. I had lost all my money in the Friday-night poker game with my three friends, Cliff, Olli, and Jack, and I was tired, and was lying on the couch, trying to sleep, regretting my loss of two hundred dollars in the game, while my wife and Auntie Reens sat on the floor in the living room, with the homemade designer popcorn between them in a large yellow plastic bowl she used for making dough for banana cake and bread.

Their words were making me relax, and were lulling me into and out of the sleep I craved.

It was about two o'clock in the morning, and their hockey team had earlier won a place in the Stanley Cup playoffs; and they were happy, and were – between my sleeping and waking – giving each other high-fives, and they had continued to sit on the floor, dipping their hands into the large plastic bowl of popcorn, and were drinking red wine and chasing it with Grand Marnier, to celebrate the victory of their team.

And in between their drinking and being merry, and in between my sleeping and waking, I heard their voices, like far-off water, becoming waves, moving in to me on the beach, and then ebbing back from me into the farther waves of the living-room floor.

"I went shopping today at lunch?" my wife said. She got up from the floor, adjusted her white silk chemise, and continuing talking, and eating popcorn, she went to the piano and took a parcel from the keyboard. It was a white cardboard box in a white shopping bag. She removed the white tissue paper, and eased the silver circle with the name of the store where she bought it from the tissue paper, and lifted from the box two pieces of clothing which she shook out, and they became two pairs of panties. One was black. One was red. They were both made of lace. "Which? Which one do you want?" she asked Auntie Reens.

Reens held both of them up, in front her face, and looked at them, and through them, and from where I was lying on the couch, I could see her face, though not her eyes, through the transparent, patterned, and delicate lace.

"I imagine this won't cover much of you . . . honey!" Auntie Reens said.

"Which one?" my wife said.

"Do you realize," Auntie Reens told my wife, "that you raise your voice at the end of what you're saying, even when you aren't asking a question?" They both laughed at this.

"Which one do you *choose*?" my wife said.

"Which one don't you want?" Reens said. "Tonight is *Friday*! Remember?"

"What little's left of it," my wife said, as she looked at me, just as I had sat up on the chaise longue, this chaise longue she had bought one Saturday at the Goodwill store on Jarvis Street for fifty dollars.

Eight months later, my wife had the chaise longue reupholstered by Simpson's, for seven hundred dollars.

"*Who* would know," she said, when it was delivered, "this came from a junk shop?"

My wife bought many things second-hand. Reens bought almost everything "new-brand-new," on her charge accounts at the Bay, at Ashley, Birks, Eaton's, Creeds, and Canadian Tire, "because I can't swear to who had their ass on my couch."

My wife said that Reens was "a spoiled, rich bitch, that's what she is!"

But she did not believe this about her best friend, not really. It was just a touch of jealousy.

As I sit up now, and walk around the living room, I look at all this luxury and pieces of furniture and things that show good taste – all the things she assembled in this apartment. This room, which leads into the larger dining room, is cluttered with photographs and memories of herself. They were taken and gathered from those days when she was ten years old, of driving from Kingston to Michigan in the Volvo station wagon with her mother and father and brothers and sister, to visit her uncle.

And there are some photographs of her, when she was attending the National Ballet School, raising her leg above her shoulder as she stands stiff, athletic and precocious at the practice bar. And some framed informal snapshots of her family: mother, dead father, mother's brother, now dead, and all of these in oval frames of silver or of brass.

There are two framed portraits of the dog. One taken in winter showing him cowed by the heavy woollen Stewart tartan, made into a dog's waistcoat. One in summer showing him yapping, naked and with his coat raised in the passion of his playfulness.

I look carefully at her family, at this family of siblings and dog, as you do at a family when you see all its members for the first time. With wonder and interest.

I do not have any family that lives even in one photograph, in this apartment. For with mother dead, father dead, and brothers, one dead from typhoid fever, and another dead from some unknown cause, but which the vicar said was a "natural cause, 'cause we don't know the cause, and we never had autopsies in this parish to cause and raise scepticisms," and a lone sister somewhere in America, in Brooklyn, New Jersey, or Queens.

I look again at her family. There is a lake behind them. Just miles and miles of grey water and distant greenish trees. The rest is skies. Skies and water. They are standing on a dock.

The dock is wooden. There is no boat in the picture. There is no sand. Only rocks. But there is a lifebelt, a red inflated thing like an inner tube, like a gigantic LifeSaver mint. They are holding on to one another in a tight, laughing knot of summer blood and bond, a family tree.

There is a snapshot of her, flat on her back, flat to the full rays of sun which at lakes can make you dark. There is another one of her sitting in a pose I have seen in portraits by Gainsborough in the Art Gallery of Ontario, with a dog in her lap.

I look at these photographs, all of them, and at other scattered snapshots in frames, on tabletops, side tables and coffee tables, and I see for the first time that there is no photograph of me amongst her collection.

How did I not notice this omission in all the three or four years I have been in this apartment? Perhaps, in a mood of newness and redecoration, she had brought them out, all of hers and her family's out, just before we left for the *Messiah* at Roy Thomson Hall, and had forgotten in her haste to lay mine out, like headstones, with the other tombs!

Perhaps hers have been here all the time, and while my time was taken up with the black American statuette, I missed them. Perhaps. Perhaps I am not seeing any photographs of her and her family and the boatless dock and the sun in Spain. Perhaps, it is all in my imagination.

Perhaps, there have always been photographs of me, like statues marking boundary and culture and civilization, and I myself threw them into the incinerator with the Friday-night garbage, in a fit of rage.

Perhaps they are here, and I cannot see them. I can offer no reason why it had not occurred to me earlier to check the photographs in this apartment, and realize there are none of me.

A pair of ballet shoes is tied by its pink laces, and hangs over the upright piano. Another pair, more worn from dancing pirouettes, hangs over the toilet bowl in the bathroom. I know this pair.

She keeps small tins and vials of Tylenol in the two tips of these shoes. I see this pair every night when I enter into communion with the black American doll, drinking from her lips the slightest suggestion and innuendo from her two-faced answers.

The bathroom is painted pink. Its walls are covered with prints. One is of a ballerina dancing in red shoes. Prints and photographs of dancers and ballerinas, torn from magazines and framed in expensive ovals and squares and rectangles. Male dancers, too.

There is one print of a man from the National Ballet of Canada. When I'd seen him the first time, the first night she brought me here, to this apartment, from the summer party when we had sat together and she talked her life to me, I hated him. And I hate him still.

For months afterwards, I would have sworn that he was that man with whom she wanted to have the child. Still, I do not know.

Later on, she explained that this man I was jealous of is a famous man, with a famous unpronounceable name in the world of dance, and that it was he who made the first real grand jeté, and broke all previous history with this move, and that he came to America, a smaller continent than the one in which he originated and was born, by running into the arms of the immigration officer, with the speed with which he ran into a grand jeté, and said, "Take me. I am political refugee." And he's now dead.

Looking around now, in this large living room, I can paint

a portrait of my wife, and her tastes, her likes, the projects she has undertaken to finish, to make herself into a better person, into a better modern woman, into a better supervisor at her office, in order to become more independent of me, and of men, "*you pricks!*"

But most of these projects she abandons, in various stages of boredom, before completion.

She keeps her membership in the Weight Watchers program for young overweight executive ladies; and Auntie Reens, who is herself a little overweight, and who does not think it bad, or a "bloody problem," goes with her for company.

On the first cold Monday night of January last year, after all the holidays and parties, they went to work off the food they had eaten and had enjoyed the previous month. They lasted two Mondays. But they were happy.

But they continue to keep their Weight Watchers memberships through every January, and dump the course through non-attendance before the end of February. Auntie Reens says each February, "I was made this way. Fat is in! Or should be!" My wife has no answer for that, which causes Reens to add, "If you're so worried about a little weight, tell people you're Italian. An Italian mama, for Chrissakes!"

I do not need a Polaroid camera to paint an instant portrait of my wife. I can draw a picture of her, better than any sidewalk artist, just from the things she has adorned the apartment with: her possessions.

A file folder is left on the coffee table. It contains a covering letter she typed with her application for admission to a graduate course in social administration at the University of Toronto, two nights a week. I remember the night she licked the stamps, and pressed them on with the heel of her right hand, lined them up with precision on each envelope.

There is a second envelope. In it is her resumé, or as she calls it, "my currickerlum vi-tay." On the folder is the name of the department in the provincial civil service where she works as a manager. It still carries the scrawled signatures and classifications and departments of civil servants who have used this same inter-office envelope. I can almost tell the mood they are in when they open this inter-department envelope with the holes, by the hand used to sign their names. The envelope is ripped in these places.

She has not yet posted these two letters. And it is five months since she licked the stamps.

A piece of black vinyl covers the typewriter. I touch the cover with my hand, and my hand is caught in invisible strands of spider's web and human hair. It is months since I brought this typewriter to the apartment from McTamney's Pawnbrokers at Church and Queen, down from Wilde Oscars where she and Reens like to have a beer.

Eleven months ago, almost to the day, on her birthday, I brought this typewriter to the apartment.

"I tried my best with the bloody Weight Watchers, and it didn't work. And what did you care? I started the course in social admin at U. of T., two nights a week, after work, to upgrade myself. Did you ever sit down once and ask me if I had any problems? With my own hands, I made new cushions and blinds for this bloody apartment. I'm tired as a dog . . . not you, nice doggy-woggy! . . . tired as a slave when I get home. What do you do to help? I started to take cooking lessons? Did you ask me *how* my courses were going? If I got the books from the library? Like bloody hell!"

Then she turns to another project.

"I want to put my thoughts which are driving me crazy? Down on paper?" she says.

Her face is beaming. She is happy. Her happiness that she expresses about such simple things causes all those other days empty of this effusion to be more sad.

"*Poems!*" she goes on to say, but her enthusiasm to write poetry capsizes upon the pages of a small beautiful blank-paged book she bought at Mirvish Books, just off Bloor Street, near Honest Ed's.

She fills this little book on weekends, with every remembered detail of her life, of the previous five days. Meals she has cooked go into it. Scrabble games and their outcomes go into it, with comments on Auntie Reens's foul temper when she loses two times in a row. Her visits to Reens's house, the dog's visits to the vet, the four times after work that she and Reens visited their favourite bar, Wilde Oscars on Church, near Maitland, and one entire sentence on her husband: "MY HUSBAND IS MY FRIEND BUT HE CAN BE SUCH A PRICK!"

This is written in green, in block letters, with her Sheaffer fountain pen.

She does not use the typewriter for this autobiography. She has used it only once. And that was to write part of a sentence which Auntie Reens, an executive legal secretary with a prestigious firm of lawyers, told her is the one sentence written all over the world by secretaries, in numerous languages, to check the touch and the movement and the function and the workings of a new machine.

"Now is the time for all men to come to . . ."

She did not complete the sentence. And I do not know, and Auntie Reens is not disposed to telling me, what to expect of those men who are supposed "to come . . ."

But who is this woman? What do I really know of my wife?

This woman who has brought passion and risk, joy and the savagery of bliss into my life, beginning with the July afternoon in the summer when we listened to the music about Southern nights and magnolia trees nourished with blood at their roots?

Three years, and almost four, have gone by. Who is this woman from that afternoon that was so blessed by the blossoming pink and red impatiens, profuse as weeds after the rains in the hot island?

What does she hide so successfully in her angry moods that swallow me up? What prevents me from understanding that there is no animosity behind her change of face and her erupting mood?

We talked once. Long into that July night and into the next morning, when we drank coffee and Grand Marnier. We talked about the need for communication, talked about openness, and agreed that it was the foundation of any meaningful relationship.

That July night, we sat in the living room of her apartment, almost completely in the dark, except for the glowing tips of Tisang Tsang incense sticks, from Beijing, in tubular boxes painted in Chinese characters and half-naked women tanned to the colour of my black American statuette, and with long flowing ribbons like clouds, sticks planted into the soil of four flowerpots with the dieffenbachias and yellow mums in green plastic pots with cellophane round them, and with a plate under each to keep the water from marking her glass-topped coffee table. She pressed the tips of her half-smoked cigarettes into the soil of the pot with the mums and got up and went into the bedroom. When she returned, she was wearing a black silk housecoat with dragons and other mystical beasts drawn on the back; and I could see the scar on her leg more easily; and I could see her legs, because the band round her waist was not tied.

She sat down opposite me, and placed one foot on the edge of my chair, and the other on the glass of the coffee table. She raised her housecoat above her knees for relaxation and informality. And the time passed, and we talked.

Hours later, with the talking, and after we had got into the thick of kissing, and my tongue was tired and sore, and Pepsodent was colouring my taste, and my hunger for her body was raging, and I was so close to satisfying it, since I had eaten nothing for the whole day; with the wine in my head, I saw this woman with such savage, beautiful rawness and lustful wonder, that I knew she had already understood the death-like stranglehold she had on me.

I could feel her strong tongue as it dug into my mouth, turning my own tongue out of its way, marking the sore roof of my mouth, rubbing my lips and my ears with the sandpaper of her raging. We were placing the pot of yellow mums, which we had knocked down, back on its plate, and the water from the pot was already a pool on the coffee table, and the ashes and cigarettes left a mark on her off-white broadloom carpet, and the mark buried itself deeper into the carpet the more I passed the paper towel over it.

"Anybody would think we were screwing on it!" she said.

While she helped me mop the glass-topped coffee table, the band of her housecoat fell, and the front of her housecoat was open, and the black dragons and other beasts were scattered with the new hang of the robe, and were making her uncomfortable, so she took it completely off. And I saw the short white silk chemise underneath.

I saw the full, seductive beauty of her body.

Seeing it, breasts and heaving belly, and her legs as if they contained muscles which were about to burst through her skin, her body which was white, whiter than her arms and legs, transferred its life into my own body and made it tick faster and tremble. We dried the water from the table.

She did not put the dragon-encrusted housecoat back on. It was late. The first streaks of dawn were coming through the large picture window, over the balcony, through the solarium. Dawn showed me the tallness of the trees that ringed the grounds of the apartment building and the red slate on the roofs of buildings nearby. I did not know where I was.

She put a cassette on the stereo, and the song about the strange fruit and blood and Southern trees filled the room with a soft, plaintive, but tense feeling. The effect was like the pain in my mouth from the violence of her tongue, mixed with the ecstasy of touch, and the taste of Pepsodent, and the smell of rosewater.

The song played and played again; and when it had outlasted both our appetites, and our attention, I asked her how long could one cassette last. And she said, "If I like a tune, I tape it, and tape and tape it . . . four or five times? . . . for hours."

Yes, it was at this time of exhaustion with the variations of kissing, when I attempted to go beyond the decency of first meeting, when she said, "Not the first time, if you don't mind?"

And with nothing more to do, my appetite already sharpened and then made dull, and satiated by the closeness of our bodies, and the accidental destruction of her things, arranged so beautifully in her large living room furnished with antiques – for in our passion, we had knocked down and almost killed one of her plants.

But the new light, the dawn of this new love, was taken up with coffee and sipped Grand Marnier, and the answers were no longer significant.

All during that night we listened to the song about the Southern nights, and we talked and talked.

She poured more coffee in demitasse cups with smaller dragons painted into their fragile bodies, and their mouths tipped in delicate rings of gold. And she patted my leg, dropped a drop of Grand Marnier into the snifter I was drinking from, and closed her eyes, with her cigarette cocked to one corner of her mouth. When she patted my leg, the touch took me back to the gesture of my mother, who did the same thing when she wanted to assure me that I was a nice little boy.

"Did you tell me that the scar . . . is it your left leg, or the right? Did you say a motorcycle accident caused it?"

"I have had accidents."

She patted my leg again.

That first night, when the night turned into morning and found us talking, there was a greyness into which I was looking that painted the buildings across the mysterious courtyard. I still did not know where I was. There was no address on the front of the building and no name on the door; and I could not remember the address she had given to the African taxi driver. But I felt safe, and new and daring.

We remained in this new light, with fresh coffee, and we drained the bottle of Grand Marnier; and when it was finished, we poured warm water from the kitchen tap into the bottle, and swirled it round, and added it to our coffee . . .

Outside, in the warm early morning, waiting for a taxi, I looked across the courtyard, the blues in my mind, and wondered what was the name of those tall, green, stately trees? I looked around me, in this courtyard, which told me only that the rich lived here.

Even the deep breath that I breathed in seemed cleaner and different from the air in the neighbourhood of Huron and Spadina and St. George, of the basement bedsitter where the Filipino woman lives.

That my curiosity went beyond the measure of decency which I myself had always understood to be the barrier against curiosity itself, the boundary between curiosity and invasion, left me shaking with remorse. But I was shaking with rage as much as I was shaking from the shock of my action.

I am rummaging through the two drawers of the bureau. Digging into the second and third drawers of this antique dresser where she keeps her things.

She is tidy. She is almost impeccable. Bordering on the immaculate. I have always liked that in her. And her cleanliness, and order, as I can see it in the arrangement of her possessions, suggest also a touch of godliness.

But I am not seeing this now, as I am driven to this desecration. And why am I being driven to this?

All her personal . . . all her . . . her panties are arranged by colour, texture, style, the demand of the occasion, and price. I handle them now, with the three fingers of my left hand, thumb, index finger, and second finger. I begin to feel, through their touch of delicacy, the reminiscence of moments of satisfaction amongst the spasmodic passion and sexuality of our lives, the three Fridays in a month; and I am not even remembering at this moment that there was a time when I touched them when they were still on her body, when she wore them under a white silk chemise two nights ago, or when they were taken off, never by me, but by herself, and pulled down, discarded, and flung onto the carpet afterwards, as we watched television.

I would always smell the dog's urine dried into the carpet, whenever we lay there.

I hold her bra now, high up before me, expecting greater light to come in from the window (but the light is good enough from the floor lamp), this window which does not even keep out the noise of the subway trains travelling south and north. This window is not protecting me from the noise of the trains as they clamber into their terminus at the end of their shift, or from the cold Yonge Street north wind.

I am surprised she is so large in her measurements, when I read the size printed into the tags of her undergarments. For when she is dressed, her chest looks flat, restrained, as if flattened by the bones in a corset.

But the cups I hold now in my hand show me her true size. And they send a thrill of strange satisfaction through my body. I have never thought that the touch of cloth worn against the flesh could bring out a sensation so similar to the touch of the flesh itself. And it brings back to me the hunger and the pain I suffered on that first night in July, in the summer, years ago, when I held her breasts in both my hands, and then had to leave their tantalizing power unrequited.

"*Not the first time?*"

She had said it both as a question, and as a reprimand. But the nuance in her voice had the same effect. And the voice she used, and the glasses of Grand Marnier, and the coffee, softened and dulled the anger in my disappointment. And it was then that I thought she was genuine. For that was the first lesson she had given me about her character and her upbringing.

It must have been this, this aristocracy, this class, this sophistication, that caused the choice I knew I had to make the following day to come through. Sacrifice must be made to ensure gain. "Tough. How ya like *them* apples?"

But what am I looking for now, amongst her personal garments? Evidence? What evidence? Evidence of what? What has driven me to this molestation and assault upon her privacy in her absence? This terrible lingering and accumulated doubt about a woman with whom I sleep, lie beside in bed every night of every week of every month of every year for the past three or four years and a few months? Falling asleep in the same bed beside the clattering noise of cars down in the visitors' parking lot, and the chattering of the parking subway trains, eight floors below, all these long years, and with the dog buried between us?

And I am going back to those many sleepless nights, those countless nights when I pretended to be asleep, when she moved my hand from its search along her thighs the moment my fingers touched the soft brown hairs in the clinking darkness, in the cold bed, and caused her to mutter, as if she was snoring and grinding her teeth at the same time, and say, "I'm *sleeping*?" She always turned her back to me, and with noise and the violent moving of her body, she would resettle herself into the trough the mattress had provided for her safety and rest. I was always the one left with a raging headache.

As time went on, a stiffness in my chest followed the headaches. And then, all that was alive during those long nights of rebuke was the movement of trains and the wheezing of the wind and a cat crawling along the wrought-iron rails of the joined balconies, crying out, and me counting sheep, and remembering lines of worthless poems:

O, Mary, go and call the cattle home,
And call the cattle home,
And call the cattle home.

Buried under one pile of underwear is a photograph. It is of her, when she was about thirteen years old. She could be ten. I have never seen this one before. It is in a frame the shape of a heart, painted silver. Her face shows even then the beauty it would take on, and the roundness as she grew older. Her legs are strong-looking, much too developed for her age, but brought about perhaps from the exercises at the ballet bar, in front of one of which she was standing. Confident and challenging, as if she is looking for a fight. And very beautiful.

This photograph must have been black and white when it was first taken in the studio whose name is printed at the bottom, in raised letters, faded out of recognition. Now, it looks the colour of sepia.

In this photograph, there is a ribbon in her hair. Her hair is plaited in the shape of a diadem. There is something about her hands in this photograph, something that has always attracted me. Her hands are older-looking hands than the hands of a thirteen-year-old child. And even now, today, they are older, longer hands for her age.

They are the hands of a woman who moulds clay into shapes, the hands of a woman who digs trenches and plants fruits and vegetables, of a woman who holds instruments for digging up and weeding, on land as vast as the fields that are now the suburb of Scarborough. Rough hands. Tough hands. Strong hands. Hands that look crooked because their fingers show joints that are prominent, and strong. Large old hands.

The smile on her face is the same as the smile I faced and surrendered to when I met her four summers ago, on the wooden deck bordered by the beds of flaming red impatiens, the deck that showed the vehemence of nails driven into its cedar planks, with some heads left showing.

I pull the photograph out of its frame. In the process, I rip a small piece off the corner. But I get it out entirely, eventually. On the back of this photograph is handwriting which says, "My Petite Orchard, This is my favourite pix of you – Uncle." Between the two pieces of cardboard backing that hold the photograph in place is a note. It is in different handwriting from that on the photograph. The date in the left-hand corner at the bottom shows it was written two years ago, one day before she and I stood in the draughty room in the Old City Hall building, in front of the judge, on our wedding day. The note had been torn in half, and then into another angry half. There are edges which were not cleanly ripped.

I read the part that remained undestroyed:

. . . and I must say that although I think I understand what is happening and has happened to make you make this decision you are about to make that after all these years I have to feel you have betrayed something that we had for your future comes first before my present and the past which is all that you have left me with but I shall always love you.

I place the pieces together on the bed. I take a deep breath to settle my trembling hands before I pry farther into her past.

The note flows undecidedly to its point and conclusion. The note had been balled up, perhaps when it was received, and its contents read first at a glance; and then flattened out; and then ripped into four.

I am able to feel and experience the emotion and the anger that went into its spontaneous destruction, when it was first received. I then realize that only part of the note had been kept. The combustion of rage must have burnt out the part that was too incriminating, or too personal, or too detestable, or too embarrassingly true.

It takes me a while to read it, without punctuation.

My first reaction is to rip the note and the photograph into shreds. But there is mystery in the note, something almost sacred, something hidden, something that only the writer and the present owner of the note are meant to understand. And this mystery burns my curiosity.

I place the note back in the heart-shaped frame, and am about to replace the two pieces of cardboard backing when a second photograph falls out onto the bed with the four piled pillows against which I am sitting. This photograph was cut roughly into the shape of a heart to fit the frame.

Two women are in this photograph. Impulsively, I throw the photograph to the floor. And immediately after doing this, I pick it up.

It seems to be out of focus. I do not see the images clearly. And then I do a strange thing. I glance over my shoulder, to make certain that no one is in the room with me. Am I making sure no one can witness my agitation? Or witness that I am a voyeur? To see, and to know, this other side to my wife's character? Her proclivities? To catch me red-handed? And to see this other side to *my* character?

There is no one.

I think of the dog. Why do I think of the dog at a time like this? Many times, when I was worrying over my wife, or over a refugee case I had to listen to on the Bench, or over women who are Tamils, or over her staying out late, and trying to learn things about her customs, I very often wished that the dog she loved so much could talk.

Today, the dog is with her mother in Kingston. I listen carefully for its noise, nevertheless. There is no one in the other rooms. All I can hear are the subway trains eight storeys below, clambering to the end of their scheduled runs, in the station swept clean by the wind, and trains banging and clanging into their berths just outside the window that is eight floors above, and the rock and roll music coming from the wall of the neighbour next door, on the left.

My thoughts pass to her now in the audience in her sparkling dress. I think of her in a collision of steel and subway trains and in the cold wind. I see her resting her hand in Reens's hand, her eyes closed, as she listens more attentively to the hallelujahs and hosannas of the *Messiah* that soothe their appetites for music played over and over, like the blues song about Southern fruit.

How many choruses have the thousand-voiced choir sung in the *Messiah* by this time? How many more hours does she have to sit in the plush red seat, one row from the front, she always liked, looking up at the hairs in the nose of the man playing first violin, into the mouths of the singers and the bells of instruments polished to a blindness? How much longer before she puts her key into the door of the apartment and calls out, "*I'm home!*"

Would she announce her arrival this time, like at other times? On this Sunday night? To put me on my guard?

Announcing her greeting while still standing outside the door, even when she was beside me, when she called out, "*I'm home!*" she was really talking to the dog. Not to me. Perhaps, if the dog could talk . . .

The photograph is not old. The second one from the heart-shaped frame. It is in colour. But I can see one woman kneeling over the other, on a bed. They appear to be wrestling with each other, and are laughing. And one woman is wearing a white chemise. The photograph shows me these two women.

Sure in their beauty, romping in a version of pillow fight, appearing as if they have just landed on a trampoline, their hands grabbing for each other, and one woman gawking at the camera. Both are laughing. In their teens, they must have practised these fights on Saturday nights leading into the whole weekend spent between alternating homes, in pyjama parties. The exercise tights that one woman wears are like white soft skin.

Sometimes, on Friday nights, when there is no hockey on the television, especially in the winter, and after my wife and I have finished our spaghetti dinner, she will disappear without warning into the bathroom, leaving the door slightly open, leaving her voice and her promise behind with her words spoken as soft as the water she bathes in. "I'll just be a minute." I can smell the fragrance moving under the door which she seldom closes tight, and inhale the perfume representing her arriving presence. "I'll just be a minute."

She makes me lie flat on my back. And she kneels over me, as if conquering me; and she grabs my wrists in the manacles of her strong-fingered grip, her fingers like pieces of steel, and nails me to the cross which her passion has drawn in an invisible, squared-off area on the carpet that is white. The carpet is now a boxing ring.

In this photograph in my hand, Reens is kneeling over my wife. And this woman, my wife, is flat on her back, her head bent back in laughter, her arms raised. I can picture her muscles playing, and her body moving in rhythm to fit the passion in the tug-o'-war of the pillow fight and the bounding trampoline. All this detail, all this magnified vision, takes place in the single second of a glance.

But who could have taken this photograph? And where was it taken?

I begin to feel the force of guilt. The same guilt as that which infuses me when I remember the first summer we spent in this apartment. A glorious summer. When we sat, barbecuing on the balcony near the wrought-iron railing closest to the neighbour whom I have not met.

Balconies in Toronto are romantic. And for me who had spent a life buried in dust, in an old house, with raccoons in the roof and attic, and mice in the basement, and shaded by maple trees which completed the shadows and the tomb of that living, this balcony of new love was rich with wine and conversation. Almost all the balconies my eyes reached were decorated with potted red plants, geraniums, and the people on them were barbecuing and drinking wine and beer; and I could see inside the neighbour's living room, on the left, as if I were following in his footsteps as he went back inside to bring out the onions and the ground beef and the wieners and the sliced tomatoes, for his fire was raging, and had reached the correct hotness, and was smelling good in its anticipation of the hot dogs and hamburger meat; so I thought he was going in for that, and I followed his movements into the room, expecting this. And instead, I was seeing him in another room mounting his wife. It was my miscalculation. He had not even taken his apron off. Seeing his hot-tempered but legitimate act with his wife did not melt the guilt of my blunder, and it did not prevent me from watching the way he stoked that fire, nor prevent me from feeling unclean to have witnessed it. I felt the guilt of my mistake and my observation. And I took my eyes off their writhing, violent, shortened movements, off the tableau of their other hunger.

It ended as fast as it had begun. Bang-bang-bang! And then, "Jesus Christ!" he said, like a curse, less as acknowledgement.

The Scotch I poured myself, with her beside me, ignorant of what my eyes had lighted on, was without ice, without water, and drunk off in one gulp. The taste of what I had seen remained on my tongue. And my steaks bought at the expensive butcher, Orliffe, turned into charcoal. She said, "What the fuck?" She did not know.

In the thickening, billowing smoke, smelling as awful as the taste of embarrassment, I could see him with his apron still on, eating four hamburgers piled on a paper plate. His wife had three hot dogs on her plate. One for each "bang."

My mind is running. Travelling back over all that time. Trying to piece the evidence to the seasons. Trying to pick out each explanation and excuse she had been giving me when she came home late from the office, after drinking with "friends." When she said she was going to get her hair permed. When she said she was going to the dentist, three times in one week, I remember now, to have a root canal. And what about that time I challenged her excuses, and she had to admit, "It is Eireene I was out with, so you won't have to be bloody suspicious all the time! And search for evidence! Call Bistro 990 and ask them and they'll tell ya!"

That explanation sealed my temper. The doubt disappeared. And I was at peace.

My mind is running back now to a Saturday afternoon. And I was eating dinner on a tray alone, in front of the television, when she called to say she was stopping off on Church Street for a drink after working late.

"With a friend. Just a girl friend."

She even gave me the name of the bar. Wilde Oscars. In those days, she did not always identify Reens as this girl friend; and I was not jealous about her girl friends. But now, with all this mystery and remembered details coming into my head, into this close-up of history, they plunged me to other harmless occasions when my temper jumped to calculated conclusions.

I can see that afternoon in summer two years ago, or three years ago, clearly now. We had planned to go to the Island on a picnic. I had prepared sliced cucumber with rosemary and avocado pears, cold chicken and slices of ham from the deli-catessen beside the cleaners. She decided to get two bottles of white wine from the liquor store, "only because it is summer and red wine leaves spots on your trousers." She had decided to have Reens join us on the Island. It turned seven o'clock and she had not returned. I knew no one to telephone. I had no telephone number of any of her friends. I could not think of who to call. I realized then that I was a complete stranger in this land. I knew no one. Suppose she was dead . . .

Eventually, the telephone rang. The woman's voice at the other end was telling me that my wife had been with her daughter. "She's been in the pool all afternoon. You want me call her?"

When my wife came to the telephone, I could see the water from the pool drifting off her legs and arms, and drops were falling in rhythm from between her legs and from her bathing suit, onto the tiled floor where she was standing in the kitchen beside the fridge.

Now, in this bedroom, I am seeing things for the first time. Things I am not supposed to see. Secrets. My wife's secrets.

I am holding a photograph in my hand and wondering who the photographer was. And how he was able to hold his camera and his equanimity so still, even though his subjects were so excited in their jumping and romping on the bed, moving all the time as a vibrating trampoline does, even when the last child has jumped off.

And suddenly I remember the tripod. The tripod that sits propped in the corner, behind the undressed Christmas tree.

There has always been this tripod leaning in the corner where the upright piano stands. The tripod is never touched, and remains simply part of the trim of the room.

And the piano stands dumb, like the tripod, a decoration with dust accumulated on its keys, which are never touched or tinkled by my wife – except once, one night in the first winter after we met. She's told me it is her grandmother's piano, which was given to her by her mother when her grandmother died. And she told me long ago and many times that she had studied photography in night classes at the Ontario College of Art, and pianoforte at the Royal Conservatory of Music. Up to grade seven.

It was ten chords she played. Touched with knowledge of someone who studied music. Ten chords which showed my wife's ability, and disclosed to me, not musical in body, the title of the tune those ten chords represented. And that she did attend the conservatory, and had had classical training. And that night, just as I got the title right, she stopped. Dropped the cover down. With a bang. It made a sharp noise that had a reverberation of a note in it. And before the note cooled, she had shouted, "I've lost it! I've lost it!"

Auntie Reens understood better than I the frustration in my wife's words and mood. "It's a long time since she practised," she said. "She's lost her touch, can't you see?"

And she went and stood beside her best friend, still sitting on the piano stool. And she stood behind the stool, and passed her hand across my wife's neck. I saw the tears settle in Reens's eyes; and when my wife was still but still not pacified and tears were streaming from her eyes, too, she ran from the stool into the bedroom, slammed the door, and shouted again, "I've lost it! I've lost it!" and her shouts came through the door to me, standing stunned beside the piano. I remained dumbfounded.

Auntie Reens saw my state and went to the bedroom door and stopped. She did not knock but entered. And then I heard the door pulled in. It was the first time our bedroom door was ever closed. And then, coming to me was the sound of their voices, and then they were laughing.

It is only now that I understand the cause of my wife's tantrum and her inability to play so little of that song.

I remember she had told me when we had been sitting on the wooden deck, when her leg was resting on my white linen trousers, and she was talking about her uncle, and how the seams in his thick worsted trousers were always pressed and were sharp enough to peel an apple, and how, all those many times sitting on his lap while he played the piano, it was always the same song he played. And I learned from her, on that July afternoon, the name of the song, the same song which on that November night she played the first ten chords of. She told me on that summer afternoon in July that when she ran from her uncle's house and sat on the cold cement at the end of the long driveway without her coat on, hiding from him and waiting for her mother to return from Vegas in the Volvo station wagon, it was the last time he played the song for her.

Almost four years it has taken me to make this connection. I had forgotten until this minute, standing now in our bedroom, that the name of the song my wife began to play one night years ago on a piano that has not been opened since was "Somewhere Over the Rainbow."

In the photograph I am holding are pillows. Pillows I have seen before, but cannot remember nor place. Pillows I seem to recognize. The white flowers in the photograph are in the same design as those carved into the head of the brass bedstead. I look at them once more, and I know. It is the head of the bed

I sleep in. My bed. Our bed. And the flowers in the design at the foot I have also seen. Many times. I have seen the four pillows in this photograph just as many times. And the pillow-cases and the flowers in the sheets which my wife and I would hold at arm's length, and make into billowing sails, and let the wind from the window facing the changing trains fill the sweet-smelling cotton sheets, and make them look like a garden in July.

My wife always had to have flowers in the design of her sheets. And in many books I took from the shelves, including the Bible, she had stuck flowers when they were alive; and when I turned the pages, the cured small branches, like mummified insects, would fall into my lap. And I would smile. She has this thing about flowers, whether they are dead or in pots. And we would let the flowers in the laundered sheets fall, and we would run our palms over them, flattening them, softening them in anticipation of the touch of our bodies on them. These things happened when there was still that kind of love.

I am now sitting on these same sheets as the sheets and the four pillows that are in the photograph that I hold in my hand. I look at the photograph again, and I see that it was taken on my wedding day. The dress that Reens is wearing is the one she was dressed in when she met us at the bottom of the cold steps in front of the Old City Hall, facing the parked white stretch limousine. I know it was taken on my wedding day because on the sheets, with their pattern of manufactured flowers, is the bouquet. The bouquet that Reens had placed in my wife's hand before she entered the limousine. It is lying on one pillow. And that pillow is on my side of the bed.

I am still dressed in my black serge. I am sitting on a river-bank. There is a highway behind me. And before me, to the left, this highway goes into the suburbs, into Scarborough and Pickering; and to my right, going into Union Station and the lake, are the steel tracks of the CNR trains and railroad. It is cold. Ice is on the ground, and on some branches of trees. I am wearing the rented tuxedo. And I have no overcoat. But I do not feel the dampness, or the sting of the wind. I cannot feel the wind which, if I were in another place and in another time, would be like icicles punching my skin against my ribs and lashing my face, as if buckets of ice water with pebbles in it are being pelted on me to wake me up.

The water barely moves. Perhaps, it is not moving at all. I wonder why I think it is moving? I wonder who fished in this river years ago when the bottom could still be seen, clear as the skin of the fish baited on a hook made from a common pin and plucked from its warm home?

Now, the water is dark and thick, and there is scum on it, almost as wide as the stream itself, floating before my eyes. The scum moves imperceptibly, taking a lifetime to travel to the captured insect struggling on a dead piece of stick. I cannot see beneath the top of the scum.

Water comes to my eyes, and I do not wipe it away. Not because my hands are cold, but because I have no strength left. The force of my shock and the violence it has caused, the anger in it, has drained my strength.

Before I left the apartment, I found a sealed envelope. I opened it and found a poem I had written to my wife a long time ago. It was never given to her. Also in the envelope was a sprig of dried flowers. I cannot remember what I did to the envelope. But the dried flowers are in the folds of my cummer-bund, which keeps slipping below my waist. And I have the white Kleenex, with her lips printed on it, and folded into four.

There will be a time to see, and a time to read, the contents of that envelope.

But how did I get from the intersection of Yonge and Davisville – and before this juncture, from the apartment through the park, between the two houses where no one lives, to the corner of Yonge and Davisville – to this cold river? How did I complete the devastation to the room? To the entire apartment. And decide that I was going to leave it behind me, and choose this place, this cold, wet, polluted bank, beside a stream, beside railroad tracks that no longer move trains, which I have seen only from the window of a speeding taxicab, or from the streetcar travelling overhead on the Bloor Street Viaduct?

And how did I disembark from whatever has brought me here to this place, to descend all these hundreds of feet below, over the cold frozen ground; and the snow is thinner here, below the road, below the bridge, below my level; I used to be an honourable Judge, an honourable man, a federal Judge in the court for refugees . . . past the bloated body of a dog, dead now for days in the ice-covered twigs, with no smell of its disintegration, because this is winter, and because the cold kills smells as it kills life; and no flies rise from its frozen carcass; how did I come to be below the level of the road, to sit stooping by this partially frozen stream of water, which never in my time in this city have I ventured close to?

I bend over, almost losing my balance, to wash my right hand in the black water. It changes colour from its former darkish green to some tint of red, or crimson. The water stings my hand. The water stings the cut in my hand. The cut is three inches, running along the bottom of my thumb, along the fat of my palm, right up to my wrist.

I cannot remember when I got this wound. But since it is the wrist, I wonder if it is *that*. If it means *that*. I wonder if I can pull back the skin of all that confusion, and see the attempt to curtail the heaviness of what I had absorbed, in an act of self-sacrifice?

I cannot remember how I got this wound. And as I go to brush the dirty water away from my hand, rubbing it against the black serge, I see that the front of my stiffened, starched white shirt, the bib, is marked by a red slash, sharp and clear as my action must have been, some time before.

I am bleeding. Is this why the two women, one from the islands, the other Canadian, sharing a seat with me, looked at me, and then lowered their eyes in such biting scorn mixed with pity, like two sides to an argument?

This reminds me now that I have travelled by streetcar. The red slash brings it back to me.

The body of the scentless dog reminds me of pig bladders that we kicked in our made-up football games back in the island, just a few hours after the pig had been killed in the backyard.

The photograph was so fragile. Like a flower. Like the kind of flower she called herself when we met the first time that night, long ago in the summer. And the glass was so brittle. I did not know my strength, as I have never in my time in this half a continent, been asked to demonstrate brawn and passion before.

"*I'm home!*"

I had heard the voice clearly. My wife's voice. But coming through the intercom. There was no laughter in her voice. I could hear another voice, with laughter in it. Her voice, and a second voice. It wrenched me from the bedroom.

I had just dumped all her clothes I could get my hands on into the bathtub, and the cold-water shower jets were at full blast. The bathroom became cold, appeasingly cold. It was as if I were about to take one of those showers which people say cool the passion, and postpone the appetite for sex.

"*I'm home!*"

And I expected the dog to run from under the bed to the door, and jump at it, and paw on it, and wag his tail, and claw the door down. But the dog is in Kingston, on his Christmas holidays.

I dropped the bundle of clothes in my hands into the water, and watched them get heavier and heavier still, and then sink. The shower tap pissed like a huge water pistol. A gun shooting. I saw the names of designers on her clothes get wet and heavy, and then sink. The shower tap pissed like a gun shooting.

This image came to mind. But I did nothing about it, as I had no gun or pistol in the apartment. But if I did . . .

The bathtub was full. I went back to the bedroom, and to the clothes closets. Both of them were already emptied of their contents. I had dumped my own clothes into the cold water as well. I wanted to purge everything I owned, everything I had seen and touched, everything she owned, the entire discovery from my memory. Everything. The long silk dresses which she would buy from a second-hand designer store in Yorkville Village; her leather purses and handbags from Holts; all her suede shoes in greater number than I ever counted, most of them red with high heels; her winter coat of fur, or skin of some animal caught in the North, given to her by her mother; everything. Wanting to drown everything I had seen and read.

And I stood listening to my wife's voice coming up into the bedroom through the intercom, and wondering how my rage would spill over and touch her. And would it touch her? And I turned the water off.

By the time I had thrown all the clothes into the water, and as I was making the five trips to do this, a thought passed through my head: Suppose it was my anger that had forced my eyes to paint pictures that did not exist? Imagination. Improvisation.

Suppose the photograph was nothing more than an anonymous photograph sent by someone to make misery. And taken in 1895 and *not* 1995, the year we got married, as I thought I had read on the back of the frame that held the photograph of Reens and my wife.

Suppose that, in my mind, and through my anger, I have transferred suspicion to fact and sight, and have placed those two innocent women guilty only of loving each other, like sisters, into this fantasy of infidelity that bears a different name?

Suppose what I saw is not what I have seen.

It terrified me to think that I had made a mistake. The photo, after all, was out of focus.

And suppose.

The photo was out of focus.

Suppose I had to take all these expensive, ruined designer clothes out, and dry them, and have them dried, and send them to the cleaners.

But today is Sunday. This city is dead. Does not function on Sundays.

Or suppose I have to replace them all, if that is possible. And before replacing them, have to explain to my wife, and the insurance adjuster, why they are not in the closet where they belong.

"*I'm home!*"

My wife's voice. It is coming up in the elevator.

I had dropped the heart-shaped frame on the sheets. I then

rose from the bed and went into the kitchen, into the cupboard above the sink, to bring down the large bottle of Ballantine's Scotch she saved there, for emergencies; and I poured a drink, twice my usual strength and size, into a crystal glass, and added soda. The cap of the soda bottle had been left unscrewed, so the soda did not fizz.

I took the drink to the chaise longue she had upholstered at such great expense, and sat in it, facing the television, which I have turned on even though I am not watching it. I poured half of the drink on one of the cushions before I took a sip. Without knowing why.

Through the window, from eight floors down, came a cold breeze each time it seemed that a subway train chugged into the station.

The room was quiet in the interval. The neighbour next door, the man I had caught lying on his wife that afternoon when the coals in his barbecue were hot and red, was now moving about in his living room. I could hear the music through the wall on his side. Rock and roll. Elvis Presley. And the breeze which turned into a wind, brought up to the eighth floor where I was, the sound of feet, and tires slowing down, and then more feet moving over the hardened path, and then the fading sound of tires driving away. I could hear the music again. I thought I heard the wailing of a distant siren.

"*I'm coming!*"

It was my wife's voice.

"*I'm coming with you!*" Auntie Reens said.

"*I'm coming!*" my wife's voice announced a second time, emphasizing the words. "*I'm coming!*"

It was my wife's voice. The same voice she used when she lay over me, as I was pinned, like a cat, sprattled on my back, with her hands holding me on the off-white carpet. Or pinned to the sheets fresh from the laundromat and still warm, with their pattern of flowers running through them, as if we were really on a picnic on the Island, on the grass, or in the nearby park when the dandelions were raging yellow and the other wildflowers were playing havoc with my allergies.

"*I'm coming!*"

Her voice was only announcing her arrival.

There was no voice speaking to me. It was not her voice. And the voice I had heard coming through the intercom earlier was not her voice. The intercom has not functioned in four months.

And the time was only six-thirty. My wife was still at the concert, listening to the one thousand voices singing hallelujahs in the *Messiah*.

Closer to me, away from the slow-moving water, is a puddle, a small pool covered with sprigs and straw, and pieces of twig and very small branches, like the dried flowers she keeps between the pages of a book that have lived their lives in other places, in the four months gone by, in summer when they were not separated from their nourishing trunks, and were growing.

I put my finger into this small pool and move the pieces of straw and bramble aside so that I might see the water and the things below the surface that the water is concealing. It is cold at my first touch. But the more I hold my fingers in the water, the colder it becomes, making my fingers numb. And this numbness curiously gives the illusion of warmth.

I remember having sex with my wife, touching her leg, touching the scar on her knee, moving my hand up and down, and feeling at the first touch the coolness of her leg; and not knowing when that coolness turned into warmth, the warmth of my appetite and of her appetite, I stopped my fingers from moving up and down.

I remember the sensation was strong and deep, and that it shook my whole body.

Now, sitting beside this river that does not move, that can no longer, through its pollution, take me to the Island, that has no clear water that would make me want to take the common pin that holds the red rose my wife pinned to the lapel of the black serge jacket and dip it into the water, and wait for the suggestive tightening of the string warning me of success. Or I can pull out the thread showing at the bottom of my jacket until it becomes a line, and feel at the end of the tightening the slimy, silver, shuddering, small body. And pull it in, and feel its small life in a struggle with my appetite. And smash its head with a rock. And eat it in olive oil, and pour lemon juice on its shrivelled body, with a smile of conquering.

When I had moved from the bathroom, trying still to control my temper, and thinking of the consequence to all this violence that I have been carrying within me, and having changed my mind about dousing my wife's sweaters and winter scarves and calf-skin gloves and jogging suits, along with the other things lying in the cold tub of water, my temper was still out of control.

I knew that I had not completely purged the anger from my system. And that it would flare up again. It was not long in erupting.

I became a man caught in thick bramble in the bush, not knowing the direction I was taking. I was entangled in this thickness to which I could not put any order to find the direction back to the point beside the parked station wagon, beside the road and the clump of bush which I had landmarked against this eventuality, before I had taken the first steps to enter the bush.

I trampled what was before me. I kicked out of my path all that was blocking my rage. I was surprised at the ease with which I broke the first two chairs that were still pushed under the dining table. And I smashed them without having to take them out. One was the chair on which Reens always sat. The other was my wife's place. They were pushed into the table, and set in front of the placemats, rectangular and green with flourishing red poinsettias that my wife had laid out for the dinner she had planned.

The four tall brass candlesticks fell. The crystal wineglasses leaned and fell over, and rolled to the edge of the white damask tablecloth.

It was as if my rage were now being fed by each piece of wood, of linen, of expensive cloth, of leaded glass and crystal, and of cardboard that I could find to lay my hands on and rip apart, because words had not done their part after that first afternoon when our words were like waves.

In the fever of my destroying these things, my act was lodged for a moment in my guilt, like contrition, like the chest pains I get. My blows to these possessions, to these things that encompassed me, and blocked my path, like encumbrances that prevented my extrication from the bush, told me something of the nature of this kind of panic and the violence it can bring about.

I thought I heard the neighbour on my left turn his music off, and stand with his ear to the thin wall, listening . . .

It was my mistake. Let my mother, who brought me up to be a man more than to be a human being, let my vocation, a Judge in the court for refugees, who listens to gruesome, despicable stories, unrelieved by a phrase of love, take the blame for this mental disintegration. It was my mistake.

It was my inability. My final refusal to swallow pain. It was the consequence of living in such close quarters, in a land that became arid through the lack of words and water.

I was brought up in the hot island to trust in deeds. "Doings," my mother called them, and said to me the third time she seated me in the Victorian chair in the front-house, our living room where sentences were pronounced, where love was told in kisses and sugar cakes, where she also always scolded with the Ten Commandments, "Doings, boy! Doings! Not talk. Talk cheap. Doings, my son!"

She was telling me about life. And schooling me in the philosophy to be used by me in my growing up.

"Doings! The things you do, and the way you carry yourself through life, those going-speak more louder than any talk you could ever make your tongue say, in the lines o' love, or in the lines o' life. 'Cause talk cheap. Remember that."

The other two times she sat me down to impart knowledge into my head was the night when the man gave her little god-child the red lollipop, the time she told me about the way the man took her godson's virginity.

And the third time was when she told me about the "perils" a man faces with women.

"Make sure you don't get mix-up with *no* woman who going-horn you. You hear me, son?"

"Yes, Ma."

But she had also said there was no friend close enough and confidential enough "for you to spill your guts to" than the woman you call your wife.

When I walked out of the apartment, it was left in a condition similar to those I had seen often in television shows of cops and robbers. Like the ravaged three-storey mansion of a drug dealer who lived in a suburb to the north of Toronto. Or the smashed bungalow of a man suspected of bringing Jamaican men and women across the border to make them illegal citizens.

This total destruction of an immigrant's independence and excursion into small business practices, this total destruction of another man's castle, was the calling card of cops and robbers I have seen on television.

On the screen, in the movies, they all happened after the stroke of three in the morning. Cock-crowing time.

And many nights, at the apartment, when I couldn't sleep, when I counted and counted sheep as they say we must do, to conquer sleep, when I would rehearse my favourite children's poem,

O, Mary, go and call the cattle home,
And call the cattle home,
And call the cattle home,
Across the sands of Dee . . .

Yes, I wrote her a poem once. I wrote a poem to my wife. I found it in the envelope with some dried flowers and a piece of Kleenex with her lips marked on it. The poem was an ode.

I dip my fingers into the small dirty pool of water, stirring it in small circles that become smaller and smaller, until I can no longer trace the measurement of the circle, for the circle is now a point. The centre.

And my fingers are no longer moving around. I can still feel the faster beating of my pulse.

I am back in the hot island, reading my elementary-school

text, *Nelson's West Indian Reader, Book Three*, which means that I am in Class 3. And I am following the multiplication tables, "Nine ones is nine! Nine twos is eighteen . . . !" I am thinking of that red-haired girl who was not allowed to play with her friends the games of hopscotch and rounders and catcher and hide-and-hoop, and was given a man's job. To bring the cattle home.

It was the season of storms and raging rivers. And it was across the tricky sands of the River Dee. . . . But this river I am sitting beside, on its bank, has no raging currents, even when it is not winter. It is not really a river. Does not move. But Mary with the red, wet, flaccid hair was told, ordered by name, "O, Mary, go and call the cattle home, and call the cattle home, and call the cattle home. . . ." Three times. Just as my mother warned me three times before she pulled my belt from the tabs of the khaki short pants I was wearing, and promised "to paint your arse in blows. You think you is a man in this house, boy?"

And all these painful commands, all these solicitations for help, always heaped on the smallest, weakest shoulders, always those of a child.

I was a child once. A child who grew up in a small hot island where at night the light is a circle of warm kerosene lamplight that throws only comforting shadows throughout the darkening house.

But now I am a man sitting beside a stream almost completely frozen of movement, in this cold place the size of a continent. Sitting here, I am hiding, trying to evade the light of the city shimmering in the background behind me.

No one knows I am here.

The two women on the streetcar earlier, who were forced into conversation by the evidence of blood on the stiff starched white dress shirt I was wearing in their presence, and which I wear now, have not followed the trail. And no detectives have yet arrived at the scene of this crime. No one looks out of his fast-moving American car going south towards the CN Tower, or going north then to travel east, speeding into Scarborough and Pickering, nor follows an empty cigarette box that is thrown from the window and floats in the wind a moment after it has left the hand. For immediately as it is thrown, the window is shut by automation. And the inside of the car returns to its warmth again, and to its silence. The box drops a few feet from where I am stooping, with my finger in the water, clearing the weeds and brambles from this intriguing little hole.

The dampness makes me shudder. The darkness makes me frightened. I put my hand into the folds of my cummerbund, which has slipped below my waist, and I touch the sprig of dried flowers. I take it out and count the flowers on it. There are three. I tuck the sprig back into the warmer darkness of my black cummerbund, for safety. I put my hand into my left breast pocket, and my hand touches a piece of paper. I pull it out, thinking it is my subway transfer. It is the poem. The ode I wrote to her. I thought it was still in the envelope I'd found in the apartment. I unfold the small piece of paper and it grows to the size of four postage stamps. I fold it up again and put it back. I do not want to read it now.

There is no embrace that this black night can promise me, or hold for me, so that I might be protected in my secret, dark act. There is no sympathy, even though no one knows I am here. No one, except the two joined women who will never think that I am here beside a stream killed of its fish, a stream that flows no more. That cannot reach the Island, that cannot reach the lake.

I am alone. And I do not want to be. I wish I could go some place, to see someone. Some place I can go to where I know someone and I can tell about these things I have done. The secrecy of my act does not give me comfort, or solace, or power. I thought it would.

I am unable to hold my crime in my thoughts, in my mind, as I can no longer go to the basement bedsitter.

I wish I could talk with my wife.

I feel the tug of conscience that pulls me back to her, as if this stagnant water, all of a sudden, is struck by a wind that gives it current and movement.

I do not even know if my wife is at home. How long can one thousand voices or one hundred take to sing the *Messiah*?

When she arrives, and sees what I have done, she will need a shoulder to support her shock.

Would my wife's shame at having Reens beside her to witness my violence be proof perhaps that she had made the wrong choice?

Can I go back to the apartment and offer my wife this three-pronged sprig, and the ode I wrote to her, and talk about love and misunderstanding, and understanding, and have her understand? And what is there to understand? And talk about redemption?

I walk up the slippery embankment and crawl under the lowest line of barbed-wire fence, with the black serge scraping the ground. And before I can straighten my body out, and stand, and extricate myself from the wire, a car roars down the highway. And in this crouched position, with my knees still dragging through the cold, short, and stiffened bush, and my hands groping, I am splattered.

I am too alone to move, to care, to want freedom from the encircling wire. And I no longer want someone to listen to me tell the story. My strength has gone. But before it collapses entirely, I see the dried three-stemmed sprig fall into the old snow and slush that is thicker here. And I try to pick it up, but it disintegrates in my fingers. I cannot save it. And I think of the ode in my pocket, and wonder what it can add to my story.

Where can a man go, if not back home? Whatever that home is, and where, and in whatever state, even when that state is one of thorough destitution, and the going back is like returning to one's vomit. Or returning to the scene.

I shall take myself up, and shake this river water from my black serge cloth, rinse the blemished white bib of the dried blood, and stand stiff in this unredeeming cold.

The train at the intersection of Bloor and Yonge has no crowd. I sit in the bright, wide, empty space, with the discarded newspapers in the aisle and on the seats and on the floor, with cans and wrappers, and I can do anything I want; I can look at my reflection in the passing windows when the subway slows down, and in the panels of glass and shiny advertising boards with messages, or in the changed light when the train pulls at a slower rate into the Rosedale station, and I can still wander in my imagination when it goes into a tunnel of darkness near the place where liquor can be bought later at night than at any ordinary liquor store, and I can shout and sing and no one on this train can hear me, unless the driver, who I cannot see, has a device for picking out disturbances. I wonder who on this subway train, man or woman, whom I cannot see, is running from some disaster? Or is riding up and down to gain courage to jump to some disaster? On this Sunday-night train I can kill a man, or a woman, and no one will be able to point me out in a lineup in a police station. No one will know. No one knows I am here.

And suddenly this freedom, this independence of being alone, of being sovereign, overcomes me. I want to be home. I want to be with my wife. And I want to be with Auntie Reens. I want to be with the dog. With the man who could have been the father of my wife's child, making me the child's uncle. I want to know *her* uncle who is back there in Mount Pleasant Cemetery, his body having been brought back, by his sister, by Amtrak from Dearborn, Michigan, to the Canadian border at Niagara Falls, and from there, by Via Rail, to Mount Pleasant, and put in the family crypt, "dust to dust."

I am still the only living being in this subway car, as we leave Summerhill station for St. Clair; and I am regaining consciousness, the consciousness that sometimes comes after a near-calamity.

The last stop. Davisville. What is there about this stop that is so significant? Is it a destination, an intersection, a context of time and place that makes it so romantic? Is it the rumble and clanking of the subway trains going into their terminus?

Through the cold alleyway off Chaplin Crescent, opposite Lascelles Boulevard, between two houses where no one seems to live, cross the pasture which has dandelions and dog mess plentiful in summer causing the young soccer players to cry out, "Fuck, man!" and slip and fall, and the younger children to cry, and which I am walking across now, at the same angle I take crossing paths and walks – across the planted grass, avoiding the paved walk. I am walking across this slice of pasture, and I am face to face with the entrance, the frozen fountain, the frozen pieces of paper and soft-drink cartons in the round garden, the frozen plants, the hard driveway, the door with glass in it, the panel of names beside the buzzers which do not work.

There is a whirring light, like the visible representation, the symbol for a sound. A cry of a siren. Police. Ambulance. Or fire truck. And I do not pay any attention to this. They are parked far from the entrance, not to block my path, not to cause a scene, far in front of the adjoining building. In our area, in our district, sirens explode frequently, on their way to tragedy and childbirth. And when the alarm in this building goes off, I remain in the warm bathroom with the black American statuette, buried in clouds and vapour and bubbles.

I walk to the elevator and press the button and watch the numbers go from 6 to 5, to 4, to 3, to 2, to 1, to L. And the doors open. I like the mathematics of this kind of travel. Then I press my number.

The elevator goes up. I wonder if my wife and Auntie Reens have come straight back from the concert. And if they have . . .

I will take my lead from my wife. And then I will tell her the things I did, the words I wrote, the action I am guilty of.

My key is in the lock; and it turns, in one direction, one time, and turns in the opposite direction, one time; and I open the door and walk in.

I hear a sound like water running. But it is only the sound of the wind, and the noise of subway cars lumbering to their berths; and I smell the smells of my home: incense and tangerines and fingernail polish . . . it is Christmas . . . and I see the small box that once held mandarin oranges wrapped in reddish tissue paper, and which my wife now uses as a stand for her red and white poinsettias. I turn the lights on, for in my mind is the beautiful large dish in which she keeps fruit. It is the basin of a matching set with a ewer she bought at a yard sale.

Destruction, like the debris left over from a construction site, hits my eyes. The mahogany dining chairs are overturned and broken like wooden matches dropped from a box, and the crystal glasses are in shards, flashing each time I step over a fallen object, a fallen adversary of my temper. My temper seems greater, more unbounded than I remembered it to be. The dining table is yawning in the middle and shows two metal strips. It lists to one side. Photograph frames are smashed, and in the light of the living room I can see where the marks of my heels touched the glass and the brass of the frames and the silver. On the chaise longue she cherished is a glass. I remember now this is the glass of whisky I poured earlier. The glass is still on the cushion where I rested it. It is only half-full. The thick, comfortable cushion on which the weight of my body has been accommodated for all these three or four years is stained.

The television screen is on, and there is a kind of shimmering snow falling, on the screen. Had I forgotten to turn it off? There is a noise, a sound I cannot decipher or describe, like a buzz, a hum.

On my way to the bathroom to check if the faucet is dripping, I come to the bedroom. I am standing now at the bedroom door. I cannot move from this spot, to enter the room. But I know I must go in. From the open door, and in spite of the dim light, I cannot help seeing the sheets, dragged back from the four pillows at the head, as if the occupant, tossing in sleep, had leapt from the bed to walk in the troubled night, deeper in her sleep in the walking than she was in her sleep and in her dreams . . . and the frames of photographs, and that one photograph which caused this . . . explosion. I can see, from where I am, at the door, the sheets, enticing as the gardens in the nearby park we use in summer; and the flowers running up and down in abandon like the violence in colours in wild gardens in the hot island.

I turn on the light and I see the tripod. I wonder how it moved from its place in the living room, beside the piano, to this place where it now stands, in this bedroom. It is standing with its legs in the posture of someone who dares an opponent to throw the first punch, like someone sure and bragging about that belligerent attitude by the stance he takes. And on the tripod is my camera . . . yes, I must have tried the experiment of taking my own picture, sitting on the bed, just as my wife and Auntie Reens must have done by using delayed action.

Inside this camera there will be a picture of me. What image of myself will emerge from the grey film? Will the film show me the truth in focus? Will it show me who I am? I am certain that it cannot help but show me exactly as I was in that second when the time ran out, and I heard the click of the shutter . . .

I turn off the bedroom light and proceed down the hall to the bathroom, and as I walk in, my eyes accustom themselves to the different light there, to the dusk inside the bathroom, the same dusk that starts out as a pink hue and turns dark, like the colour of dirt itself, the dusk that back home brings out mosquitoes and ghosts.

I turn on the light, and I am blinded by this new brightness. The light is harsh and blinding and strong, and, with no scent of oils or incense, deodorants or lotions, and no sight of the black American statuette, all I am aware of is the giant-sized bathtub, and my wife's body lying in the tub, which is a watery grave like those in books about women buried in water with flowers floating through their legs and in their hair and on their white dresses, flowers floating in harmony with the printed flowers already in the pattern of the dress and in the water. It is a dress I am looking at. And at the flowers in the pattern of this dress. This dress, which I have seen her wear, and which is now floating at the top of this tub full of clothes, makes me think I am seeing her.

The bathroom is congested with too many dresses, too many undergarments, too many memories which come alive, and are strangers in my private place, in my bathroom of this large apartment. I am suddenly overcome by fatigue. I want to lie down, and I start to walk to the bedroom. I can hear the sound of a siren. Police. Ambulance. Or fire truck. There is no other sound.

Just then, I hear a key in the door. It turns in one direction once, then once again in the other direction. I hear the door handle turn, and then I hear my wife call out, in her usual exuberant voice, "*I'm home!*"

I do not answer, as I never do. I stay where I am.

I hear the door open, and I feel the draught from the hallway. I hear the jingle of keys, then I hear the door close. The draught from the hallway is cut off. I hear my wife's footsteps on the bare parqueted floor of the entrance hall. She is just inside the door.

"*I'm home!*" she says a second time.